DISCARDED

The Return

Center Point
Large Print

Also by James D. Best and available from
Center Point Large Print:

The Steve Dancy Tales
Murder at Thumb Butte

**This Large Print Book carries the
Seal of Approval of N.A.V.H.**

The Return

A Steve Dancy Tale

James D. Best

CENTER POINT LARGE PRINT
THORNDIKE, MAINE

This Center Point Large Print edition
is published in the year 2014
by arrangement with the author.

The text of this Large Print edition is unabridged.
In other aspects, this book may vary
from the original edition.
Printed in the United States of America
on permanent paper.
Set in 16-point Times New Roman type.

ISBN: 978-1-62899-014-0

Library of Congress Cataloging-in-Publication Data

Best, James D., 1945–
  The return : a Steve Dancy tale / James D. Best. — Center Point Large
Print edition.
    pages cm
  ISBN 978-1-62899-014-0 (Library binding : alk. paper)
  1. Large type books. I. Title.
  PS3602.E785R48 2014
  813′.6—dc23
                                                    2013046967

For Diane

The Return

Chapter 1

"Five."

My partner, Jeff Sharp, whistled. "I sure hope ya got good cards, 'cuz mine ain't gonna help."

A hand shot out from each player to steady the suitcase lying across our four sets of knees. We had all felt the narrow-gauge Denver & Rio Grande begin a bend along the mountainous route to Leadville, Colorado. The whist game had been going on for an hour, and we had gotten used to the routine. When the train began rolling to the side, we each grabbed a corner of our makeshift table to keep our cards from sliding to the floor. Jeff Sharp and I had discovered eager opponents in facing seats and quickly settled on a wager of two bits a point. Our opponents had won the first game by five points, and Sharp had been in a funk ever since. He didn't like to lose, even for small stakes. Our luck was about to change.

Five seemed like a foolhardy bid, but my seven trumps included all of the face cards. After a couple of hands, I had collected everyone else's trumps and started gathering up tricks with high cards in other suits. We went up six to win the second game. Now each team had won a game by five points, so we were tied.

As we gathered up the cards, I heard a disgusted snort. "How 'bout a dollar a point?"

The young man speaking sported a neatly trimmed beard, a tailored suit, and expensive shoes shined to a high gloss. His soft hands had never used a tool more blister-raising than a fountain pen. He had also proved to be an obnoxious sort. He gloated every time he won a trick and whined incessantly when he lost. Beyond the game, he regally issued curt orders to attendants and talked loud enough to share his opinions with everyone in the railcar. In fact, he yammered endlessly, which I knew would set Sharp's teeth on edge.

Without hesitation, Sharp answered for both of us.

"A dollar a point it is."

A smug expression grew on the bearded gent's face. He probably thought I'd never get a hand that good again. Probably not, but I wouldn't put it past Sharp to call on Lady Luck now that the bet was serious. I knew my friend well enough to tell that our bearded opponent had gotten under his skin. Since we were what others would consider rich, the money was a minor matter to us, but Sharp would make an effort to put this man and his traveling companion in their place—which was probably anywhere out of his sight.

Jeff Sharp was a good friend and sometime business partner. He had traveled the world, built a huge personal fortune, and displayed the confidence of someone who had bossed tough men in dangerous situations. When I met him the previous year, he owned numerous high-producing silver mines in Nevada. Now, at around fifty years of age, he had sold everything except the Leadville general store we owned together. He now claimed to be fancy-free, but in truth, he had never been anchored to a place or things.

Nearly two years earlier, on my thirtieth birthday, I had sold my gun shop in New York City and ventured west for adventure and fame. My adventures had involved far too much violence for my taste. Although I had been around guns my entire life, I had never shot at anyone until coming west. After I had helped save Sharp from a hanging in Prescott, Arizona, I had resolved to stay out of any more trouble. Fame was another matter. I hoped it would come from a novel I had written about my adventures in the Wild West, due to be published in a few months.

As we swayed and lurched our way to Leadville, Sharp and I were free of earthly possessions—except for our general store in Leadville. I wanted to sell it, but Sharp had cast a lecherous eye on Mrs. Baker, our third partner and the store manager. Mrs. Baker was an attractive, high-spirited woman from Philadelphia, whose engineer husband had died in a mining accident. Like me, Mrs. Baker had abandoned membership in high society to experience the excitement of the raw frontier. Our respective status-conscious families had ostracized us. I suppose they felt it was punishment, but neither of us felt injured.

Our bearded opponent finally quit shuffling and dealt. I was not a big gambler. I liked an occasional evening of faro but seldom played poker. My face or mannerisms gave me up, and everyone at a poker table knew my hand before I played it. I was as competitive as Sharp, so I avoided games that made me look foolish.

"Three," Sharp said evenly.

The bid meant Sharp had a strong hand, and I seldom got in the way of a partner with good cards. When the man on my right passed, so did I.

The bearded gent wasn't as eager to cede the bid. He alternated between looking at his cards and gazing at the ceiling as if he could foretell how the cards would play out. In the end, he passed.

Sharp controlled the play, and I went along for the ride. We were up four after the first hand.

Without cards to endlessly shuffle, the beard got talkative. "Why are you gentlemen traveling to Leadville?"

"Business," I answered as I helped gather up cards.

He laughed. "Is there any other reason to venture to that icebox? What kind of business? If it's mining, I might be of assistance."

"It's not," Sharp said, dealing all fifty-two cards.

The beard looked puzzled. "What other possible business can there be in Leadville?"

"Shop keeping," I answered.

"As luck would have it, I know of a fine establishment available on Chestnut Street."

"I'll bet ya help lots of newcomers," Sharp said with a bit of an edge.

The beard ignored Sharp's tone. "That I have. All have been grateful for my services. Some very generously, I might add."

"We're not in the market . . . for an establishment or yer services," Sharp said.

"Not in the market for an establishment? How do you intend to keep shop without a store?"

"We already have a store," I said matter-of-factly.

The beard ignored his cards. "Where's your store? Perhaps I'm familiar with it."

"End of State Street," I answered.

"With the whores? My God, have you seen it? That's a terrible district. Who sold it to you? Maybe I can intercede on your behalf."

"No, thank ya." Sharp sounded distracted as he studied his hand. "We like whores."

"Sir, that wasn't meant as a joke. You've been bamboozled. That is a perfectly awful part of town. Whores, drunks, savages. Bad men and worse women. Hell, the Indian encampment is just up the hill. The men who frequent that misbegotten neighborhood are looking for cheap liquor and cheaper women. No, no. This will never do. You seem like fine gentlemen. I might be able to set things right. I have an excellent attorney on retainer and a discreet relationship with the police and town council. You'll find my fee reasonable."

"I won't," answered Sharp. "Play, or pay the four dollars ya owe."

"There's no reason to be rude. I was only offering help." The man huffed like a church lady stepping out of the way of a soiled dove.

"Mister, we ain't lookin' for help," Sharp said. "We like our store right where it is."

We had originally bought the store to entrap a bad man who had abducted our friend's daughter. We had aimed purposely for a raunchy part of town because that was where our quarry went for goods. Although Mrs. Baker had done a fine job of turning a profit with the store, the reason we had bought it was now dead.

"Thought you men said you were newcomers." The beard had still not picked up his cards.

"Not what I said. Now, are we playin' cards, or are ya gonna continue drummin' up business?"

We won the next three hands and were up eleven points. The bearded man's travel companion hadn't said a word, but I had the impression they worked together. My guess was they rode this train back and forth between Denver and Leadville to pick off suckers on their way to make a fast fortune. Leadville may have been the richest ore field in the high Rocky Mountains, but most newcomers deposited more wealth in the town than they extracted. Thieving was a prevailing trait of mining camps. During our last trip to Leadville, a shyster had circled us like a vulture until he discovered that Sharp was an experienced mine owner. Then he skedaddled before we discovered he was a fraud. Booming silver towns were like the circus; there was always somebody ready to fleece you while you were distracted by all the hoopla going on around you. I was going to enjoy making this pair pay up.

We lost the next hand. Sharp slowly lifted his eyes until he was staring at our opponent.

"I'll take that eleven dollars now."

His voice was low and even. I recognized it as the tone he used just before he exploded.

"We haven't finished," the beard said. "Besides, we went up two points on that last hand. You're only ahead by nine."

"We have finished." Sharp waited a long second. "I don't play cards with cheats."

"Cheats! Sir, that is a grave insult."

"On that last hand, ya threw a trump on the second trick. That last card ya threw was a spade. That means ya weren't short spades on that second trick. I consider that grave."

15

Although I didn't sense danger from these two dandies, I shifted so I could easily grab my gun from the shoulder holster under my coat.

The beard threw his cards into the center of the table.

"I never cheat . . . never. I don't remember the second trick, but I doubt it was spades. If it was, I merely made a mistake. No cause to get your feathers ruffled."

"Are ya gonna pay me?"

He snapped a "No" just before Sharp's fist hit him straight on the nose.

The beard yelped like he had been stung by a wasp, then blood gushed between the fingers of the hand he'd thrown up to his face. "Good God, man, look what you've done."

He shook a handkerchief from his pocket to staunch the bleeding. "You son of a bitch, you broke my nose. I'm going to sue and take that horrible store away from you."

"I hope you do sue," I said, shaking my head. "That'll mean you're still alive." I jerked a thumb at Sharp. "When he punches someone, they tend to end up dead in short order."

After a sideways glance at Sharp, I added, "Jeff, I'm not stopping them from hanging you this time."

The beard swung out of his seat, grabbing his suitcase with one hand as he held the kerchief over his nose with the other. "I mistook you ruffians for gentlemen. I made a serious error. Good day."

As he turned to walk away, Sharp said, "I'll let ya go 'cuz yer bleedin', but if we see each other again, ya better have eleven dollars in yer hand . . . or I'll take a second punch."

The bearded man and his companion scurried out of the railcar. When the door slammed behind them, several men in the car nodded approval at Sharp.

Chapter 2

We had made it through the mountain passes to a large valley high up in the Rocky Mountains. The railway hadn't been completed the prior autumn during our last visit to Leadville, so we had ridden horses through the mountain trails. A train ride was much easier but required renting a buggy and driver to get us to our hotel.

The cobalt blue sky was not as expansive as I had come to expect in the West. Leadville was over ten thousand feet, but even higher peaks hemmed in the valley from every side. Two- and three-story brick buildings lined intersecting streets, and construction on every block confirmed booming mine operations. The buildings weren't the hasty clapboard variety I had encountered in other mining settlements; instead, the materials of choice seemed to be brick and mortar. Construction was difficult in winter, so Leadville hadn't changed much since last fall. Countless workmen were making up for the hiatus, and every last one of them seemed to be yelling. Foremen screamed orders at their crews, bricklayers shouted for materials, teamsters yelled at pedestrians or their horses, and others just bellowed obscenities for no apparent reason.

Despite exterior appearances, the Carbonate was

the best hotel in Leadville. The sidewalk fronting the plain three-story, square brick structure was too narrow to accommodate even a chair. Hotels in the West usually had a porch or balcony, but Leadville weather dictated indoor living. The nondescript exterior hid a lavish, heavily masculine interior that hadn't changed since the previous fall— except that they had cleaned the bloodstain from the dining room carpet where Captain Joseph McAllen had shot Mrs. Bolton just before she could fire a double-barreled shotgun at me. Prior to that, she had poisoned my horse and twice tried to kill me. I was grateful all trace of her was gone.

The manager recognized us from our previous visit and welcomed us with the phony familiarity innkeepers use to make guests feel important. The last time, we had had to bribe our way into rooms, but we had learned our lesson and made reservations this trip. The cost of the rooms was still outrageous, however. Everything in a mining town was priced as if money lay on the ground just waiting to be picked up.

We settled into our rooms and then met downstairs to enjoy a few drinks and eat a good meal. I had an excellent trout, and Sharp ate grilled lamb chops. After our meals and several whiskeys, we were full, content, and very relaxed.

A steward appeared at my shoulder.

"May I bring you gentlemen dessert?"

"No, thank you," I answered. "We've been

sitting on a train all day and need to walk off this meal. Perhaps when we return."

"I'll save you some of our lemon cake. Just the thing to go with a fine cognac prior to retiring."

"You do that," I said as I got up to leave.

Sharp remained seated. He waved me back into my chair and told the steward to bring us coffee. "What's on your mind?"

"Mrs. Baker."

We had agreed ahead of time to visit our store manager after the meal. That was to be the destination of our walk. Evidently, Sharp wanted to discuss something before we left the hotel.

"What about her?"

"Ya promised her another ten percent interest if she doubled the first year's profits. I know it's only been eight months, but she's already made us a pile of money. I think she deserves a full twenty percent ownership now."

"Agreed."

Sharp lifted his head in surprise. "I didn't expect yer agreement. Leastways, not so easy."

"We have different reasons. I want to increase her ownership because she'll be motivated to sell the store. You want to make her happy."

"What's wrong with makin' a woman happy?"

"Because you want her to celebrate with you."

Sharp laughed. "Yep. So?"

"So nothing. Since we agree, why are we sitting here?"

20

"Beyond likin' coffee after a good meal, I thought we oughta have paperwork drawn up before we visit Mrs. Baker."

I pulled some folded sheets from my pocket and slid them over to Sharp.

"What did you think I was doing in Prescott while you were gallivanting with Mrs. Cunningham? Mac Castle drew up the papers."

The steward arranged two china cups and saucers in front of us, lifted a silver pot, and poured steaming coffee from a great height. I suppose he meant to impress us with his skill, but my irritation with Sharp distracted me. I had stayed at Mrs. Cunningham's boardinghouse while I worked to get Sharp released from the Prescott jail. He was being held for murder, and his chances didn't look good. I hired Mac Castle to defend him in court. With our mutual friend Captain McAllen of the Pinkertons, we eventually proved his innocence and found the real murderers, saving Mr. Jeffery Sharp from hanging.

During that time, my relationship with Mrs. Cunningham had been testy, but Sharp sauntered into her house after being released from jail and effortlessly took her to bed. Now he wanted to seduce Mrs. Baker. He treated women like socks, switching whenever he felt he needed something fresh. Worse, the women never felt discarded and retained affection for him even after he left them for a new adventure. How did he do it? It puzzled me because I had never been easy with women. Sipping coffee, I realized that my irritation came mostly from jealousy. The realization did not alleviate the irritation.

"You weren't gonna tell me?" Sharp put on a hurt expression.

"Not until after I saw the store and books. If everything was in order, then I was going to suggest we enlarge her interest."

"We own equal shares. Ya should've told me yer intentions."

"I want to sell. You don't. We'd been arguing about it, and I didn't see a need to throw more wood on the fire."

"Well, ya shoulda told me. We're more than partners—we're friends."

I was taken aback by his offended tone until I realized something.

"Wait a minute. You're not going to tell me you came up with this idea when dessert was offered. We both waited. I just waited a bit longer."

Sharp studied his coffee. When he lifted his head, he wore an honest smile.

"Yer right. Hell, don't mean a damn thing. We both want to enlarge her interest. Bygones be bygones."

"Fine by me, but we need to discuss the sale. Why do you want to hold on?"

"It's my only connection to a right smart woman. But, hell, with a surprise bump in her interest, things'll work out or they won't. Can't hang around pinin' for somethin' I can't have."

He took a long swallow and snapped the cup back in the saucer.

"We sell."

Chapter 3

After putting on coats, gloves, and hats, we started walking to the far end of State Street. Leadville was bone-numbing cold in winter and in summer could be downright chilly at night. This end of town had fewer buildings, and the sun having set while we ate, it was as dark as the bottom of a well. We saw the store from a block away. A lantern glowing outside the door and soft light spilling from the front windows made it downright inviting. We entered to find it toasty warm and bright as a summer day. By the last time we had visited, Mrs. Baker had already white-washed the raw lumber walls, hanging more lanterns and a couple of bright paintings to cheer up the place during the long winters. Originally, I thought her decorating would make no difference to the male clientele, but I had never lived through a Leadville winter, with its dirty snow and almost constant overhang of gray clouds.

The store became an oasis of cheer in a brutal world that held few comforts for struggling miners. She circled chairs around a warm stove and served fresh coffee for a nickel. The store became a gathering place, where the miners could talk and keep warm until they decided to visit a saloon or brothel before heading to some dreary bunkhouse. The store prospered, because anything the miners needed, they bought on the way out.

There were about a half dozen men talking and laughing in the center of the store. I didn't see Mrs. Baker, but I did see a neat, slight man behind the counter. A huge lout sitting in one of the chairs eyed us with more curiosity than we warranted. We walked over to the counter.

"Is Mrs. Baker around?"

"Naw. She left for the day. Can I help?"

I held out my hand. "Steve Dancy. This is Jeff Sharp."

He nodded and shook our hands, but I detected no note of recognition.

"And your name?" I asked.

"Just call me Henry. What can I do for you gents?"

I gave Sharp a glance, but he seemed to be in a staring contest with the big man by the stove. I turned back to Henry.

"Has Mrs. Baker ever mentioned us?"

"Not that I can recall."

The big man got up and sauntered in our direction.

"Then we'll come back in the morning."

The big man leaned against a support post. "If you got business, you can deal with Henry and me."

I felt Sharp bristle. For some reason this man had set him off.

"No need," I said quickly. "We can wait until morning. We're friends of Mrs. Baker."

"I'll be here when you come back." The voice was casual and the posture nonthreatening, but the big man still conveyed an air of menace.

"Do ya work for Mrs. Baker?" Sharp asked in an equally casual tone.

"Ah do."

"Then ya work for—"

I jumped in to interrupt Sharp. "Tell her we'll come around after breakfast. We sent a telegram, so she's expecting us."

I nudged Sharp, and he reluctantly quit glaring at the big man. I didn't need him hitting anyone else, especially one of our employees. Gently taking his elbow, I guided him toward the door. As we turned to leave, I noticed Henry's hand had fallen below the counter, presumably close to a gun. Mrs. Baker must be expecting trouble. Sharp and I would need to find out why.

When we got outside, Sharp said, "Why did ya interrupt me? That big jackass works for us."

"If Mrs. Baker hasn't told them she has partners, I think we should keep it to ourselves until we talk to her. Besides, what'd he do to get your dander up?"

"He challenged us from the moment we entered the store. Eyes, posture. Like he thought we were robbers . . . or worse. Then he sidles on up to us and acts way too casual. Did ya see he carries a gun an' a sap? A sap ain't common. It's used to knock people unconscious."

"I know what a sap is for. Seen plenty of them in New York. Nasty weapon in the right hands."

"Damn right. Why does she keep a thug like that around?"

I thought about it for a few seconds and then asked, "You agree Mrs. Baker does a good job running the store?"

"Hell, yes."

"Then she has a reason for having a giant ruffian confront strangers. We'd better find out what it is."

Chapter 4

The store was more crowded the next morning. We had slept late and eaten a leisurely breakfast, so it was already past ten o'clock. I expected everybody to be working at one of the mines or prospecting, but I counted six seated around the stove and another two standing because there were no more chairs. Everyone held a china mug of coffee, and the conversation was animated. A couple of men in the back and another two at the counter explored the merchandise. Even during the day, the numerous lanterns made the store seem brighter than outside. It was also a very noisy establishment. Everyone seemed to be talking at once, drawers banged, and the bell on the door kept tinkling as men walked in and out.

The big bruiser who had challenged us the night before leaned nonchalantly against the same support beam. This time, instead of glaring at us, he wore an expression of appraisal. I assumed Mrs. Baker had assured him we meant her no harm.

One of the customers at the counter moved a bit, and I could see Mrs. Baker. I was stunned. She was prettier than I remembered. The floral dress that covered her completely from the chin down was so tight that I suspected someone had helped her into it. I hoped it was not a man. I remembered her as generally attractive but not stunning. As far as I could tell, she wore no makeup, and her auburn hair was pulled straight back into a bun. Maybe the simplicity showed off her features. She was probably in her late twenties, trim, and a bit alluring. From our previous encounters, I knew she could be frustratingly strong-willed. Then I realized why I was struck by her appearance. She was smiling. When we first met, we had argued. She had remained stern through our negotiation of her salary and ownership interest. To my recollection, I had never seen her smile. What a difference.

I glanced at Sharp and saw a smitten man. Damn, that might make things complicated.

"She looks pretty today," I offered.

"She was always pretty. Ya never looked before 'cuz ya were lovesick over Jenny."

As usual, Sharp was right. I had been infatuated with a girl in Nevada who had muddled my thinking until I came to see who she really was, instead of who I imagined her to be. Jenny was a young girl, while Mrs. Baker was definitely a woman—once married, but now widowed. Then I remembered that she came from an eastern social register family and was the type of woman I had come out west to escape. If Sharp wanted to chase her, he would get no interference from me.

Suddenly, I grew anxious. Sharp had walked

over to the big man. I followed, intent on stopping any trouble.

"Ya mention us to Mrs. Baker?" Sharp asked.

"Ah did."

"What'd she tell ya?"

He let a smirk slowly encompass his face.

"Said ah should leave you alone." His tone was arrogant.

"Too bad. Ain't been—"

"Jeff, let it be."

I offered my hand to the big man. "Steve Dancy."

He shook.

"This rude gent is Jeff Sharp."

"Ah'm Michael, but everybody calls me Tree."

"I can see why. What do you do for Mrs. Baker?"

"Ah protect her."

"Ya here all the time?" Sharp asked.

"Mostly. How else ah gonna protect her?"

"Much trouble hereabouts?"

"Nothin' I can't handle."

Tree wore a six-shooter in a cross-draw holster that allowed a long leather sap to hang along his right side. My bet was that he tended to club troublemakers rather than shoot them. He probably then unceremoniously dumped them in the street.

"Michael, can you handle the customers?" Mrs. Baker had come up from behind.

"Yes, ma'am." He nodded in my direction,

smiled provocatively at Sharp, and walked over to the counter.

She held out her hand to me and made steady eye contact.

"It's good to see you gentlemen again."

I shook her proffered hand and received a faint imitation of the smile I had admired earlier.

"I was hoping your return would not be delayed."

When she turned to Sharp, he leaned over and made a show of kissing her hand.

"I can assure ya, ma'am, the pleasure's all ours."

She pulled her hand back, but not in anger. "I hope you haven't gone soft, Mr. Sharp. I need a capable man, not some dandy."

Sharp chuckled. "I can assure ya, ma'am, I ain't gone soft . . . an' I'm thoroughly capable."

"Good. Because you need to protect your property."

She turned away from Sharp and gave me a purposeful look, but I had no idea to what purpose.

"There's a café around the corner on Chestnut Street. I suggest we talk there," she said.

As soon as I nodded, she yelled in the general direction of the counter. "Michael, take care of the shop. Henry should be here shortly." Then she whirled around and headed straight toward the door, grabbed a shawl from a hook, and threw it around her shoulders, without the slightest hesitation in her step.

We scrambled to catch up. Damn, she hadn't changed a bit. When we had first met, she was chief clerk at the best haberdashery in Leadville. She was sharp-witted, highly efficient, and above all, well organized. Her erect posture and stern bearing kept men at bay. Sharp saw a challenge in piercing that off-putting demeanor. I thought he should leave the woman alone and was a bit irked that he had made a sexual reference. It seems she had chosen to ignore it—or perhaps it simply didn't register with her businesslike mind.

We were wearing sheepskin coats, but I still braced against the chill. I wondered how Mrs. Baker kept warm with only a wool shawl, but her pace provided part of the answer.

After we caught up, she said, "What a beautiful summer day. It's good to feel the sun at last."

Officially, it was summer, but I sure didn't feel the sun. Since I had a bad habit of arguing with women, I kept my thoughts to myself. Sharp had sidled up beside her, so I walked behind on the narrow boardwalk. She walked fast, which was fine with me because I was eager to get to a private spot to ask about her curious comment. If someone was threatening the shop, I had even more reason to sell it. Damn it, I didn't need any more fights.

Although only a short block away, Chestnut Street was another world, where people with money lived, shopped, and found entertainment.

The brothels had been quarantined to State Street and respectable people kept away—or snuck over after dark. Our shop catered to prospectors instead of mine owners, Indians instead of gentry, and madams instead of church ladies. Mrs. Baker obviously was a draw for men, and I bet many spent more than they intended.

At mid-morning, the café was nearly empty. I had discovered that in the West, high-end cafés had square tables with chairs, while working-class eateries used long tables with benches. This was a high-end café. It was bright, cheery, and colorful, its light blue walls and blue-patterned china prearranged on the white covered tables. If the tables hadn't tipped me off, the carpet and gaslights would have. In fact, it may have been the first carpet I had encountered outside of an expensive hotel. In the East, good restaurants used carpet to soften the noise of people walking, but in the West—where men often wore jangly spurs—carpet was rare. On the plus side, hardwood floors made it difficult for a man to sneak up on you.

"Ya look radiant, Mrs. Baker," Sharp said as we scooted our chairs up to the table. "This high climate suits ya."

She gave an exasperated sigh and addressed me. "I'm glad you've come. I was afraid you were off on another adventure, and I might not see you again. I presume you've been pleased with my monthly reports and deposits."

"We have. Mrs. Baker, I'd like to continue with pleasantries, but your earlier comment bothered me. What did you mean when you said we needed to protect our property?"

"After we order."

She waved at a middle-aged woman wearing a full apron over a cheerful gingham dress.

"Mrs. Paul, I'd like a cup of tea and a plate of apple fritters."

Since we had already eaten breakfast, we just ordered coffee.

Sharp leaned toward Mrs. Baker and smiled conspiringly. "How do ya keep your fine figure eatin' fritters?"

"Mr. Sharp, if you think I normally take time off in the middle of the day, you're mistaken. I open the shop before daybreak and stay until late afternoon. On Henry's day off, I work until closing. We're here to discuss business, but that doesn't mean I can't enjoy a small pleasure while we talk." She eyed the kitchen door. "For your information, Mrs. Paul is a very good cook. You two could save a lot of money by eating here instead of that highfalutin hotel. And the shop is right around the corner, which will be convenient because I want to see more of you inside the shop until this business is behind us."

"What business?" I asked, exasperated with her delays.

She started to speak but turned to Sharp.

"Before we get to that, we might as well settle something else. Mr. Sharp, your flirtatious remarks are wasted on me. Despite your innumerable charms, you should know that I've heard every advance possible since my husband's death. I normally ignore them, but in your case, I believe you will persist until I become cross. I assure you, you do not want to see me cross, so please quit this silliness."

"Mrs. Baker, I can assure ya, I intended no silliness."

"You prove my point. Let me be blunt. You don't appeal to me. I'm sorry to say this, but even if you were twenty years younger, you still wouldn't appeal to me. I have no interest in having you court me . . . and I certainly do not want a liaison." She gave him a withering look. "Do I need to become rude?"

"No, ma'am." He looked genuinely contrite. "I'll respect yer wishes."

"Good."

I started laughing. It took me a moment to recover my composure. Finally, I said, "Jeff, I never saw you cowed by a woman before."

"Well, ya ain't known me all that long." He smiled shyly and nodded his head in my direction. "Please excuse my friend. He finds humor in the most inappropriate places."

Damn. He hadn't given up. He might no longer make crude innuendos, but he was still going to apply whatever charm he possessed to get what he wanted. I thought that "twenty years" comment would have taken him aback, but the man was intractable.

I wanted to get to business.

"Mrs. Baker, can you explain your comments about our mutual property?"

She glanced over my shoulder. "In a moment."

Mrs. Paul arrived with a tray. After she distributed cups, she placed a small plate in front of Mrs. Baker. The aroma from the apple fritters made me want to grab one. They looked as good as they smelled: three round, crispy pastries showered with a generous amount of powdered sugar. Sharp and I immediately ordered our own plates.

Mrs. Paul grinned. "All I have to do is bring one plate to any table in the room, and the aroma gets me orders from every customer. That's why I cook each order fresh."

After she left to fill our order, I said, "You're both good businesswomen."

"Thank you. We're friends, by the way." After pouring cream and then tea into her cup, she shifted in her chair to turn slightly in my direction.

"Mr. Dancy, you ran a shop in New York City. Did you ever encounter protection gangs?"

"Of course."

"That problem has been exported to our fine city. There's a gang led by a man named Hugo

Kelly. They demand weekly payments for their supposed protection." She nibbled at a fritter and waited to see my reaction.

"I never paid in New York. My family was tightly connected to Tammany Hall. Gangs preyed on the weak . . . shopkeepers without any other recourse."

"Like myself," she responded.

I sipped my coffee to stall a moment. I didn't want to get into another fight to protect something I no longer wanted to own. On the other hand, running away seemed cowardly. I discarded that thought immediately. I had proved my mettle. Now it was time to prove my smarts.

"Jeff and I have been talking about selling the store."

"Steve's done all the talkin'," Sharp quickly said. "I argued to keep the store. Steve—"

"Oh, no you don't." Mrs. Baker crossed her arms and glared at me. "I put too much hard work into that store. We have a deal. I could have waited until the second year to make improvements, but I jumped right in. I made it more difficult to double profits the second year, but I can still do it. Now you tell me you want to sell. You're taking advantage of me . . . worse than those gangs. What am I supposed to do? Beg for my old job at that haberdashery?"

"Mrs. Baker, I apologize, but I don't want to get into a brawl with a gang." I pulled the papers from my pocket. "But you're right about the fine way you managed the store." I handed the papers to her. "This contract assigns an additional ten percent of the store to you. Jeff and I believe you've already earned it and shouldn't have to wait another year."

She looked askance at me and then read the document carefully. Laying it aside, she seemed thoughtful.

"That's a generous gesture, but the store will never sell for enough that even twenty percent would let me do what I want. Kelly has State Street in a vise. It's his personal fiefdom. After the brothels, he captured the more legitimate businesses on State. Now he's moving up from the bottom of Chestnut Street toward the rich end of town." She gestured toward the kitchen. "Almost everything Mrs. Paul earns goes to Kelly and his thugs. I started by paying him fifteen dollars a week, and then he upped it to twenty-five. Now he wants seventy. If I pay that, he'll want a hundred. Michael has helped me hold his thugs at bay, but most of the other businesses have already caved to higher fees."

She looked me directly in the eye.

"The point is, gentlemen, everybody in town knows about Kelly, so no one will pay a reasonable price for the store."

I wondered what she wanted to do and how much money it would take. Sharp interrupted my thoughts by asking, "Ya mean yer already payin' the bastard?"

She gave him an exasperated look. "I pay him twenty-five dollars a week. I stalled as long as I could, but in the end, I didn't have a choice."

She sat back and put her hands on her hips.

"Neither of you were around to help."

"So Tree ain't as tough as he looks." Sharp sounded triumphant.

The glare she turned on Sharp would have wilted freshly cut flowers.

"Mr. Sharp, this is our store, not his. He wants to take on the Kelly people, but I refuse to send a man to an early grave for seven dollars a week. His sole job is to protect me from physical harm. The store is not his concern." She started to shift toward me, then whirled back on him. "And do not use foul language with me. Do you understand?"

"Yes, ma'am."

Sharp looked embarrassed. She had already read the contract, and I was sure this was not going the way he had intended.

To avoid further argument, I said, "Mrs. Baker, I'm beginning to understand. Kelly's plan from the beginning was to head up Chestnut Street. He started where it would be easy—where good people would ignore what was happening. Unfortunately, if he's going to make the rich pay, he can't let anyone off the hook."

"Correct. The real money is with the expensive hotels, saloons, and shops." She shook her head. "You've got to give him credit. Kelly figured a way to get rich without getting his hands dirty from digging in black soil."

"Police?"

"The police are paid off . . . as well as the town council. He used the easy money from the brothels to finance his early moves. Now he needs better men, so he's squeezing us for more cash. It's a good plan. His gang gets stronger by the day."

"Surely the Chestnut Street business owners see him coming," I said. "They must be taking action."

She shrugged. "They don't confide in me, but I suspect you're right. If they have a plan, it doesn't include helping us on State Street. My strategy has been to stall until Kelly got in over his head and stronger men took him to task."

I looked at Sharp. "Jeff?"

"With Tree, there's three of us. Let's give that small-time bandit a dose of his own medicine. Hell . . . I mean heck, I haven't had a good fight since we handled that last gang in Leadville."

"Fisticuffs don't count?"

He chuckled. "Not if they don't fight back."

"Make no mistake," Mrs. Baker said. "Hugo Kelly will fight back."

Chapter 5

The three of us signed the contract for her additional ownership interest, and over fritters and coffee, we agreed to resist the Kelly gang. I was reluctant at first, but in the end, I couldn't allow some small-time crook to steal my property. Kelly knew the routine for a protection racket: Early on, make an example of a few, and then other merchants will fear resisting. So far, there had been property damage, a few beatings, and the rumored murder of a brothel madam. I was afraid this could turn frightening for Mrs. Baker, but she seemed as eager as Sharp for a fight.

She told us the collector came on Wednesdays, which was the next day, and we decided to pay up this week to gain time to strike some kind of arrangement with the merchants on Chestnut Street. If I could convince them to unite, a fight might be avoided, especially if we had a strong show of force. My first task would be to send a telegram to Captain Joseph McAllen of the Pinkerton National Detective Agency. Sharp and I agreed to hire a team of six Pinkertons, even if it meant cutting deep into our profits from selling the store. We told ourselves it was principle that drove us, but we both knew we just didn't like losing to a bunch of shiftless ruffians.

Mrs. Baker accompanied us over to the Western Union office. When we returned to the store, Tree was talking angrily to two mean-looking men. I noticed that Henry, looking frightened, kept both hands flat on the counter. He didn't want to provoke the thugs. As we approached the knot of men, Sharp gently pushed Mrs. Baker in the opposite direction.

"Have the rest of it tomorrow, or we take it out in trade with yer boss. No more stallin'."

"Do that, and I'll have to kill ya," Sharp said evenly.

The man who had been talking went for his gun handle as he whipped around. Lucky for him he didn't pull it, because I had my gun in his face before he had completed the turn. The click of the cocking hammer sounded as loud as a church bell on a quiet Sunday morning.

For a moment, nobody moved. The two men were tall, trim, and young—probably not much older than twenty. They would be no match for Tree in close quarters, but my guess was they would stay out of arm's reach and fight with guns. They both needed haircuts, shaves, and a bath. They stunk up the store. What bothered me was their eyes, which showed no fear. They probably weren't brave; their fearlessness almost certainly came from being members of a dangerous gang. In fact, that was the purpose of a gang. You didn't need to be brave because you brutalized ordinary citizens with overpowering numbers. If you were a coward, being in a gang made you feel protected. At least, I preferred to think that these men were really cowards behind the bravado.

"Put that gun away, greenhorn. Ya don't have the guts to use it."

"That would be news to some," Sharp said with a chuckle.

Sharp seemed amused, but I was annoyed that even these thickheaded toughs could tell I wasn't native to the West. Hell, I had been out here nearly two years and felt more like a westerner than a city dweller.

Irritated, I put the gun under his chin and tilted his head up. "Take the twenty-five dollars. You don't get any more money until the summer trade is stronger. If that's not good enough for you, I can solve the problem with lead instead of silver."

"Who the hell do ya think ya are?" he asked, still unafraid.

"A nightmare, my friend," Sharp answered. "We have an interest in this store, an' our money comes first. Tell yer boss he's at the back of the line."

Tree took a half step. "Wait a min—"

"Shut up." Sharp pointed at Tree to emphasis his point. He turned back to the two men. "Git the hell out of this shop. And tell ol' Hugo we want to see him."

"Hugo ain't old." This came from the one without a gun under his chin.

"Then tell yer youngster boss we want to see him. We gotta make an arrangement. Both of us can't milk the same cow."

"Mr. Kelly don't share."

"Hell, ya say."

Sharp pretended to think that over as he rubbed his chin.

"Since he don't share, hand me back that twenty-five dollars. We'll keep it all."

"No . . . and we'll be back tomorrow for forty-five dollars more. If it ain't forthcomin', we can't protect you. Who knows, maybe some irate miner will toss lit dynamite into this here store."

"Steve, put yer gun under this man's chin and see if he still talks brave."

Before I could react, Tree swung his sap and hit the man in the temple. He went down like a marionette with its strings cut. Tree looked at Sharp and said, "Shuts him up faster."

"Indeed," Sharp said.

I holstered my gun with my right hand as I used my left to slip the gun out of my opponent's holster. He actually reached for it. I held it in front of his face to show him why his holster was empty. In the West, stealing a man's gun was a major offense, but taking his bullets was seen as just being cautious. Using two hands, I cycled the ejector rod so fast, bullets fell to the floor like a broken jar of jawbreakers. I shoved the empty gun into his chest, and his hands automatically came up to grab it.

"Now pick up yer partner and git," Sharp said.

He holstered his empty gun and dragged the unconscious man by the armpits out the door.

"Hold on there," I yelled. The man hesitated at the door. "Tell Mr. Kelly we'll be by to see him tomorrow. We'll work out a deal for the summer. No need to start a war over a few dollars."

When the door closed behind them, I told Tree, "That was theater. We're on Mrs. Baker's side."

He looked satisfied.

"Will they come back?" I asked.

He thought about it. "Ah think Kelly will wait until he talks to you. He'll want to keep any rebellion quiet. But when you meet, he'll have more men than you can handle." Tree looked almost sympathetic. "You'll be walkin' into a beatin' at the very least."

"That's the way I figure it," Sharp added. "They can't let this stand."

Mrs. Baker joined us. "I'm not sure that was the best way to handle the situation."

"Maybe not." I looked at the closed door and then back at Sharp. "Jeff, what should we do?"

"Stall until we get reinforcements."

"How?"

45

"Buy our way out tomorrow. Pay the whole seventy dollars. Do it in a way so that it's a victory for Kelly. It's only five hours by train from Denver. McAllen can be here tomorrow afternoon."

"Assuming he's in Denver."

"Assuming he's in Denver," Sharp agreed.

Chapter 6

The next day we headed for Kelly's office. After asking around, we discovered it was less than a block from the Carbonate Hotel. He was sending a message by placing his office in the heart of the wealthiest district in Leadville. Since we didn't expect serious trouble, Sharp and I left Tree to protect Mrs. Baker. On this visit, both parties would be gauging each other. Real trouble would come later. At least, that was our hope.

Kelly's office was on the first floor of a four-story brick building. An unadorned private entrance displayed only a brass address number on a black lacquered door. The remainder of the building front was a woman's apparel shop, its large windows filled with the latest fashions.

A thug we hadn't seen before leaned against a lamppost, obviously watching the comings and goings on the street. Sharp walked right up to him.

"Tell Mr. Kelly the fellas from the general store on State Street are here to see him."

After an appraising look, he entered the building without a word. He returned shortly, held the lacquered door open, and waved us through. The small front and side windows were shaded, but the inside was bright with gaslights. There must have been six lamps, and the hiss from the jets reminded me of a rattlesnake ready to strike.

On the other side of a waist-high barrier sat a red-headed man in his twenties. Even seated, I could tell he was tall, but he was lanky rather than thick like Tree. Two other men sat attentively nearby on office chairs, while a third walked forward to open the gate for us. He smirked as he nodded for us to pass through. I did not have the feeling this was a welcoming gesture.

Dispensing with niceties, the redhead said, "You two are either dumb as a rock or foolhardy. I should beat you to within an inch of your lives."

"We're new to town," Sharp said. "Came to see ya because we don't want trouble."

Kelly's accent was familiar. It was New York Irish, probably second generation. He was just another young man come west, but he had brought a rotten piece of New York culture with him. A protection racket was one of the common ways the strong preyed on the weak or vulnerable. Shopkeepers were not necessarily weak, but they were vulnerable because they owned exposed property. Thugs threatened to destroy years of work and accumulated savings unless they received a cut of the profits. These lazy louts demanded that they be given what another man had earned. Even worse, police became accomplices for a little cash slipped into their outstretched hands.

"Did you bring the rest of my seventy dollars?" Kelly demanded.

Sharp shook his head in bewilderment. "No, sir. We agreed upon twenty-five. Seventy seems a sharp increase."

"Your end of town is a hotbed of crime. Murderers, robbers, Indians, swindlers, whores . . . God knows what else. We keep your property safe and your limbs unbroken. No one messes with a business we protect."

"We ain't had any problems," Sharp said.

"Because Mrs. Baker wisely bought our services. But it's expensive to protect a rough-and-tumble town like this, so we need an adjustment." He stood to show us his full size. "What's this to you, anyway?"

"We loaned Mrs. Baker money," Sharp answered. "She's been short in her payments. Says she's gotta pay ya first."

"Smart woman. Leadville's dangerous. She's an attractive woman in a town full of lonely men. We protect her . . . and your investment."

"With this sloppy bunch?" I spoke for the first time.

The two seated men were instantly on their feet, and I could feel the one behind us take a step forward. The room was suddenly tense.

Kelly held up the flat of his hand. "Relax, boys. These are clients." He turned his attention to me.

"I apologize for being impolite. I'm Hugo

Kelly. What're your names?" His voice was non-threatening, but he made no attempt to shake hands.

"Steve Dancy." I nodded to my left. "This is Jeff Sharp."

"Well, Mr. Dancy, I understand you were unkind to my men yesterday. I'm going to let that go because they were errand boys, and you were unfamiliar with our arrangement. This town has attracted a nasty element that preys on hard-working folk. The police are useless. They arrive late, and they have no interest in chasing down criminals after the fact. It's really quite dis-heartening. That's where we step in. We work hard to maintain a highly professional reputation—professional, but tough. Wrongdoers do not want to face us, so they assault someone outside our protective circle." His condescending expression turned hard. "No one in his right mind wants to go to war with my marshals."

Sharp responded. "Please excuse my hotheaded young friend. We want no war. But twenty-five dollars a week seems fair for keepin' trouble from knockin' on our door."

"The price is seventy dollars." Kelly walked over to me. When we stood nose to nose, he said, "Seventy dollars. Bargaining ended when you put a gun to my man's head."

I wanted to put my gun in his gut, but we had agreed to stall for time. After McAllen arrived, we could easily take care of Kelly. No sense getting him overly riled until then.

I tried to look cowed. "Jeff, I've got forty dollars. You?"

"Yep, I got five."

"You have a hearing problem. I want seventy dollars. The twenty-five I got yesterday was a fine for busting my man's head open."

Without further comment, we handed over the money to Kelly, who painstakingly counted it, then relished passing the money back and forth between his left and right hand as he stared at us.

"Are you from New York?" I asked, to break the silence.

"Born and bred. On the hard streets. Why?"

"I'm from New York also. You went to Catholic school?" His expression turned quizzical, so I added, "Your diction."

"The sisters taught me well."

"It seems you didn't pay attention to all of the sisters' lessons."

There was a flash of anger. He glanced over my shoulder and made the slightest of nods. It was enough to give me warning, and I dodged a blow from behind. I grabbed the swinging arm up high and pulled him forward, using his momentum to throw him to the floor. He was holding a nasty looking blackjack.

We all stood around staring at each other. I felt relief no one had gone for a gun, but that didn't mean we would be allowed to leave the office unscathed. Sharp had a knack for fighting. He unerringly read opponents, and in a fistfight, he usually put them on the ground with a single blow. I had been in my share of scrapes in New York City, but I didn't have Sharp's strength to end a match quickly. What happened next would be Kelly's decision.

It took him a long time to come to a decision, but he finally said, "Go." It was a command.

As we approached the door, Kelly added, "Seventy dollars each week. If you accost any of my men again, very unpleasant things will happen to you, your store . . . and Mrs. Baker."

We left his office without rebuttal.

Chapter 7

As soon as we were on the street, Sharp snapped, "Did ya need to challenge him so direct?"

"I wanted to find out how tough he was . . . and how smart."

"What'd ya learn?"

"He's a pretty standard bully, but smarter. He wanted to teach us a lesson. When the first attempt didn't work, he could have overwhelmed us, but didn't. I don't think he wanted to risk gunplay in his office. He keeps his emotions in check."

"Agreed. There's more than brute force in that man." Sharp pointed at a saloon. "Parched. How 'bout a beer?"

There was a large window on one side of the saloon door painted with the words *Lucky Prospector*. The other window was boarded up with fresh lumber. I wanted to find out if the window had been shattered in a brawl or by Kelly's men as a warning.

"Sounds good. We better drink fast or Mrs. Baker will worry."

Sharp laughed. "I can finish two before ya see the bottom of yer glass."

He was right, of course. I had never seen anyone who could gulp down a beer faster than Sharp. It was like he never swallowed, just poured it straight down. As Sharp ordered three beers, two for him and one for me, I looked around. The large room seemed dark, but I guessed that was partly due to the boarded-up window. The owners probably waited until dark to turn on the gaslights. The saloon was expensively finished with dark wood, bright brass, and huge mirrors, but the centerpiece was the long bar, a masterwork of wood carved with lion heads, palmettes, and curlicues. The brass boot rail glistened as if polished each time a customer removed his foot. In no time at all, three beers slid down the bar's oiled surface into our waiting hands. I took my first sip, thinking this was a refined establishment.

When the barkeep wiped his way to our end of the bar, I asked, "May I see the owner?"

"Owners. The three of them are sitting at that table." He nodded behind us.

I saluted the barkeep with my glass. "Thanks."

Sharp emptied his first glass, gave a big sigh, and wiped his mouth on his sleeve. As I turned around, he followed holding his second beer.

I walked around the table to the empty chair on the other side and noticed the barkeep keeping a wary eye on us.

"Gentlemen, my name is Steve Dancy and this is Jeff Sharp. We own an interest in the general store at the end of State Street. Could we have a few moments of your time?"

"On what subject?"

The man who spoke wore an expensive suit that could have been tailored in the East. The other two were similarly dressed, but their suits had shiny elbows, and their vests showed stains from meals long gone by. I heard a chair scrape behind me and realized these men had more than a barkeep watching out for them.

I decided not to beat around the bush.

"Hugo Kelly."

"What's your interest in that general store? I thought Mrs. Baker owned it."

"Not entirely."

"Have a seat. Your friend can grab a chair from another table."

We sat down with our beers, and I noticed the three owners were drinking black coffee. There was a general round of introductions. The well-dressed man was named White, and the other two were Carter and Wilson. There were several ways to approach the subject, but since directness had worked so far, I decided to continue to be straightforward.

"We just arrived in town to check on our investment with Mrs. Baker. Two men came into the store and demanded protection money—seventy dollars a week. Mrs. Brown had been paying them twenty-five. Evidently, once you show a willingness to pay, the tariff goes up."

There was a knowing glance between White and

the other two. White directed his question at me. "Why do you want to talk to us?"

"Have you heard about Kelly's protection racket?" After receiving a nod, I continued. "We understand he's moving from State to Chestnut Street. If we band together, we should be able to send them all packing."

"We have enough protection of our own."

Sharp pointed at the boarded-up window. "Looks like ya had some trouble already."

"Probably a drunk."

"Perhaps," I said noncommittally. I made a point of looking at the unbroken window on the other side of the door. It was painted with the saloon name in an arc with the words *Dancing Girls* underneath. "Glass that large is hard to come by. Then you'll need a skilled letter painter."

White suddenly looked suspicious. "Do you work for Kelly?"

"No." This came from Carter. "I recognize these men. They bought that general store last fall. Mrs. Baker took it over a bit later."

He leaned over the table toward us. "You two captured Bob Grant and his gang of ore thieves. Killed a bunch too."

"No more than we had to." Sharp got testy when accused of killing.

"Didn't say you did." He settled back in his chair. "You were town heroes."

"We didn't do it for the town," Sharp answered, with only a little less irritation.

Everyone stared at everyone else. Finally, White said, "You think Kelly's boys broke our window?"

"Yes . . . and so do you."

"That's why we're sitting here." White took a drink of his coffee. "We're trying to figure out if we could handle them. He's got lots of men. Mean brutes. Maybe eight or ten work for Kelly, but he hires shiftless miners to do small jobs. People have even whispered about a murder. A woman. The rumor is the madam at the Nuptial House refused to pay, and they killed her as an example. Supposedly she was shot by an angry miner, but he did jobs for Kelly. Got clean away. Somehow there was a fresh horse waiting just outside the door. He was never known to own a horse before."

"I'm from New York, like Kelly," I said. "He's running a standard protection racket. They make an example out of someone early. Scare the hell out of all the other merchants. Breaking windows is a calling card. Just a little incentive to listen when they come to call." I took a sip of beer. "By the way, that will be today. They probably would have been here already, but we caused a bit of a problem and messed up their schedule."

"What'd you do?"

"Yesterday, we clubbed one of their errand boys. We just returned from seeing Kelly at his office. He was less than cordial."

All three faces showed surprise. White spun around and checked the door and then scanned the rest of the saloon. "You attacked one of his men? Damn it, they'll take retribution against you and anyone associated with you. Please leave. Now!"

I stood slowly. "Come and see us when you get tired of working for Kelly. Once you give in, he *will* bleed you dry."

I calmly finished the last swallow of my beer and set the glass down on the table.

Sharp gulped a half glass and snapped his heavy mug onto the table. "Yer fools. Ain't no talkin' with this bunch. Fight or pay. Those are yer choices."

We walked out knowing every eye in the saloon was following us. When we got to the street, it suddenly occurred to me that Kelly might be inclined to bushwhack us. I looked nervously around but didn't see anything threatening. I wanted to get off the street anyway, so I started walking at a fast pace in the direction of the store.

"They'll join us," Sharp said, a little out of breath as he sprinted to keep up.

"Right. After their greed overcomes their fear. That may be too late for us. We need to talk to other merchants. If they're going after saloons that have hired enforcers, they've already gotten others to knuckle under. This has gone further than I thought."

Sharp remained quiet a few paces and then said,

"Steve, we need a better plan. Kelly's not goin' to give us enough time for McAllen to arrive."

"My thoughts exactly." I gave him a glance. "Think you can hire some decent men?"

"Yep. Get to it right after we see Mrs. Baker."

"Start carrying your rifle." Sharp always preferred a Winchester to a pistol.

"Been thinkin' on that. It's back at the hotel."

"We'll check on the store, borrow you a rifle, and go back to the hotel to get your Winchester."

"Mrs. Baker?"

"Thinking on it."

Chapter 8

The shop was busy when we returned, and my first thought was that more people meant safety. Then I noticed tension. Sharp did as well and immediately moved away from me to the other side of the store. The more we were spread apart, the harder it would be to get the drop on both of us. Henry was behind the counter helping a tough-looking man. Two others were doing a poor job of pretending to examine merchandise. Tree leaned against his support post as usual but failed to acknowledge us. That had to be a signal. More worrisome, Mrs. Baker was nowhere to be seen.

As I approached the counter, Sharp walked up the aisle where soft goods were displayed. I wore my Colt in a holster at my side, but Sharp was unarmed unless he was carrying his knife, which he normally concealed in the small of his back.

When I reached Henry, I noticed that he was not talking to the supposed customer, confirming that these men worked for Kelly. I stepped behind the counter like I owned the place. The sawed-off shotgun was not in its normal position under the counter. I scooted behind Henry, picked up a box of shells, and then pulled a Winchester from a rack behind the counter. I had the attention of every man in the store except Sharp, who continued to walk toward the blanket-covered door that led to a storage room.

The man on the other side of the counter said, "You try to load that rifle, I'll kill you."

I laid the rifle and box of ammunition on the counter. "Not a chance in hell. Maybe one of your friends over there . . . but not you. If you move, I'm the one who'll be doing the killing."

His left eye flinched but otherwise, he remained as still as the wooden Indian outside. These were not errand boys like the first two men. This was an ambush. In fact, I had a strong dislike for the man in front of me. He was the worst type of bully. He enjoyed causing fear.

Now what? I had a rifle, but Sharp was forty feet away . . . and the rifle was unloaded. This supposed gunman wouldn't hesitate for long, and although Sharp held the attention of the other two, they wouldn't remain distracted if the man yelled out or they heard gunfire. I had to divert the attention of the man in front of me.

In a loud voice, I called, "Tree, where's Mrs. Baker?"

He didn't answer. He looked nervous, too nervous for a man who claimed he could handle any trouble. The man in front of me turned his head and gave Tree what I presumed was a warning glance. As he returned his attention to me, I grabbed him by the hair and slammed his face onto the counter. As his head bounced up, I grabbed the rifle and rammed the barrel into the middle of his chest. He immediately bent forward, holding his face with both hands as he gasped for breath. I flipped the rifle over and drove the butt into his forehead. He collapsed to the floor.

When I looked up, somehow Sharp had moved ten feet from where I had last seen him. He held a knife to the throat of a second man. That left only the third. He and I stared at each other. He was alone now and unsure what to do. While I held his eyes, I inserted three cartridges into the rifle that was still in my hands. I continued to lock eyes with this third man as I chambered a round by cocking the rifle. I slowly lifted the Winchester until the butt was seated to my shoulder.

Sharp whispered, "Tree?"

Tree pointed to the back room and held up two fingers. Next, he stepped over to the man I had the rifle trained on and deftly smacked him with his sap. He caught the unconscious man under both armpits and noiselessly lowered him to the floor. Sharp used his knife butt to do the same to his man. Those on the other side of the blanket must have heard a racket and some odd noises, but since no one had called out, they probably weren't sure what had happened out here.

I lowered the hammer on the Winchester and threw the rifle to Tree. I pointed at Sharp. He understood and tossed it on to Sharp, who caught it with both hands. I held up three fingers, and he nodded understanding that there were only three cartridges loaded in the rifle. He slid close to the blanket-covered doorway. I saw the blanket move. Someone was peeking out to see what had happened. He got a rifle butt in the head. Before he hit the ground, Sharp brought the rifle around and used the barrel to shove the curtain aside. He stepped into the doorway, rifle at the ready.

"Let her go an' ya live," he said.

"Tree!" I pointed at the men on the floor as I rushed toward the backroom door. He drew his pistol, loaded it, and took a position where he could see all of the men. Evidently, they had made him unload his revolver as part of the ambush. They must not have known that his most lethal weapon was the sap.

When I got to the doorway, I held back. Sharp had not entered the storeroom, and the entryway was too small for both of us. I moved to the side but couldn't get a look inside. Damn. I saw no way to help.

"Let the hammer down an' drop it. Ya can leave with yer friends."

"Move back. I'm coming out with her."

"No."

"What da ya mean, no? I'll kill her."

"Maybe, but yer brains'll be splattered all over our merchandise. Don't really want that." He hesitated. "Do you?"

There was a long silence. Then, "How do I know you'll let me go?"

"We didn't kill none of yer friends."

"I don't know that."

"I'm not in a talkin' mood," Sharp said. "Decide."

It was so quiet, I heard the hammer release and then the gun clatter to the floor. I was surprised by the intensity of my relief.

Sharp lowered the rifle and slowly backed up. The man who came out of the storeroom was thick but not much over five feet. He looked warily between us. I holstered my gun and hooked a thumb toward the door. That was all he needed. With barely a glance at his fallen brethren, he raced out of the shop.

Sharp entered the storeroom, finally giving me enough room to get a look at the situation. Mrs. Baker was ashen. He leaned the rifle against the wall and started to extend an arm toward her. With a quick motion, she ducked his arm and ran to me. Before I realized what was happening, her head lay on my shoulder, and our arms encircled one another. Sharp first looked bewildered, then annoyed. I was just confused.

Chapter 9

Mrs. Baker lifted her head from my shoulder, but our arms were still around each other. There were no tears, but she looked terrified. I asked if she was all right. She nodded and then surprised me by saying, "I discovered I may not be ready for war. Is it too late to buy peace?"

"That's not yer decision," Sharp said irritably.

"It's twenty percent my decision. What do you think, Steve?"

Was she trying to play the two of us against each other? If so, this was a side of Mrs. Baker I had never seen before. She had always been tough, but never manipulative.

"Jeff and I are together," I answered.

She pushed me away. "No . . . I . . . you misunderstood. I just want to know what you think."

"I think it's too late. Kelly has to bring us to heel, or he's done in this town. He won't back down for money."

"What'll we do?" she asked. "He has more men. Some are killers. Ruthless. Like the one who held a gun to my head."

"He was a ruthless killer?" Sharp asked derisively. "That little man who ran away without even givin' his friends a glance?"

Mrs. Baker whirled around. "How many killers

65

do you know with a sterling character? He bossed those men. And they were afraid of him. That man enjoys killing . . . especially women. Some believe he murdered a good customer of mine who ran one of the houses down the street."

"That's why you're so scared?" I asked. "I heard the murderer was a hardscrabble miner."

She spun back toward me. "He was a scapegoat. The girls told me that little man did the shooting, and the miner was paid to run so he'd look like the killer."

She pushed herself away from me. "Don't you think I had good reason to be scared? He held a gun to my head, whispering vile things. If you hadn't come along, no telling what would've happened."

She swung back to Sharp. "What the hell took you so long anyway?"

"We talked to some merchants," I answered quickly. I didn't want Sharp to say we stopped for beer. "Tried to get allies. This will be easier with friends."

"Besides, they were waitin' for us," Sharp added. "Nothin' was gonna happen till we got here."

She whirled again toward Sharp but sputtered for a moment. We had to get out of this tight storage room. I exited, assuming they would follow, but instead I heard her angry stammer.

"You call fondling nothing!"

"No, ma'am. I didn't know. I apologize."

"You damn well should." She stormed out, cursing under her breath.

Tree was still keeping an eye on the men we had bludgeoned. They were either playing possum or still unconscious. She looked them over, and I had the impression she was disappointed they were still breathing. She used her foot to nudge the one Tree had sapped, but he wasn't getting off the floor anytime soon.

"Michael, what do you think we should do with these three?"

"Kill 'em." But he was smiling to show he wasn't entirely serious.

"Not his decision," Sharp said sharply.

"Well, isn't this great? You abandoned the store to my care, then suddenly come riding back into town, demanding to make all the decisions." She almost charged at him. "Okay, Mr. Sharp, what do we do with these men?"

Sharp unconsciously backed up half a step. If the situation hadn't been serious, I would have laughed at his discomfort. I expected him to be at a loss for words, but he immediately came back with an answer.

"We strip 'em naked an' throw 'em in the street."

Now I did laugh. All three of them turned on me. There didn't appear to be much appreciation for the absurdity of Sharp's suggestion. Then I caught his expression and realized he was serious. After a moment's thought, I decided it was a good idea. It would do no good to deliver them over to the police, because the chief and constables were in Kelly's pocket. They were trying to intimidate us—or possibly worse. We might as well send a return message. These three might even be embarrassed enough to leave town or withdraw from the fight.

"I'll take the one by the counter," I said, smiling.

I leaned down, unhooked his holster, and unbuttoned his braces. After I got his boots, pants, and shirt off, I yelled, "Long johns or buck naked?"

"Buck naked," Sharp answered. Then I heard him laugh, which meant we had overcome the tension of the prior moment.

In short order, we had all three of the desperados completely undressed. Looking up, I noticed that Mrs. Baker was unembarrassed. She collected the lice-ridden clothes, boots, holsters, and other articles, except for the guns and knives, and threw them all in a heap by the storeroom. Then she stood arms akimbo and examined the three men still lying on her floor. None had yet regained consciousness.

"Michael, please drag these good-for-nothings into the middle of the street. Let the whole town gawk at them. Then burn their things before they smell up my store."

"With pleasure, ma'am."

As Tree busied himself with his task, I approached Mrs. Baker.

"We need to talk."

"Now?"

"Yes, now. Before Kelly makes his next move."

"I think we're well beyond talking." There was still a lot of anger in her voice.

I tried to look sympathetic but firm.

"We're in the thick of it and we need a plan. For the plan to work, we need to know what's gone on up till now. All of it."

She walked over to the stove in the center of the store, shook a teakettle to see if it held water, and placed it on the hot plate. She opened the cast iron door and threw in a couple of pieces of wood. When Tree returned for another of the unconscious men, she told him to put out the closed sign and lock the door. After she had settled into one of the wooden captain chairs, Sharp and I followed suit.

"Why didn't you tell anyone you had co-owners?" I asked.

"What? Why's that important?" she asked.

"Everybody in town thinks you own this store outright. If we are going to convince the other business owners to band together, they need to know we have a stake in this fight. Just tell us, so we understand."

Looking exasperated, she explained.

"Unless you're running one of the houses down the street, you get no respect as a woman in business, at least not in this town. If men thought I owned this store, they didn't question my orders for merchandise or prices." She glanced toward the door, where Tree kept an eye on the street . . . and probably the crowd gathering around the curiosities. "And I got more respect from my employees."

"When did this business with Kelly start?" Sharp asked.

"About six weeks ago. Kelly's men came to see me. They offered to protect the store and my person for fifteen dollars a week. I didn't like it, but the price was low so I went along. Next thing I know, they wanted twenty-five dollars. Now seventy. They'll never quit until they've sucked all the profit out of the store." She looked between us. "That's about it."

"Has anyone successfully resisted Kelly?" I asked.

"Not that I'm aware of. Early on, one of the madams told him to go to hell, and she ended up dead. No one protested after that . . . until now."

"How many Leadville businesses are under his thumb?" Sharp asked.

"My guess is all of State Street and some on Chestnut. He started with the whorehouses. Nobody cared. Then the liveries, general stores, and cafés. I think he's ready to go after the saloons, hotels, and restaurants."

"Judgin' by the reaction we got at the Lucky

Prospector, I think yer right," Sharp said. "Do ya know how many men he's got?"

"I'm not sure. It seems like the number keeps growing. I'd guess about a dozen of what he calls marshals . . . maybe another dozen down-and-out miners."

"Have you talked to anyone else who's fed up with Kelly?" I asked.

"Mrs. Paul."

"Does Mrs. Paul have a husband?"

"No."

"Then I don't think she can help," I said off-handedly.

She immediately bristled. "If that's your attitude, you're out of luck. Almost all the businesses already under Kelly's thumb are run by women."

"You mean brothels?" I asked.

"The brothels, this store, Mrs. Paul's café, the seamstresses next door, the fortune-tellers, and even the ice cream parlor. All women."

She looked ready to explode. For some reason, she was offended that I thought Mrs. Paul couldn't help. What did she think a bunch of women could do? Her comment held another surprise for me. It seemed that most of the State Street businesses were run by women. This was supposed to be the dangerous part of town. Raunchy men looking for cheap goods and cheap women. How did these women survive?

"The brothels hire men to keep order, right?" Sharp asked.

"That's right. Many have an interest in the house."

"Ya have Tree. Any other businesses hire men?" Sharp asked.

She thought a minute. "Mrs. Paul's son and another man help in the kitchen. George works the desk for the fortune-tellers. I think only the seamstresses work alone."

This sounded more promising to me. "These men might make a small army. Kelly will move fast. I don't have time to make convincing arguments to saloon owners. Do you think these men will fight?"

"Mr. Steve Dancy, the women are ready to fight. Do you think only men can take on Kelly?"

"It's going to get rough. Possibly even gunplay."

"If you remember, you gave me shooting lessons. I kept up my practicing."

"Damn it, you could get hurt."

She became rigid as a plank. "Bravery is not the exclusive domain of men."

I thought about what she had said and how she said it.

"You've already held meetings and organized the women, haven't you?"

"Did you expect me to wait for you to wander into town and save the day for us helpless females?"

"How many men will join?" Sharp asked.

"Tree, some of the men in the brothels, Mrs. Paul's son."

"How many?" Sharp repeated.

"Ten . . . counting the two of you. Many of the women know how to handle a rifle or six-shooter, and we can all wield a club."

We needed a meeting of everyone who was willing to fight. Speed was crucial. We spent the next ten minutes making a rough plan and deciding who would alert which business. Sharp would escort Mrs. Baker to the brothels, while Tree and I would start on Chestnut Street and then move up State until we ran into each other.

"Any last questions?" I asked.

"Yep," Sharp said. "Mrs. Baker, are ya sweet on Steve?"

At first she looked startled by the question and then somehow relieved. As she stood to leave, she looked directly at me. "Perhaps. Let's go."

Chapter 10

Before we left, I grabbed Sharp by the elbow and guided him to the back of the store. He looked amused.

"Why did you ask her that?" I demanded.

" 'Cuz yer too dumb to ask yerself. 'Sides, I needed to know before I made a fool of myself. Don't do any good to chase a woman that's got her eye on someone else."

"She doesn't have her eye on me."

"I think she just said she did." He seemed very pleased with himself.

"She said perhaps."

"There's no perhaps in love."

"Love!"

I paced back and forth in the narrow aisle between the soft goods and canned food. Finally, I stopped in front of Sharp.

"She's a moneyed easterner from a damn socialite family. I came west to get away from that type of woman."

"The West scrubbed the gentleman off ya. Ya ain't the same no more. Same can be said for her. 'Sides, she alienated her family. Sound familiar?"

This was perplexing. Sharp had great instincts for women. I had none. The one thing I knew for sure was that I had enjoyed her arms around me in the back room. There was intimacy in the stillness of her body that I had never experienced before. Sharp was also accurate in saying she was as estranged from her family as I was from mine. Should I hold her upbringing against her? Too much to think about. Kelly was not sitting around befuddled by a woman. He was taking action. We needed to do the same.

"We need to get moving. I'll deal with this later." I pointed at the Winchester in Sharp's hand. "You need to finish loading that rifle."

"Yep." He looked at it. "Rather have my own, but I guess goin' back to the hotel'll take too long."

As we walked to the counter to get cartridges, I noticed Mrs. Baker and Tree at the door, looking very impatient. They were right to be impatient. Time was not on our side. Sharp nimbly emptied the rifle and dry shot several times. After an affirmative grunt, he loaded the Winchester and emptied the rest of the box of cartridges into his coat pocket.

At the door, I asked Mrs. Baker, "What are you carrying?"

In answer, she lifted an axe handle.

"I meant, what's in your coat pocket?"

She drew out a .38 caliber Colt Lightning. From a prior visit, I knew that her deceased husband had given her this gun for protection. The Lightning was a compact double-action, small-caliber pistol.

It had a long, hard pull, which made it difficult to fire accidentally. Her husband had made a good choice for her. On my last visit to Leadville, Mrs. Baker had insisted that I teach her to shoot. Although she had shown no natural ability, she had plenty of earnest determination. After several hours, she had become somewhat proficient, but only at extremely close range. That was probably good enough inside the store; on the street, however, she would be safer using the axe handle. Kelly's men would not hesitate to shoot a woman pointing a gun at them, but they might be reluctant to shoot a woman wielding a club—at least until she got close.

"Keep that pistol in your pocket. Don't use it unless they knock the axe handle away from you . . . and you fear for your life."

"I can shoot."

"Close range. I'd rather see you swing that club if you're that close. You've seen Tree work. Does he go for his gun or his sap?"

She didn't answer, so I lifted an eyebrow at Tree.

"He's right, Mrs. Baker. Hit 'em on the head. They'll go down, and no one seeks revenge."

I took another look at Tree. That was smart. The man knew how to deal with a misbehaving lout without getting his friends riled. I returned my attention to Mrs. Baker. She nodded understanding. With that, we opened the door to leave the store. Mrs. Paul blocked our exit. She looked frightened, and her son, behind her, looked scared as well.

"They're coming," she said. "A dozen or more. They mean business."

I grabbed Mrs. Baker's elbow.

"Go sound the alarm up State. We'll hold them off until you get back."

"I'm not standing in front of that crowd," Mrs. Paul cried. "They'll be here any minute."

"We have to, Ma," her son replied. "It's now or never."

He was a brave boy, obviously scared yet ready to stand his ground. I gave Mrs. Baker a gentle nudge, and she bolted in the direction of the brothels. I stuck my head out the doorway but saw no men in the street. Waving everyone inside, I directed them to the gun rack behind the counter. I handed shotguns to the boy, Tree, and Mrs. Paul. I was more comfortable with a sidearm but took a rifle for myself. Moving as fast as I could, I grabbed ammunition for the Winchester and shotguns, throwing it onto the counter. Without instructions, everybody loaded their weapons.

"Jeff, what do you think? Do we hole up in the store or meet them in the street?"

He looked around. "We're near blind inside this store." He brow crinkled in thought. "They can set this tinderbox on fire easier than a haystack. I say street."

"Okay."

"When we git out there, everyone spread out," Sharp instructed. "Start backin' up the street away from the store. When they appear, we want room between us an' them, so move away from the corner. Steve an' I'll take the center, an' the rest of ya spread to either side of us. Stop all movement when ya see 'em. We need to look formidable, but don't point your guns at them. Point straight up. This's probably a big bluff, but if shootin' starts, drop to a knee an' empty those shotguns right at their chests. Got it?"

We saw nods all around and moved toward the door. A quick glance verified that Kelly and his men had not yet appeared on State Street. But the wind had made an appearance. Leadville was a town covered with soot from the lead pulverized by silver mining. The wind had kicked up enough black powder to obscure our sight, and I expected the devil to emerge from a black cloud at any moment. As we walked out one by one, I smelled smoke and saw an ominous plume rising above what had once been Mrs. Paul's café on the next block. Damn. That's where they were: burning down her business. Despite feeling sorry for her loss, I realized that their stopping to put fire to her place had bought us precious minutes. I vowed to buy her a new café if we survived.

We spread out across the width of the road and backed up together. We had taken no more than four steps when I heard voices—gruff, commanding voices. They were coming. I glanced behind me but didn't see Mrs. Baker or any others coming to help. Sharp looked as calm as the sea off Cape Cod on a windless morning. He carried the Winchester as naturally as a housekeeper would hold a broom.

"Are you doing the talking?" I asked.

"Yep, if there's talkin' to be done."

I felt comfortable with that. Although I had handled some tough situations since coming west, I had never encountered a mob. Although he'd never mentioned it, I had no doubt that Sharp had at one time or another faced down a challenge from a group of angry men.

We had taken a few more steps backward when Kelly and his men rounded the corner. They were bunched up but quickly spread out after seeing the five of us stretched across the entire street. I counted sixteen men. Two of them had been our whist partners on the train. Many held guns in their hands, but Kelly repeatedly smacked a wooden club against his palm.

They stopped marching. We all stared at each other for a few moments as black dust whirled around our feet. I considered pulling my hand-kerchief over my mouth but feared I might be distracted at a bad moment.

"Ya think ya can wield that club with a rifle hole in yer chest?" Sharp asked calmly.

The pounding in Kelly's palm stopped. "Don't even think about it," he said. "If you move the rifle, you'll be dead."

Sharp smiled. "I'm pretty fast."

"Not as fast as my boys."

The two men who flanked him were obviously gunmen. They advertised their prowess with fancy gear and dark, menacing clothing. I had grabbed a Winchester to look intimidating, but I was confident I could draw my pistol faster than I could lower the rifle from pointing at the sky. I had drawn and fired my Colt thousands of times but seldom practiced swinging a rifle around on a target.

When Sharp didn't respond, Kelly added, "Even in the unlikely event you kill me, my boys have instructions to never quit putting lead into you until their guns are empty."

"That assumes they survive a shotgun blast." Sharp remained chillingly calm. He was scary as hell.

A black dust devil wound around the street, suddenly collapsing into a pile of grime at Kelly's feet. I had a bad feeling about this standoff—any erratic motion could ignite a bloodbath. I caught a flicker of concern in Kelly's eyes, and then I heard a rustle behind me. Soon Mrs. Baker stood next to me, and the street was shoulder to shoulder with women and a few men brandishing all sorts of weapons. We outnumbered Kelly and his gang.

"You hiding behind skirts now?" Kelly snarled. "Don't think that'll save you. Women die as easy as men."

"Not these women."

The voice came from my left, at least three or four people away. I didn't take my eyes off Kelly to see who had spoken. I liked her next words.

"Hugo Kelly, ya started this fight, but by God, we'll finish it. There'll be a lot of dead and some hurt, but we'll be the ones standin' at the end."

"You talk big, gal, but these are professional gunmen. Go back to your whorehouses and save yourself. My beef is with these two."

"Your beef's with all of us. We're tired of givin' ya our hard-earned money."

"Ain't all that hard earned from what I've seen." The man on Kelly's left chuckled at his quip.

"I got news for ya, buster, when ya make a visit, it's agonizin' work."

I felt rather than saw her step out in front of our line.

"Maybe I should put this here maple stick up yer behind."

This powder keg could explode at any second. I was grateful when Sharp calmed things a bit.

"Mr. Kelly, let's not let this get outta hand. There are hot feelings on both sides. Why don't ya just wander on back to yer office? Think on it a bit."

"No. We settle this now. You're interfering with my business, and I can't allow that."

It was time for me to speak. "We're not interfering with your business . . . we're ending it. I presume you asked around about us. We put an end to one gang in this town, now we're getting rid of you. It's time for you to leave Leadville."

"You're dead men." He resumed pounding his club against his palm.

"Have you heard of Captain Joseph McAllen?" I asked.

He recoiled. "You mean that coward who shot an old woman in the back?"

I smiled. McAllen had shot Mrs. Bolton to save my life, but Kelly's tone said that he found a man ruthless enough to kill an old woman frightening.

"The very same. Perhaps you'd like to meet him."

"A woman back shooter don't scare me."

"Then you're a fool."

He looked ready to explode, so I added quickly, "A man in a fight ought to keep an eye on his backside."

It took a second for Kelly to get my drift, and then he slowly turned to look to his rear. What he saw must have seemed like an apparition from hell. A breeze had blown lead dust in every direction, obscuring the far end of the street. Six black-clad men sat astride six black horses in a mist of swirling darkness. Each held a Winchester straight up, the butt resting against his thigh.

"Captain McAllen's here to escort you out of town," I said.

Kelly laughed. "No one sends Kelly packing." He waved behind him. "Your so-called captain has no authority here. Come on, boys, we'll finish this another day."

Kelly started to retreat. McAllen and all of his detectives cocked their Winchesters in unison, stopping Kelly and his gang in their tracks.

I yelled over their heads, "Would you explain your engagement, Captain McAllen?"

McAllen rode his horse forward exactly two steps.

"If Mr. Dancy or any of his friends are harmed in any way, I have been paid to hunt you down and kill you. Anywhere in the nation."

"That's illegal," Kelly stammered.

"Not the way I'll do it." He opened his jacket to show a badge. "I've been deputized by the governor in this state and deputized as a United States marshal." He paused to let that sink in. "I know enough judges; the paperwork'll be no problem. I'll make it legal."

I wanted to emphasize McAllen's point. "Kelly, if you keep up this fight, you will die . . . or be hunted down like a murdering Orange in Ireland. You're a marked man. Make no mistake, I'm a vengeful son of a bitch . . . even from the grave."

He looked away from McAllen and examined my face to gauge my seriousness.

"I suggest you drop those weapons."

His demeanor slowly changed. I had been right. He was more than a bully. He was shrewd.

"Listen, bloodshed's bad for business," Kelly said in a friendly tone. "If we part peaceably, I'll leave State Street alone."

"No, leave town," Sharp said. "We've already talked to the saloon owners on Chestnut. They won't abide yer racket, an' they got tough men to back 'em up. The Pinkertons will help, an' their fee's been paid in advance. Even if ya wait until they leave, they'll come after ya. Yer through. Time to git."

Kelly started to walk away. "This ain't over."

"Yes, it is," I said.

"Hold it," Sharp ordered. He pointed at the pair we had played cards with on the train. "They stay."

"No!" the bearded one yelled. "Hugo, you got to protect us. That man's a brute."

Kelly looked at the two on the far side of his line of men. "They're just a couple of leeches. If you want 'em, be my guest."

He turned and walked away without looking to see who followed.

Kelly's men reluctantly trailed after their leader. The two card players tried to follow suit, but Sharp marched right up, his rifle pointed dead at their midsections. They stopped.

"What'd I tell ya last time?" Sharp asked.

"I don't remember." The bearded man's voice quivered.

"I said if I ever saw ya again, ya better have eleven dollars in yer hand, or I was gonna punch ya."

The bearded man hurriedly ransacked his pockets, pulling out a wad of bills. He handed the whole roll to Sharp.

Sharp peeled off eleven dollars and handed the roll back.

"Now git."

They did.

Chapter 11

It was hard to believe the confrontation was over. For a while, I had been sure it would end in a bloodbath. I patted Sharp's shoulder and turned to Mrs. Baker to thank her for marshaling her forces. Before I said a word, she threw her arms around my neck and kissed me. It was startling and intense. I resisted for a moment, then dropped my rifle and heartily joined in the embrace. Suddenly, I heard raucous applause. I'm not sure if they were applauding us or the end of the crisis. It didn't matter. I felt good.

When we quit kissing, she cocked her head at me as if appraising me for the first time. Then I got the smile—the one that made her as pretty as a newly bloomed rose.

We still had our arms around each other as she said, "You were wonderful."

"As were you."

She stepped back, glancing down before meeting my eyes again.

"Steve, I've been too forward. I've never done this before, and it feels unnatural. I need to know. Are you ready to take the lead, or are we parting here?"

"I can't think of a worse course of events."

The smile faded. "Leading or parting?"

"Parting." The smile not only returned but engaged every element of her face. She looked radiant.

"Then you're okay with an eastern socialite?"

I rubbed my chin before saying, "Hum, perhaps I'll need to think about that."

She slapped me on the arm.

"I meant, yes, ma'am."

"Now we're getting this relationship on the right course."

She went up on her toes and kissed me again, this time lightly, but for some reason it seemed more intimate.

There was no applause this time, but when I looked around, there were a couple dozen people intently watching our little drama. I was surprised to see Sharp looking especially pleased with himself. I had just come to some kind of romantic agreement with the woman he had come to Leadville to seduce. Some kind of romantic agreement? I wasn't sure what kind, but when I examined my feelings, I was happy. I knew little about her personal life: her likes, her dislikes, her ambitions, or even when she had become attracted to me. Did she want to continue living in the West? What about Leadville? The store? I didn't know. Partly because we had argued from the day we met. I only knew her as a tough, capable businesswoman. She seemed to have friends from every walk of life. People liked her. She was hardworking, honest, and congenial—except with me. How did all of this translate into romance? To hell with thinking about it. I was ready to cheerfully go down this road.

Chapter 12

The next morning, Sharp, Mrs. Baker, and I ate breakfast at the Carbonate Hotel. I should say Virginia, because I had finally learned her first name. It was not the only new thing I learned about her. Sharp was polite enough to keep questions to himself.

As the three of us bantered, a rough gentleman in a well-worn black suit came into the dining room. He looked around with a stern expression and then approached us. His unbuttoned coat flapped as he walked, exposing a holstered Smith and Wesson .44 Model 3. I stood to meet him head-on.

"Good morning, Captain," I said. "It's not like you to sleep late."

"I've been workin' for several hours already," McAllen responded. "Steve, you aren't my only client."

McAllen reached around me to shake Sharp's hand and made an abbreviated bow to Virginia. After taking the fourth seat at the table, he said, "Mr. Kelly has departed on the train with a couple of his followers. He's gone." He laid his white napkin on his lap and signaled for a steward. "Jeff, it's good to see you again. Especially since you aren't in jail and nobody's tryin' to kill you."

Sharp laughed. "Flapjacks an' eggs is all that's on my agenda for the day."

"Glad to hear it. By the way, Steve, you owe me for six round-trip train tickets, transportation for our horses, three hotel rooms, meals, and twelve days of service from the Pinkerton agency. However, I won't be needin' that retainer to avenge your death."

"It's good to see you again as well, Captain."

"I didn't think you telegraphed me because you were in need of pleasantries." His tight-lipped smile showed that he wasn't entirely serious.

The taciturn McAllen didn't make friends easily. In fact, Sharp might have been his sole real friend. They went back many years, while I had known McAllen for less than two years. I had previously employed him as a Pinkerton, but we had also worked together without a professional relationship. Sharp and I had helped McAllen rescue his abducted daughter, and on another occasion, McAllen and I had proved Sharp innocent of a murder that was about to get him hanged. Shared danger might have made McAllen my friend, but I would probably never get a direct confirmation from him.

"Are you returning this evening?" I asked.

"I am. I pulled men from active engagements to respond to your telegram. I need to get them back to Denver."

"Write us up a bill and we'll issue you a draft . . . and thank you for coming so fast."

McAllen had rounded up a crew so quickly, he had caught the next train out of Denver. That was highly professional, but I preferred to think it was a friend responding to a call for help.

"In truth," I added, "I couldn't be happier that I no longer need your services. After Prescott, I vowed to avoid violence, and this time not a shot was fired. I'm a happy man."

McAllen glanced at Virginia. "I see that."

Her unabashed smile embarrassed him, so he quickly returned his attention to me.

"I'm glad it worked out this time. But in the future, try to resolve problems without riskin' a full-scale riot. Seemed like half the population was faced off against each other. Street brawls can be bloody as hell."

"Duly noted. Next time, I'll tell the bad men to behave in a more civilized manner."

"Next time, figure out a way to stall." He gave me a hard look. "Steve, you have a habit of going off half-cocked. Use your head. You won't always be lucky."

"Is this how you butter up your best clients?"

"I tell the truth to clients I want to keep . . . and to my friends."

"Which am I?"

"Guess."

We all smiled. We had already shared many battles together, so it was pleasant to share a quiet breakfast with no trouble on the horizon.

After we finished our meal, I asked Virginia, "What about the store?"

"We could sell it to Michael," she answered. "I've already negotiated a price for you and Jeff to approve."

Michael? To my knowledge, Tree didn't have money, so I presumed she meant for us to allow him to pay us over time. I wanted to be completely clear of Leadville, but I had kept that to myself so far. Leadville had been Virginia's home for four years. This was where her engineer husband had been killed in a mining accident. This was where he was buried. This is where she had made a life for herself, a good, successful life with many friends. I worried she might want to stay. I didn't. Furthermore, I hadn't even thought about how to discuss it with her. Damn.

"Tree got money?" Sharp asked. Unlike me, he always went right at his questions.

"His brother does. He owns a good claim, and he's offered to loan Michael the money . . . but only to buy this store."

"Why only this one?" Sharp asked.

"Because it's where he spends his winters. Comes by every day to chew the fat with his pals. It's like his second home." She paused, obviously pleased with what she was about to say next. "They'll pay thirty thousand."

"Thirty thousand?" Sharp whistled. "We paid eighteen. That's darn near double."

"It *is* double if you count the profits while we owned it," she added with a grin.

"I say sell," Sharp snapped.

"Virginia, what do you want to do?" I asked.

"I want to sell. I took on the store to get enough money to leave this town with a little style. My six thousand share of the sale price, plus my savings, does the job."

"You want to leave Leadville?" My anxiousness over her response probably showed in my voice.

"I do." I was further rewarded with a smile.

"What about you, Jeff? You came here to search for mining investments."

He rubbed his chin. "Give me a month or so . . . then I'll be ready to go to New Jersey."

"New Jersey?" Virginia's response was more of an exclamation than a question.

"Jeff and I had a prior agreement. We would come to Leadville, sell the store, and search for claims that he thought could make more money. Afterwards, we'd go to Menlo Park to see if we could get a license to use Edison's inventions for mining. At least, that was our plan before I met you."

"I like that plan. Can I go with you?" She glanced at McAllen and blushed. "Separate berths, of course."

I was stunned at my good fortune, but apprehensive. "How far?"

"All the way. I want to see this miraculous light

that comes from a mysterious fluid. I've read articles about his discoveries. My husband was an engineer. I've always loved inventions and clever devices. I also want to hear his phonograph . . . speak into his carbon telephone." She almost jumped up and down in her seat. "His inventions will change the world. I have to see them."

"Virginia, you could not have said anything that would have made me happier. I want you to come with us. The four of us will have a grand time, and I bet we'll all be awestruck by the Wizard of Menlo Park."

"Four of us?" McAllen demanded. "What the hell are you talkin' about, Steve?"

"I'm hoping you'll come with us, Joseph. I've been in communication with Tom, and he suspects somebody is sabotaging his work. I promised to bring him the best detective in the world."

McAllen pushed his coffee cup away, wiped his mouth, and threw his napkin in his lap. "Lots of problems with that. I work for the Pinkerton National Detective Agency, but I'm not really a detective. I don't solve puzzles; I pound them into the earth. I work out of Denver, and the New York office will want to handle this. Last, I already have an active engagement."

"I want you," I said. "And Allan Pinkerton says I can have you if you're willing to work the case."

McAllen plopped against the back of his chair.

"You call Edison by his nickname and you communicate with Allan Pinkerton?"

"Guilty."

"Damn."

I gave him a moment and then asked my question.

"Will you join us?"

"Wouldn't miss it if I was bludgeoned and hog-tied."

Chapter 13

In my opinion, first-class trains were the very best way to travel. Some preferred steamships, but staying on solid ground suited me just fine. Trains were fast and comfortable, and traveling from Denver to New York took only a week. The secret to this astonishing speed was twenty-four-hour travel. Instead of being fatiguing, a Pullman sleeping car made this relentless trek as comfortable as relaxing in a well-appointed parlor. Pullman's carpets, drapes, upholstery, and card tables were more luxurious than those found in many high-priced hotels. The chairs and ceiling converted into comfortable night beds, one above the other, and curtains gave passengers a modicum of privacy. Library, bar, and dining cars provided a diversion and an excuse to move around and get a little exercise. Others could have the vast expanses of ocean on a transatlantic voyage; I preferred to see America whooshing by the windows as I played cards, ate, read, or conversed.

After a preliminary narrow-gauge ride out of the mountains, we traveled in the comfort of a Pullman car on the largest railway in the nation, its service as smooth as the practiced staff at my mother's home. We had boarded a Union Pacific train in Denver and were well on our way to Omaha, Nebraska. Our horses, which we transported from Leadville in a stock car, would remain in Denver with a rancher McAllen had used for many years.

Over the past weeks, Sharp hadn't found a mining investment worth putting money into. That hadn't surprised me. Sharp liked mines that were supposedly played out so he could use his knowledge to get them producing again. Leadville had the extraction of precious metals from lead developed to a science that offered little opportunity for improvement. The rich owners, called the Carbonate Kings, had long ago sealed up all the good claims, and extraction costs escalated the further a claim was from town. Several prospectors had suggested a partnership, but that wasn't Sharp's way of doing business. So with the store sold, the three of us, including Virginia, were free of anything that could tie us down to one locale. The fourth in our party was Joseph McAllen.

Everybody was in a good mood. Virginia seemed happy to be with me and thrilled at the prospect of revisiting New York. I say visit, because neither of us could imagine settling again in the East. We were going for a holiday, and then we expected our frontier adventure to continue. Sharp generally enjoyed whatever he was doing, but McAllen could be a grump. While Virginia and I had waited for Sharp to search for mining opportunities, McAllen had returned to Denver and finished his prior engagement. He had also traded a series of telegrams with the Pinkerton New York office and someone working at Edison's operations. He concluded that something was indeed amiss. There would be real work for him at Menlo Park, which made him agreeable.

Edison had been working on a major electrification project that seemed to go well and then suddenly failed for no apparent reason. Competition to bring incandescent light to New York City was fierce, and sabotage by another company was not unknown. The random failures were perplexing enough that McAllen thought there might be skullduggery involved. Most men would have enjoyed a paid holiday to see the wonders of electricity, but McAllen felt more at ease when he earned his keep. His skills weren't needed for a week yet, so he was content to enjoy a modern train ride, where a porter was always at hand to serve him a fresh glass of the finest Scotch whiskey.

I was happy as well because my book would come out while I was in New York. My publisher wanted me to do book parties in New York, Boston, Philadelphia, and Baltimore. Virginia said it was my decision, but she wouldn't join me in Philadelphia, so I had agreed only to New York and Boston. I hadn't reconciled with my family but felt I could handle them more easily than she could handle hers, although if I were really confident, I would have informed my mother I was coming to town. I probably should have felt guilty for not telegraphing, but I knew she would take over my schedule and try to manage my every minute. I couldn't keep it secret, however. Sooner or later, I would run into someone who knew me, and my publisher was a distant relative. It may have been avoidance, but I decided to deal with my mother as it happened.

Perhaps I could talk my publisher into Chicago and St. Louis. It would be fun to sell books on the way home. Home? I thought about that a moment. I had no home. At least no abode I could call home. But I knew my home was the West. After all, I had just experienced the two best years of my life. I saw no reason to quit my adventure for the staid life of New York society.

Our red velour seats faced each other, and a mahogany table separated us. Virginia hooked her hand through my arm.

"I like this," she said. "Too much, perhaps. I don't want to overindulge. I might be tempted to reconcile with my family and their money."

I wanted to tell her that I had plenty of money, but I still wasn't sure about the seriousness of our relationship. Or at least, I wasn't sure how serious she was about me. I said, "Most people would consider six thousand dollars a tidy fortune."

"For a couple years, perhaps, but not a lifetime." She made a point of looking around the Pullman car. "And not even a couple years living like this."

McAllen harrumphed. "I could make six thousand last a lifetime."

"How?" I asked.

"Buy a ranch and raise horses. To hell with cows. I prefer wranglers to drovers anyway. I'd raise the best team west of the Mississippi."

McAllen had imbibed enough to make him uncharacteristically talkative.

"Joseph, you'd still be working if you owned a horse ranch . . . and that would be using money as capital. I think Virginia is saying she doesn't think her stake is big enough for her not to continue earning."

"The three of you have a different idea about money. You think you gotta make it grow. I'd use it to buy what would make me happy . . . and I'll tell you, a horse ranch outside of Durango would make me happy."

I understood. McAllen's daughter lived in Durango with his ex-wife, and his daughter loved horses more than anything else. Maggie boarded her horse at her aunt and uncle's ranch, but it was a couple days' ride from Durango, which meant she visited only during school breaks. I bet McAllen intended to buy his ranch within an easy ride to Durango.

"Captain McAllen, how much does a horse

ranch in that part of the country cost?" Virginia asked.

"Hell, I already own the land. I bought six sections of prime horse country a couple years ago. Since then, I've probably saved enough to build a ranch house and sturdy barn. Need another year or two with the agency before I can afford the right horseflesh. I want to breed Spanish Barb and Indian horses. Got some ideas."

"What kind of ideas?" Sharp asked, suddenly interested. "What are ya lookin' to breed?"

"A travelin' horse. One that can go long distances carryin' a man and his gear." He tapped the card table between our facing seats. "I'll tell you, Steve, I want to breed a string like Chestnut. That was a fine horse."

That surprised me. He had never said anything when Chestnut was alive. In fact, I didn't think he liked Chestnut, because my horse wasn't fast like a quarter horse or agile like a cowboy pony. Chestnut was more like a train engine. He could go long distances at a brisk pace, carrying a heavy load. Give him enough room and he could outrun any horse, but it had to be an endurance run. One time, I had raced McAllen uphill over a long distance, and he seemed upset to have lost rather than impressed with Chestnut's strength. Mrs. Bolton had poisoned my horse to get even with me for imagined wrongs. In truth, her son's murder had resulted from my convincing him to run for governor of Nevada, so maybe the wrongs weren't imagined. At any rate, McAllen had never expressed an admiration for Chestnut. Now he wanted to breed a string with the same characteristics.

"After you get your ranch going and breed the kind of horse you want, I'd like to be your first buyer," I said.

"Second. Maggie's first."

"Hell, ya say!" Sharp exclaimed. "Yer gonna make yer daughter buy her horse from ya?"

"Of course not. Said it wrong. Steve, you can be my first buyer . . . but you can't have any horse Maggie claims as her own."

"I'd consider that an honor, Captain."

He reached across and shook my hand like we had concluded a deal. Then I remembered McAllen's character and realized that in his mind, we had just agreed on a deal—a deal he would honor come what may. I looked between him and Sharp and marveled that I had fallen in with such good men.

McAllen gave me a rare smile, showing teeth.

"Steve, you better learn how to take care of yourself, because I don't intend on doin' this kind of work much longer."

Chapter 14

Grand Central Terminal resembled a carp pond during a feeding frenzy. I had forgotten New York City's frenetic pace, which now assaulted my senses and struck me as feigned and unnatural. I had gotten used to the measured pace in the West, and our train ride had been so reserved that I now felt like we had been dumped out of a quiet library into the middle of a world exposition. Where were all these people going in such a hurry?

Our porters seemed to have magical powers to divide the sea of people as they led us to a waiting carriage. Three things hit me as I stepped outdoors: bright light from a high summer sun, even more people hustling about, and the awful odor of rotting garbage, unwashed people, and horse excrement.

Virginia squeezed my arm. "Welcome back, Steve. I'm sure you missed all this."

"Good God!" McAllen exclaimed. "Why are all these people cramped in tight together?" He looked up at the multistoried buildings. "Stacked atop one another, like cans of peas. Don't they know there are wide-open spaces just over the horizon? Hell, I can show them places where they won't see another soul for days."

Sharp laughed. "City people like this. It makes 'em feel alive an' connected to the world."

"Connected?" McAllen looked genuinely puzzled. "Hell, the rest of the world doesn't even care if they exist."

"Oh, the world cares," I interjected. "They care because amongst all these ordinary people, a few geniuses are creating miracles. People like Edison, Vanderbilt, and Bell are changing the world—helping people get from place to place at unbelievable speeds, allowing instant communication across oceans or the Great Plains, and stretching the day as long as they want with light that instantly appears like magic." I looked around. "I used to find this energy and excitement invigorating, even normal."

McAllen pointed up. "Normal?" He sounded uneasy. "You call this crowded livin' normal? Look at that hodgepodge of wires. They go every which way. Damn, Denver's a rat's nest, but nothin' like this. When I'm on the trail, I don't like even a single telegraph wire messin' up my view." He waved his arm. "Steve, this ain't normal."

He was right. The city had grown ugly since I had been gone. Tall wooden poles were planted everywhere, each sprouting wires in every possible direction. It looked like a giant spider had made New York City home.

McAllen grabbed his bag and threw it up to the

coachman standing on the roof of our carriage. The porter took umbrage at McAllen's interference with his duties and scooted sideways to block us from our baggage. He needn't have worried. The rest of our party were used to the habits of the East and climbed aboard to let the porter and coachman sort it out.

The porter stuck his head through the door window to say everything was secure and we needn't worry. The remark, of course, was meant to solicit a tip, so I handed him a handful of coins. He grinned and nodded a thank you, and the coachman snapped his whip.

"This town stinks of horse piss and horse shit," McAllen said as the carriage rocked with the sudden pull of the horses.

"Captain, watch yer language," Sharp nodded at Virginia. "Mrs. Baker already lectured me to not use bad language in front of her."

"It's all right," Virginia said. "I was trying to unbalance you, Mr. Sharp. You had designs I was unwilling to fulfill. The captain's words are neither foreign to me nor inaccurate."

We all had a pleasant laugh. I wasn't sure if it was due to her remarks or relief at being away from the terminal mayhem.

The coachman must have heard McAllen's complaint because he slid back the communication glass behind his head and yelled, "There's over one hundred and fifty thousand horses in

New York pulling trams, trucks, stages, and private carriages! Guess how much manure?"

"Too much!" I yelled back.

"You got that right, sir. Each day, horses leave over two million pounds of manure in the city streets. Nobody knows how much urine . . . but avoid stepping in puddles." He laughed so heartily, a person would have thought he had told a joke. "Keeps my no-account brothers in work, so I'm not complaining. That other smell is sour beer. The sawdust in the bucket shops gets soaked with it. But don't you worry; where you're going, it'll smell like sweet flowers."

I was wondering how to politely ask our talkative new friend to be quiet, when McAllen reached up and slammed the communication window shut. Ever since we had stepped off the train, he had seemed edgy, which was strange, because he normally remained calm.

Our destination was the Fifth Avenue Hotel, at the intersection of Fifth Avenue, Broadway, and Twenty-Third Street. The hotel faced Madison Square Park. The intersection of three streets and a six-acre park protected the hotel from the seamier aspects of the city. The Fifth Avenue Hotel was the social, cultural, and political hub for elite New Yorkers. Family or friends were sure to run into me there. I had considered hiding in an obscure hotel, but my dealings with Edison were sure to alert my family to my presence anyway.

Besides, I wasn't afraid of them, just disgusted with their business and social practices.

A more difficult decision was what to do about rooms. In Leadville and Denver, Virginia and I had shared a room without causing a raised eyebrow, but we were back in the haughty neighborhoods of our upbringing. Both of us felt a need to revert to the appearance of decorum expected in polite society. The key word was *appearance,* so we decided on adjoining rooms with a connecting door.

Through the glass behind the coachman's head, I saw the hotel well before the carriage pulled up. The Fifth Avenue Hotel was a five-story brick building with white marble facing at ground level. We had reserved rooms on the top floor because it was quieter and the air clear of road dust if you wanted to open a window. Climbing four flights several times a day would be daunting, but this hotel had a device unique in the entire world. Otis Tufts had installed a steam-powered "vertical screw railway" to effortlessly lift passengers to the floor they desired.

We climbed from the carriage with helping hands and welcomes from every side. I'm sure we presented an odd sight to the hotel staff. I was wearing a reasonably well-tailored suit that I had bought in Prescott, Arizona, but I was sure it was not the sort of thing their stylish clientele wore. I was right. As I looked around, I saw that most of the men wore long coats that hung almost to the knee, stiff collars, cravats, and shiny silk top hats.

Virginia wore a presentable dress that was probably also out of fashion. The women around us wore dresses that were relatively simple above the waist, but elaborately detailed below, especially in back. In fact, I wondered if women were allowed to sit any longer. A few sported dresses with massive protrusions that grossly exaggerated the derrière. I couldn't believe men found this attractive. I glanced at Virginia and could tell by her expression that she was appalled at how ridiculous some of the women looked.

A small crowd of onlookers had gathered around us, and my guess was that Sharp and McAllen were drawing their attention. McAllen wore a well-worn, ill-fitting black suit that had seen many years of use on the trail as well as in towns. His unbuttoned coat exposed the big Smith and Wesson holstered at his waist. He also wore western-style boots not frequently seen in the city. His suit had been thoroughly cleaned, but his white shirt retained a grayish tinge that probably could never be removed. However, McAllen's attire was only a curiosity. His demeanor was what commanded attention. He looked angry at what he saw and fully capable of singlehandedly sweeping it from his sight.

Sharp's attire was worse. He indifferently wore

a tattered suit that obviously had fit him better when he was twenty pounds lighter. He did not appear threatening like McAllen. His wide-open, curious expression made him look like a simple bumpkin rather than a ruffian. No one around us would believe that he could buy and sell almost anyone registered at this expensive hotel.

Stepping past the onlookers, we entered a handsome lobby adorned with lush carpet, brocatelle upholstery, crimson curtains, and rosewood accented with heavy gilt trim. Large windows made the lobby gay, and gaslights were strategically placed to cast light into the darkest corners. The hotel—one of the world's finest—employed over four hundred people to serve guests. Each room had a fireplace, and each was equipped with an indoor bathroom.

I went immediately to the registration desk and waited behind another gentleman. Sharp poked his nose into the reading room and then into the bar. I thought he wanted a drink, but when he moved on to the massive dining room, I realized he was just inspecting the public rooms.

When my turn came, the clerk asked, "How can I help you, sir?"

"Steve Dancy. I have four rooms reserved on the fifth floor."

"Let me see." He ran two fingers down a ledger. "Ah, yes. Your rooms are ready."

He looked quizzically at the three of us, and I

pointed at Sharp, who was engaged in conversation with an elderly woman.

"That's the fourth member of your party?" There was a note of concern in his query.

"Yes, that's my friend."

"Oh dear, I hope he's not bothering Mrs. Chilton. She doesn't take well to strangers."

I followed his stare and realized that I was acquainted with Mrs. Chilton. In fact, I had once dated her granddaughter. The woman was the worst sort of snob. Her family was running out of money, but she remained snooty nonetheless. I was about to ask McAllen to rescue the old biddy, when I saw her laugh and place a hand on Sharp's forearm. I guess age did not hamper Sharp's appealing ways with women.

I looked back at the sheepish clerk. "I apologize. They evidently know each other."

"Actually, no. Mr. Sharp seduces rich old women. I'll go over after we finish here and inform him that Mrs. Chilton has run into a bit of a rough patch."

"Excuse me, sir?"

Virginia stifled a giggle.

"I'm not serious . . . except about the rough patch. Now, can we proceed with the rooms?"

"Of course, sir. I see you reserved two adjoining rooms . . . with a connecting door. I presume that's for your bodyguard." He nodded at McAllen, who had never quit scowling.

"Hotel staff should not presume," I answered. "The adjoining room is for the lady." I hesitated a beat. "We find it convenient."

I had succeeded in embarrassing him, but when I glanced at Virginia, she seemed amused. He stammered some apologetic sounds and busied himself making notations. When he looked up, he said, "One moment, sir. I have a letter for you."

He pulled a letter from one of the pigeonholes behind him and handed it to me. I thought it might be from my mother, but the envelope did not include her engraved name and residence.

"Should all the rooms be charged to your account, sir?"

"Yes, except for Mr. Sharp's. He'll take care of his own room and charges." I waved him over to sign the register.

With that, we were all issued keys and a condescending smile.

"Where is the Tufts lift?" Virginia asked with a note of excitement.

"Right there." The clerk pointed to a grated gate. "It will be back down in a moment."

As we approached the gate, I could hear the steam engine in the basement. I wondered if it was safe, then reminded myself that hundreds or possibly thousands of people had already used the device. Most elevators used a rope and pulley system, but that design had safety issues, and passengers had been killed when such lifts broke from their moorings and plummeted to the ground. Elisha Otis had invented an automatic brake that supposedly made rope and pulley elevators safe, but Tufts used a screw mechanism that made it impossible for the car to fall. I was grateful the hotel had selected Tufts's design.

As we waited, Virginia squeezed my arm and whispered, "Steve, that was very wicked. I should remain in my room to punish you for embarrassing me." Her smile said she was not embarrassed at all.

The elevator noisily arrived. When the gate slide open, a boy in a neat burgundy uniform beckoned us to step into a small box lit by an oil lantern. Virginia's expression of anticipation reminded me of a young girl on Christmas morning. We instructed the operator to take us to the fifth floor, and Virginia uselessly peppered him with questions the entire ride. I say uselessly because the young boy had no idea how the elevator's mechanism functioned. I was certain, however, that Virginia would thoroughly understand its operation before our visit was over.

The rooms were as elegant as expected. I had a suite, and the adjoining room was a single designed for a family with children old enough to be in a separate but connected room. Normally, McAllen would be instructed by his employer to find less expensive quarters, but I had insisted that I required him close by. There was a knock on the door, and I opened it, expecting luggage. It was McAllen.

"Steve, how long are we goin' to stay in this confounded hotel?"

"That depends on Mr. Edison. If my understanding is correct, much of the work he needs done is in the city. We'll know more tomorrow."

McAllen turned to leave without a further word.

"Joseph, what's the problem?"

At first he gestured dismissively, but then he turned to face me. "I don't like that contraption we rode up. It feels tight."

I suppressed a laugh at his expression. McAllen had seemed to enjoy the train ride but had been out of sorts since we had arrived at the terminal. He obviously didn't like New York, but there was something more. He actually seemed frightened. But that wasn't possible. I had seen him calm and calculating when bullets flew all around him. Nothing scared this man.

"Joseph, I can get you a first-floor room, but that's not really the problem, is it?"

"No." He turned to leave and then paused, his back to me. Without turning, he said, "Crowds terrify me. I hate being penned in by throngs of people. Makes no sense, but there it is."

He opened the door and left.

Chapter 15

A half hour after checking in, I received a telegram from Menlo Park. It consisted of only two words: "Come today." Virginia and I had planned to relax in the hotel a bit and then do some shopping. I figured Edison could wait until tomorrow or the next day. Then I remembered what my lawyer had told me about him. Every minute was invaluable, and everyone was expected to be at his immediate disposal. Edison had probably requested a telegram from the hotel upon our arrival so he could beckon us at once.

I snapped the telegram against the wrist of my other hand and turned toward Virginia. "I'm afraid you'll have to shop alone. Edison wants to see me immediately."

"Are you changing?" she asked.

"No."

"Then neither will I."

"Virginia, you don't need to go."

"You are dense sometimes, Mr. Dancy. I want to go. I'm eager to go. I've been looking forward to going. If that's not clear, let me add one more thing: I won't let you go without me."

"I believe that's settled then. Let's gather up Jeff and Joseph."

"Will we spend the night?"

I hadn't thought about that. It was already after noon. Menlo Park was about thirty-five miles away. If we had luck with the ferry and train, we might make it in two hours. It would be more like three if we did any waiting. We could meet for a couple hours and return before dark, but how likely was that?

I looked at our three pieces of luggage and pointed to the smallest. "Could you pack us enough for two days in that bag? I'll round up Jeff and Joseph."

"Maybe we'll get to stay in his home."

I thought that was doubtful as I bolted from the room. I had been told that Edison seldom went home. He spent all of his time in his lab or office. I doubted he would inflict four guests on his wife. I had also heard there was a boardinghouse across from the lab. If we couldn't return to the city, we could stay there for the night. I hoped they could accommodate women.

I found my friends together in McAllen's room. Sharp lay on the bed, sipping a whiskey; McAllen drank his as he paced. Both jumped at the chance to leave immediately, Sharp because he was curious about anything new, and McAllen because it meant getting away from the press of people he feared.

We took a cab to the Cortlandt Street dock. If possible, it was more chaotic than Grand Central Terminal, partly because it was a much more varied assortment of people and animals. Horses were everywhere, but this time their odor was overwhelmed by sea creatures, both alive and rotting. Yelling teamsters wheeled around heavy wagons full of every imaginable type of cargo. Passengers for the ferry, many well dressed, stepped lively to keep from being run over or bumped by hand carts. Street vendors filled every free space and hocked their wares at the top of their lungs to be heard over the yells and curses of the longshoremen. Most of the travelers were destined for Jersey City, but first they had to cross the Hudson River on the Pennsylvania Railroad ferry.

McAllen looked not only befuddled but anxious about all the activity. This was a turn of events. McAllen had taught me how to survive in the West and enjoyed scoffing at my ignorance of the frontier. Now he was in my element. With Virginia on my arm, I walked briskly to an outside window in a large building and bought four ferry tickets. When I turned around, I noticed McAllen had brushed his coat aside so it didn't interfere with his six-shooter.

I handed him his ferry ticket. "Joseph, you have only five cartridges in that pistol. There are hundreds of people on this dock." He looked at me curiously, so I added, "You can't kill them all."

"I can clear a space around me." His awkward grin was supposed to let me know he was joking.

"Relax. We'll be on the ferry soon, and when we get to the other side, all these people will head in a different direction."

Suddenly he looked even more anxious. He waved his arm. "All of this on one ferry? Is it the size of a small ranch?"

Virginia laughed and then explained. "No. But we'll be on the top deck with these finely dressed people. Everyone else and all these wagons will be on the deck below us. We'll have lots of fresh air . . . with room to walk around."

"How long do we wait?"

"The ticket seller said about twenty minutes." I pointed to the Hudson River. "That's the ferry coming in now."

"Looks to be less than five minutes out."

"Joseph, it's got to unload before we can board." I thought a minute. "See that vendor? He's selling fresh oysters. Let's buy some while the ferry docks and unloads."

He looked dubious.

"It's out of the way. Hordes of people and wagons will be disembarking in a few moments."

He nodded, his worried eyes on the ferry pulling closer to the dock.

I looked around for Sharp and spotted him talking to someone who looked like a foreman. The three of us walked over, and I handed him his ticket as he listened to the other man explain that this dock was active throughout the night. During a break in the conversation, I pointed at the oyster vendor, but Sharp said he would meet us on board.

The oyster stand was situated to the side of the ferry building. After the ferry opened its barrier, people burst onto the dock but didn't start fanning out until they were away from the building. We had a perfect vantage point to watch the spectacle without being subjected to the crush of people. The oysters were also very good.

Partly to distract McAllen, I handed him the letter the desk clerk had given me at the hotel. It was from Thomas Edison, and he read it carefully.

Dear Mr. Dancy,

The situation has grown worse. In District 1, I have wired fifty homes and office buildings for electricity with a promise to bring them illumination. Due to labor and material shortages, only half of the fourteen miles of subway is in place. I know someone is interfering.

I have built an unequaled generating station on Pearl Street. I have illuminated J. Pierpont Morgan's house, my Manhattan headquarters, and all of Menlo Park. Everything has been tested thoroughly. It should be going smoothly, but my competitors are well ahead.

In District 1, there are 1,500 coal-gas customers with 20,000 jets waiting for clean illumination. We must get this job completed. Enormous profits await, which can be used to electrify the rest of Manhattan and then the world. I eagerly await your arrival.

The letter was signed simply with an E.

After reading the letter, McAllen asked, "What's a subway?"

"A two-foot trench to bury electrical wires. Edison insists on burying his insulated wire inside iron pipes. Many think it's foolish. Manhattan is already a nest of overhead wiring for telegraphs, telephones, stock tickers, alarms, and even some for delivering electricity to small businesses. Edison believes buried wire is safer and more reliable."

"And more attractive," Virginia added. "I hope Philadelphia doesn't look like this now."

Many of the overhead wires had been strung by companies that were now out of business. The abandoned wiring frequently fell and shorted active wires or even shocked people. Some were high voltage and dangerous. Edison wanted no part of that.

McAllen handed the letter back to me. "Why does he suspect someone is interferin'?"

"I'm not sure. Ego? Perhaps he can't believe anything he contrived wouldn't work. His insistence on burying the wires might be the real problem. It's a hell of a lot slower than stringing wire overhead. But he also might be right. There is a lot of money involved. We'll know more after we meet with him."

A barker yelled for all to board. From our position, we were among the first to the ferry. I asked McAllen to protect Virginia's other side, and he seemed grateful for an assignment. I wondered if he was going to start a fight when he roughly shouldered away two rushing men. I needn't have worried. They automatically veered away from the glowering sentinel who appeared to be escorting a lady. After we climbed the stairs to the top deck, McAllen looked more comfortable. I didn't have the heart to tell him that this vast open space would become congested after everyone boarded.

Virginia hooked one hand in each of her escorts' arms and led us to the railing. "I like to watch the boats and commerce on the river," she said.

She was a clever woman. McAllen would be more at ease with his back to the crowds and nothing but open water in front of him. Sharp soon joined us, and McAllen pulled a flask from his coat pocket. Soon we were passing the flask back and forth and pointing out three-masted clippers, side-wheel steamers, brigs, schooners, and countless barges. It was a glorious summer day, and commerce on the Hudson was booming.

When the ferry arrived with a light thud on the

other side, we waited for the deck to clear before we climbed down and walked over to the nearby train station.

As we waited on the platform, Sharp casually said, "I learned somethin' from that foreman." He looked at me.

"Edison's in trouble."

Chapter 16

The train was designed to transport a large number of people to and from the ferry crossing. The wood seats all faced in the same direction and were supposed to accommodate three people on each bench. If six men were forced to sit abreast, I presumed McAllen would have found a horse. The mid-afternoon train was not crowded, so we spread out onto three seats, Virginia and I sharing.

McAllen sat across the aisle, and Sharp in the seat in front. I tapped Sharp on the shoulder.

"What did that foreman say?"

McAllen leaned over to hear as well.

"Edison's way behind. He promised electricity to the first district before winter. His investors are gettin' nervous 'cuz his competitors are well ahead. The Brush Company used arc lights to illuminate Broadway from Union Square to Delmonico's restaurant. Now people call it the Great White Way. Ya can imagine the amount of free publicity that's gettin' Brush. Maxim illuminated the Mercantile Safe Deposit an' Trust Company. Lewis, another competitor, electrified the Hamilton Hotel. Needless to say, all the kingpins visit these buildings to see what Edison has so far failed to deliver. Edison's supposed to illuminate District 1, which includes Wall Street an' Newspaper Row." Sharp gave me a long look. "Steve, he can't afford to lose the confidence of those two."

"A foreman on the docks told you all this?" McAllen asked from the other side of the aisle.

"Accordin' to him, electricity is the rage an' all anyone talks about. It's like a parlor trick made so big the whole city can watch. He said stevedores, porters, teamsters, clerks, an' everyone else is making bets on who'll win. Hell, supposedly Vanderbilt wanted his house electrified before Morgan, but Morgan took a trip an' gave Edison his entire house to work on for months. Now people travel for miles just to see his house lit up at night. It's a favorite for courtin' couples: dinner an' a stroll past Morgan's house. Men who can barely feed their families buy stock in the company they believe'll win. Edison was the favorite for a long time, but now people are abandonin' him."

"What about real investors? The Wall Street barons?" I asked.

"That foreman wouldn't know that." Sharp looked thoughtful. "Ya know, the speed of our summons tells me the Wall Street crowd is threatenin' to jump ship."

"There have been some bad newspaper stories," McAllen said. "I read he might lose investors."

"You've read newspaper stories about Edison?" I asked.

McAllen gave me the look he used when I said something stupid.

"Yes. And I've read reports from our New York office. I don't go into an engagement blind."

"Did you know what Sharp just told us?"

"More or less."

"Anything more?" I asked Sharp.

"Yep, but it's engineerin'. Too complicated for me. There are more pieces to an electric system than a navy war ship. Lots of things can go wrong."

McAllen leaned back in his seat.

"What's wrong?" I asked.

"This ain't my kind of work."

His expression didn't invite argument.

Chapter 17

It was twenty miles from the ferry to Menlo Park, so the ride took almost an hour. When we arrived, we found no station, just a bare platform. Two hours earlier, we'd been surrounded by teeming masses. Now we were in a bucolic setting without another soul in sight. The wooden platform, a telegraph line, and a few grazing cows were the only signs of civilization.

Sharp was grinning. "It appears Edison's fantastic creations are bein' invented in a pasture."

"I like the man already," McAllen said.

"I certainly hope I do," Virginia said. "I already like his work."

"I guess we march up this hill." Sharp led us off the platform and up some crude stone steps to a dirt road.

"I'm surprised he didn't send a buggy," I said, wondering how long a walk we'd have.

Just as I finished speaking, a buggy came bouncing down the road. The driver could not have been more than fourteen. He reined up and leaped out. "Are you the Mr. Dancy party?"

"We are," I answered.

"Mr. Edison has instructed me to take you to him promptly."

"Where is he?" I asked.

The boy looked startled by the question.

"In the lab. He's always in his lab . . . well, until recently. Now he spends time at his headquarters in Manhattan . . . unless he's on the street overlooking the work. But right now he's in Menlo Park . . . so that means he's in his lab."

Sharp smiled at McAllen. "I may like the man as well. An owner needs to be where the work's getting done."

"Then I'm surprised you don't own a brothel," McAllen said. Then he remembered Virginia was present. He tipped his western-style hat. "Beg pardon, ma'am."

She clambered aboard the buggy. "You haven't forgotten State Street have you, Captain?"

"No, ma'am, but we ain't in the West no more."

She settled into her seat. "How could you tell?"

We followed her into the buggy. McAllen sat with the driver, and the rest of us snuggled together in back. It was a short ride, partly because the compound was close, but mostly because the boy drove the buggy fast enough that we all searched for a handhold.

We reached a plateau with a cluster of buildings, most of them grouped into a compound surrounded by a white picket fence. Our young driver explained that these buildings were the laboratories and Edison's office. Edison's home was outside the fence alongside the road. The few other buildings gathered outside the fence barely qualified as a village. Forests fell away from the plateau in every direction, providing a pleasant view for several miles. If Edison wanted a research site with no distractions, he had found it.

The light gray buildings were plain and of simple construction. The one running down the center of the complex was a very long, two-story clapboard structure. Edison intended this to be an idea factory. A newspaper story had explained that Edison wanted to develop "a minor invention every ten days and a big thing every six months or so." We were gazing at the first village ever built dedicated solely to inventions.

Telegraph poles running in a line back toward Manhattan—symbolic of Edison's first big invention—provided his investors an open line of communication. He had devised a way to send four telegraph messages simultaneously over the same wire. At only twenty-seven, he had sold this "quadruplex telegraph system" to Western Union for thirty thousand dollars and continued to get a four-hundred-dollar-per-month retainer from the company. He had used much of the funding to finance this isolated laboratory, which was really only a short distance from Manhattan. The thought reminded me of McAllen's comment about being able to show New Yorkers wide-open country. Edison had found wooded isolation relatively close to his biggest market.

The driver led us through a gate in the picket

fence and then into the long two-story building. The inside startled me. One room extended the entire length of the building. At the near end sat clerks making notations in ledgers, while the far side appeared to be a complete machine shop with a forge, lathes, drills, and benches. A dozen or so workers were creating things out of metal. The most prominent noises were the clank of hammer against anvil and the screech of metal as it was turned on a lathe. A large array of hand tools hung neatly above the benches. The smell of scorched cutting oil pervaded the long room.

I made a quick count of twenty windows, but they had nothing to do with the bright light that pervaded every corner. The illumination came from strings of electric lamps that extended down the entire length of the room. Edison had captured that mysterious element called electricity and magically turned it into light. This was the first time I had actually seen his invention. If this was any indication, Edison's electric lamps worked, and worked incredibly well.

Steam engines, railroads, and the telegraph had shattered commonly held views of power, space, and time. Gaslight had changed human rhythms. According to Robert Louis Stevenson, because of gaslight, "the day was lengthened out to every man's fancy." This room proved that Edison was about to transform the world once again. The light was soft, odor free, flicker free, clean, cool, and soundless. All the things gaslight was not. Gaslights had to be lit and snuffed out one at a time; Edison could light a building at the flick of a switch. Rooms did not become overheated, the ever-present hiss was absent, walls were not smoke stained, and electric lamps did not need to be cleaned like blackened gaslight globes. Gaslights burned what Edison called a "vile poison" of ammonia, sulfur, and carbon dioxide which made some people feel ill after only a few hours. Edison claimed his light was healthier because it gave off no noxious fumes or smoke. Best of all, the light looked as natural as sunlight. An Edison-lit room was truly miraculous.

As the four of us stood gawking, the boy seemed anxious to move on and beckoned us to climb the stairs to the second floor. The top floor was as long as the building, the walls painted white and lined with shelving holding what must have been thousands of apothecary jars of various sizes and colors. The center of the room was a series of worktables with burners, microscopes, batteries, glass bulbs, wire, magnifying glasses, and all sorts of electrical devices. The two floors contained all the machines and chemistry apparatus needed to construct nearly anything. I hadn't counted, but I was sure there were well over fifty men working in the building.

The boy led us directly to Edison, who I recognized from photographs. He was wearing unkempt blue flannel workman's overalls, heavy boots, and a skullcap. The browned teeth chewing on an unlit cigar betrayed a regular habit. He certainly didn't look like one of the most famous men in the world. I knew from newspaper accounts that he was thirty-four years old, but gray already tinged his hair. We might have been of a similar age, but that was probably the only trait we shared. I was born to wealth; he was self-made. I'd attended Columbia University; he was self-educated. I had a stable home life; he ran away from home at sixteen. I left New York for the frontier; he remained within thirty miles of Manhattan. I was a businessman; he was an inventor. Despite our differences, I hoped we could work well together.

I held out my hand. Knowing Edison was partially deaf, I spoke loudly. "Mr. Edison, it is an honor to meet you. I'm Steve Dancy." I turned to my companions. "This is Mrs. Virginia Baker, Jeff Sharp, and Captain Joseph McAllen of the Pinkerton National Detective Agency."

"Yes, my pleasure, of course." He wiped his hands on a rough cloth he pulled from his back pocket before shaking. For a moment, he just stood there. He seemed to be assessing me. "I don't have a favorable opinion of the Dancy family, but William speaks highly of you." He returned the cloth to his back pocket. "I mean William Vanderbilt, of course."

"William has enormous faith in you. He talked me into buying shares in your company."

"Yes, he told me, but—" He looked McAllen up and down and seemed intrigued by his Smith and Wesson. "Well . . . unless the captain here can discover who's sabotaging my work, your shares may become worthless."

"Explain the problem," McAllen responded matter-of-factly.

Edison puffed his chest. "I'm bringing incandescent light to Manhattan, starting with District 1, which is bound by Nassau, Wall, South, and Spruce streets. I've bought and equipped a building on Pearl Street for a generator that can distribute electricity for a half mile in any direction. It's the subways that are the problem—first here, then in Manhattan. I believe someone is sabotaging my company, and I want you to find out who is behind it. This must be done very quietly, of course."

"Why quietly?" McAllen asked.

"I have important backers: Drexel, Morgan, the New York Times, Vanderbilt, Western Union . . . and others." He threw a glance my way, which told me I fell into the "other" category. "If they learn of a saboteur, they'll feel their investment is at greater risk. On the other hand, if no one is disrupting my work, they'll think I'm making excuses. Neither is acceptable. I need an answer, I need it fast, and I need the investigation kept quiet."

When McAllen didn't respond, Edison asked, "What do you know about electricity?"

"Nothin'," McAllen answered. "I know men."

Edison turned to me. "You told me he was the right man for the job."

"He is," I answered.

"I surround myself with only the best men," Edison said.

McAllen made a point of looking around the large room. "Then I shall look elsewhere."

"I was speaking about you. Are you the best?"

"I am the best west of the Mississippi." He shrugged. "I have no idea about this side of the river."

Edison looked exasperated at McAllen's apparent indifference. I had had similar feelings in the past. He could prove frustrating.

"Can you find the saboteur?" Edison asked. "Fast and quietly?"

"If there's a saboteur, I'll find him. It may not be as fast as you'd like, but I can keep it quiet." He looked around again. "Can these people?"

"They know nothing of this, and I escort people around all the time. They won't see anything out of the ordinary."

"They will," McAllen said. "I need to talk to some of them."

"No." Edison offered no explanation.

"Then I take back what I said about findin' him." McAllen's voice was completely neutral.

"In my experience, saboteurs come from inside or have an inside contact."

I could almost see Edison thinking.

Finally, he said, "See me before you talk to anyone . . . and you'll need to give me a reason. Always remember, speed is crucial. I have schedules to meet."

"Who wants you to fail?"

"What? That's a ridiculous question. Everyone. All my competitors want to see me fail. Hell, you can add criminals who want to work in the dark, religious nuts who accuse me of disturbing God's order, and every lamplighter afraid of losing his job."

"Who wants you to fail?" McAllen repeated. "If you want me to work this investigation, you need to answer my questions." His expression was completely blank. "I know what I need to know."

"A lot of people would enjoy seeing me fail," Edison answered in a bit of a huff. "I'm not shy about bragging about my inventions. That's how I got investors to back building this lab. People say I'm cocky, a blowhard; they want to be proven right. A smaller but still substantial number would actually profit from my failure. First would be the gaslight companies. After I illuminated the whole of Menlo Park on New Year's Eve, their stocks plummeted . . . here and in Britain. Then there are my competitors. Brush, Maxim, Jablochkoff, Sawyer, Lewis, and Fuller are the big ones. The money for whoever is first will be more than your imagination can conjure. And don't forget the British. The whole empire wants me to fail. Parliament created a committee to review my claims and dismissed them as 'unworthy.' They're highly motivated to protect their gaslight industries." He looked pleased with himself. "Does that give you enough suspects?"

"I thought you invented and patented the light bulb," I blurted. "How can these others use your invention?"

"I invented the incandescent bulb. Most of my competitors use arc lights. Except Hiram Maxim. He stole both my incandescent design and Ludwig Boehm, one of my best men." He jabbed his unlit cigar at McAllen. "I suggest you start with him."

"Any problems with Tammany?" I asked.

"No. The city made me hire five inspectors. I thought they might make trouble, but they only come around on Saturdays to collect their pay envelopes."

"Tell me about your first problems with the subways," McAllen asked, regaining control of the conversation. "Here, at Menlo Park."

I could tell from Edison's expression that he appreciated the astute question.

"When we dug the five-mile subway here, we had to dig up the entire length three times because the lines kept shorting. We tried different insulations. All of them were tested and should have worked. We were delayed digging our trenches in District 1 until we got it working properly here. That's when I became suspicious that something other than nature was interfering with my work."

"I want a list of all of your employees from a month prior to diggin' this subway until now. Start dates for everyone and end dates for those no longer in your employ. If you have it, I want their prior employer, especially if it was one of the six competitors you mentioned. Can I get it today?"

Edison shoved his cigar in his mouth and walked over to the boy who had driven us from the train. After a whispered conversation, the boy ran down the stairs, I presumed to one of the clerks we had seen on the first floor.

When Edison returned to our little group, he said, "You'll have it within the hour."

"Thank you," McAllen said.

Virginia stepped forward. "I'm hesitant to appear forward, but would a demonstration of your inventions be possible?"

Edison smiled as he met Virginia's eyes. "That can be arranged, but not by me. I apologize, but I have something I must do. I presume you want a demonstration of my phonograph. All the ladies want to hear themselves."

"That would be wonderful. I'm also interested in the carbon microphone you invented for Bell's telephone." She looked out over the room.

"Actually, I'd like to see it all." She returned his smile. "Perhaps at a later time, you could explain your quadruplex. It seems like it should be impossible to send four messages at once. It must be quite clever."

"You seem very informed for a woman."

"My late husband was an engineer. I've always found inventions fascinating . . . especially yours. Your work is truly heroic."

Edison's self-satisfied expression showed that Virginia had made a new friend.

"The only other woman to show such keen interest was Sarah Bernhardt. I had the pleasure of escorting her through my laboratories." He made a little bow. "I will have someone see to a tour . . . and then if you can join us, we can talk at dinner."

McAllen cleared his throat and spoke almost rudely. "I understand Brush has lighted up Broadway, Lewis the Hamilton Hotel, and Maxim the Mercantile Buildin'. Who else is ahead of you in Manhattan?"

Edison nearly bit off the end of his cigar. "No one is ahead of me. Brush only installed street lights. Lewis and Maxim only fitted indoor illumination. I'll do both in District 1, just as I have at Menlo Park. They strung their wires on existing polls . . . and Brush's arc lights required high voltage . . . high enough to kill when his wires fall to the ground. I'm burying my wires."

He waved his arm to encompass the room. "This is a small part of my operations. Beyond those rail tracks you came in on is a factory that produces over a thousand light bulbs a day. A thousand! My Pearl Street Station is the most advanced electricity-generating facility in the world. I electrified Morgan's home and a Fifth Avenue brownstone I use as headquarters for operations. My accomplishments may not have the visibility of the Mercantile or Broadway, but they're far more advanced than any of my competitors'."

McAllen seemed indifferent to Edison's ire. "One more question, for now. Who supplies your copper wire and iron pipes?"

I looked at Sharp, but he gestured that he had no idea where the question came from. I could tell from Edison's face that McAllen had struck a nerve.

"For the most part, my copper wire comes from Thomas Doolittle in Connecticut. I order iron pipe from several different foundries in New Jersey and Pennsylvania."

"Although you had delays, you perfected the insulated subway process here at Menlo Park. The biggest delays in Manhattan, however, have been labor and material shortages. Is that not true?"

"It is." Edison looked intrigued by the line of questioning.

"May I have the names of your procurement people, the executives at your suppliers, and the head of the express company you use? I would also appreciate it if you would let Mr. Dancy read your supply contracts."

"Of course. Anything further?"

"Two desks downstairs."

Edison looked at Sharp and Virginia. "Will you all require sleeping accommodations?"

"Tonight only," McAllen said. "We'll be returnin' to Manhattan sometime tomorrow."

Edison walked off looking more at ease.

Sharp gave McAllen an odd look.

"What?" McAllen asked.

"I was tryin' to remember. Didn't ya say this wasn't your type of work?"

Chapter 18

Edison arranged a tour with demonstrations for Virginia and Sharp. Before he left us, he invited Virginia to stay at his home and informed the rest of us we could spend the night in the boarding-house on the other side of the dirt road. Virginia seemed excited to sleep away from me. I was disappointed.

McAllen and I went downstairs to find that two desks had already been cleared. While McAllen examined the lists of employees and suppliers, I read purchase agreements, making notations by company and totaling the dollars spent with each. Other than the large sums of money, I noticed nothing unusual about the contracts or the companies. William Vanderbilt had told me it would cost half a million dollars to illuminate District 1. Now I could see why.

When I finished, I stepped over to the supervising clerk and asked if he had a record of actual delivery dates compared to scheduled delivery dates. After a moment's hesitation, he wordlessly handed me a ledger from his desk.

The ledger was meticulously maintained, with a page for each commodity. I concentrated on iron pipe and wire. After an hour, I sat back in my chair and looked over my notes. Could this be coincidence? As I pondered, something else occurred to me. I returned to the supervising clerk and asked if he had a record of labor stoppages and shortages. He directed me to a clerk several desks away. Soon I was back at my assigned desk, with both ledgers open to the same dates. After comparing the information in both, I returned them to the clerks. The supervising clerk seemed enormously relieved. He had been instructed to cooperate with us but obviously felt uncomfortable with having his precious records in someone else's hands.

Instead of returning to my desk, I walked over to McAllen. "Care for a walk?" I asked.

He nodded, and without further discussion, we left the building. When we got outside the picket fence, McAllen turned left.

I jerked a thumb in the direction of the rail tracks. "Don't you want to see a factory that can manufacture a thousand light bulbs a day?"

McAllen shook his head. "The guard has been instructed to admit no one without Edison."

"How do you know that?"

"I asked the New York office to investigate security. It was in their report."

"When did you ask for this investigation?"

"Before I left Leadville . . . Actually right after you told me about this engagement."

"What else was in the report?"

"The factory is guarded, but security for the

laboratory depends on those clerks. Not bad. Clerks may not be armed guards, but six men would certainly notice someone enterin' that didn't belong. The agency team recommended a guard at the Manhattan headquarters building and Pearl Street Station. Edison agreed and engaged Pinkerton services around the clock."

"That must have taken weeks to coordinate."

McAllen shrugged. "Sharp was searching for a silver claim, and you were busy with Mrs. Baker."

I turned left and started walking in the direction opposite the train platform. McAllen silently kept pace beside me.

When we were well beyond the small cluster of buildings, I said, "I found something interesting."

"Figured."

"Deliveries have been late, but not uniformly late. If you look individually at the wire or iron pipe, there seems to be no pattern." I looked at McAllen to gauge his reaction. "But if you look at them in combination with the labor problems, then something is always short."

"Different clerks."

"That wasn't a question, was it?"

"I saw you take a ledger from that other clerk." He sounded distracted.

Since McAllen seemed to be thinking, I kept quiet. Soon the dirt road narrowed until it was not much wider than a horse path. I could hear nothing but nature sounds, and not even many of those. It was very peaceful.

"We have a conspiracy."

I glanced at McAllen, but he just looked off into the distance. I kept silent while he remained deep in thought.

Suddenly, he turned around and walked back toward the laboratory. When I caught up, he said, "Steve, I want you to estimate how much money is involved with this illumination thing. Say, over the next ten years."

"Okay, but it'll be a guess. What else do you know?" I asked.

"I know it's difficult to corrupt a dozen men, especially successful men eager to sell their product to what will be the biggest industrial endeavor of all time. The pattern you found was not produced by company owners; it could be done only by teamsters. Material delivery and intimidation of laborers . . . teamsters are a rough sort, so they could handle both. The puzzle is, who's behind the teamsters? They didn't come up with this on their own. They're doin' someone else's biddin'."

"Any clue?"

"Not yet. But I know where to look."

Chapter 19

By the time the village came into sight, we heard a dinner bell and saw scores of people crossing to the boardinghouse. Since we hadn't seen a restaurant, we quickened our pace so we wouldn't be late for supper. As we got closer, I saw Virginia's back as she strolled down the road with Edison. I presumed she would eat with the wizard and his family. Then I spotted Sharp marching in our direction.

"What's up the road?" Sharp asked as if it had any relevance to our sojourn in Menlo Park.

"Nothin' . . . just a trail," McAllen answered. "What's the practice here?" He nodded at the men rushing toward the boardinghouse.

"Everyone eats together downstairs. I heard the food's pretty good, but we've been invited to supper with Mr. Edison an' his family. For sleepin', they assigned us a guest room upstairs in the boardin'house. I've moved our things in."

"Do we have time to clean up?"

"Mr. Edison said to come right over just as we are."

As we started down the road, Sharp asked, "What'd ya learn?"

McAllen responded. "We learned Edison is probably not makin' excuses. Nothin' certain, but it appears he has a saboteur."

We had already reached the Edison home, and McAllen stopped before entering the fenced yard.

"Jeff, we need to talk. Privately. I think you can help."

Sharp looked at the house as if thinking. "After supper. I understand it will be a quick meal 'cuz Edison likes to return to the lab." He pointed to a small building. "That's a tavern. We can talk there."

"Is it private?" McAllen sounded doubtful.

Sharp smiled. "I already tested their wares. It may not look it, but they offer a fine selection of Scotch whiskeys. There are benches in back under a tree where we can talk privately."

"I'm glad the captain found you work," I said. "We need something that'll keep you out of disreputable establishments."

"Not exactly," McAllen said. "In fact, what I have in mind may require visits to many more disreputable establishments."

"Do say." Sharp smiled and sounded intrigued.

"After supper. We don't want to keep our host waitin'."

Mary Edison opened the door and greeted us with an awkward smile. She looked to be in her mid-twenties, and my first impression was of an unhappy woman. I wondered if the rumors were true that after their wedding, Edison had returned to his lab and worked late into the night, forgetting about his new bride. Two youngsters clutching her skirt peeked around at us like we were strange creatures. After some perfunctory introductions and pleasantries, she bid us into her home with a wave of the hand.

"These are our two children," she said. "Marion and Thomas. Tom calls them Dot and Dash. Please, come into the parlor."

The home was expensively decorated in the latest fashion, and although a couple of more hours of summer sun remained, the house was extensively lit with the invention of its owner. We found Edison and Virginia waiting in the parlor, sipping red wine.

"Ah, I see you got the message. We'll dine in a few moments, but first tell me what you've found. Mary, please serve our guests wine, and then I'm sure you'll need to assist Sara with our meal."

As Mary Edison poured wine, he added in the overly loud voice of the partially deaf, "It has been such a pleasure conversing with Mrs. Baker. She's quite astute about engineering. I'd hire her as a lab assistant except she's too beautiful." He smiled roguishly. "She'd disrupt the work of my men. Can't have that." He patted her arm. "You're the type of woman I should have married. Clever enough to invent on your own." Mary set my wine down with a little more force than required. The snap of the glass drew the attention of her husband.

"Thank you, dear. Now please see to dinner."

The dismissal was almost cruel. No, it was cruel, especially considering his tone of voice. After she had left the room, Edison looked at McAllen and said, "Well?"

"How much time do you spend at the subway sites?" McAllen asked in a loud voice.

Edison looked annoyed at the lack of an answer but said, "I spend four or more days a week in the city, and about half of that time, I'm inspecting work. I do many of the electrical connections myself. Why?"

"Do you know the men on the work crews?"

"Of course. They're good men. I told you I hire the best."

"Have you seen anyone watchin' the work that didn't belong?"

"Mr. McAllen, I'm famous, and this project is in the newspapers almost daily. There are always sightseers."

"I want to put a Pinkerton at the scene. If you're being sabotaged, then someone is keepin' an eye on your progress. A professional can spot him or her."

"Are you aware that late projects cost more than they should? You already made me hire Pinks to guard my Fifth Avenue headquarters and Pearl Street Station. I'm trying to electrify the first district, not employ everyone in your New York office." Edison spoke this last as if it settled the subject. "Did you discover *anything* today?"

I thought McAllen would reassure him that his suspicions were valid, but instead he said, "It's too preliminary to speculate. I'll inform you immediately if I discover anything important and include all of my findin's in weekly reports. Until then, we watch for a person checkin' on your progress."

"No."

When I had hired McAllen, and we disagreed, he threatened to resign if I didn't relent. I expected a similar reaction.

Instead, he said, "I'll post a person and pay for it out of my fee on the followin' condition: you pay for the man if he proves instrumental in advancin' the case."

A short staring contest ensued, then Edison said, "Agreed. Anything else?"

"How are supplies delivered to the work site?"

"What? Wagons, of course."

"Always the same hauler?"

"Adams Express Company. They're one of my investors. Small, but faithful." He looked puzzled. "Why?"

McAllen gestured, showing indifference. "Procedure. If they're normally at the site, I'll instruct my agent to look elsewhere. One last piece of advice; don't change anything. Don't act any different. If we're gonna find this supposed saboteur, nothin' can change. We can't raise suspicions."

"I wouldn't have hired you if I had thought the saboteur was 'supposed.' He's quite real, and I expect you to proceed with the same conviction."

"Of course. We'll find him . . . or her."

Edison appeared a bit puzzled by McAllen's final remark but let it go. Before we finished our wine, he led us to dinner. The meal was ordinary. Mary Edison probably had received little notice that she would be serving guests, but I had a feeling that roasted beef, boiled potatoes, and string beans were normal fare for this house. Edison seemed oblivious to the kind of comforts many strived to obtain. I suspected he viewed food as mere fuel. He spent money freely, but only across the road at his laboratories.

Virginia was to remain after the meal, but she interrupted our departure to have a whispered conversation with McAllen. I wondered what they were talking about but figured one or the other would let me know soon enough.

It was twilight as we walked along the dirt road. The entire world seemed still in this village surrounded by forest. Not even the slightest breeze rustled the leaves. The fading light made colors subtle and shadows pronounced. A drink outside seemed like a grand idea, but McAllen had indicated that he wanted to first send a telegram to the Pinkerton office so they would immediately station a guard at the work site. After McAllen used the telegraph in the laboratory, we followed

Sharp back to the tavern. I asked McAllen why he hadn't told Edison about our discoveries.

"Edison's impaired hearin' causes us to talk loud. I'd rather put our discoveries in writin' than shout it out."

"He wants speed. Why not give him a hint of our suspicions?"

"Because when Edison listed the people eager to see him fail, he forgot to mention his wife."

Chapter 20

The tiny tavern was crowded, but it wasn't difficult to find privacy outdoors. We pulled one of the benches around so we could sit facing each other. As we sipped our whiskey, we explained to Sharp that there were always shortages at the subway work site. Nothing in particular seemed to be a consistent problem, but laborers, iron pipe, copper wire, or something else always seemed to be missing to slow down progress.

"Jeff, you're the closest of us to an engineer," McAllen said. "I know the light bulb works, but do you think Edison's whole installation will work? It seems complicated as hell."

"Yep. Saw it with my own eyes on the tour. Yer right, it's not just a light bulb. To deliver electricity to an entire district takes all kinds of devices an' lots of plannin'. Edison's not just an inventor. He's a businessman. He doesn't move somethin' forward until it can make a profit. He put a lot of thought about how to deliver illumination cheaper than gaslight. I have absolute faith in his work . . . an' the work of his people. As far as I can tell, they're the best." He looked at me. "Virginia agrees."

"If this contrivance works," McAllen said, "then someone *is* sabotagin' his project. His clerks are cautious, his contracts coordinated, and his deliveries are carefully scheduled. Yet deliveries are late, or key skills are absent, or supplies have gone missin'. No one has a string of bad luck that long."

"Do ya think it's one of his clerks?" Sharp asked.

"I considered the supervisin' clerk, but it would be hard for him to coordinate it all from here," McAllen answered. "Besides, he saw Steve lookin' at material deliveries and seemed unperturbed at what he might find. He also doesn't operate a telegraph. I asked in front of his men, and none looked surprised at his denial. The telegraph is against the wall in their area, so if he used it, someone would notice. We won't rule out anyone yet, but my bet would be someone at the project site."

Sharp rubbed his chin. "It would need to be a foreman or possibly the superintendent. Seems unlikely with Edison always hangin' around."

"There's another possibility." McAllen paused for effect. "The teamsters could be behind the delays."

"Damn." Sharp quit rubbing his chin and smiled at McAllen. "Ya want me find the pub where those teamsters drink. Get friendly. Now I get that 'disreputable establishment' remark."

"I love a man I don't have to explain things to. If you went with that dock foreman, you'd look real natural."

Sharp rubbed his chin again. "Well, Captain, I don't care to use my friends that way, especially new ones."

"Then I'll add him to the suspect list so you won't be takin' advantage of a friend."

Sharp and I laughed because McAllen seldom made a humorous remark. Then we looked at each other, each wondering if he had meant to be humorous. McAllen smiled, which he also did rarely, and I knew he was ribbing us.

"Steve, I want you to talk to the men on this list."

He handed me a piece of paper. I recognized some of the names from the contracts I had read.

"Ask why their shipments were late. Check their shipment records from their side. Look for overlong transports. Ask if they received orders different from the ledger notations. Find out who hires teamsters at Adams Express. Look for a common thread."

"You said talk. You don't want me to telegraph?"

"No. Take the train." He pointed at the paper. "None of those men are far away. We'll discuss it further if it looks like you'll need to go to Pennsylvania, but I doubt it. If there's somethin' to be found, you'll probably find it in Connecticut or New Jersey."

"What will you do?"

"Check out the Pinkerton records for these businesses and the owners. I also intend to spend some time at the diggin'." He looked across the road at the laboratory. "I don't believe there is anything to be discovered in that buildin'. Edison claimed he hires only good men, and I think he does."

I thought a minute. "I'm going north first. There's only one wire supplier, so I'm more likely to find something at the Connecticut manufactory. I can go and be back on the same day. Virginia will be happy to shop without me."

"Steve, Virginia stays here . . . with Mary Edison. At least for a few days."

I didn't like that idea on a number of levels. "Joseph, it might be dangerous. She's not trained for that type of work."

"She handled herself in one of the roughest districts in a coarse minin' town. She can handle one lonely woman. Besides, it was her idea."

"Her idea? Why would she get an idea like that in her head?"

"I'm not sure. I think she wants to spend more time in the laboratory. It could help to have someone inside the Edison household."

"But have they invited her?"

"Both of the Edisons invited her to stay in their home. They like her, especially Thomas."

Should I be jealous? No, I decided. Virginia was fascinated with Edison's inventions, not the man. He was married and his wife would be in the house. No need to worry. I still didn't like the notion, but it was Virginia's, and I didn't want to be the one to tell her no. Actually, I did want to but knew I'd better hold my tongue. She could be stubborn, and if I told her where she could go and not go, she would probably tell me where to go. I couldn't risk losing her over something as innocent as her staying in the home of one of the most famous people in the world.

"Joseph, after I finish in Connecticut, I'm stopping back here to see if she's comfortable. Besides, I'll probably need to examine the ledgers again."

"Sounds reasonable."

McAllen took a big swallow to drain the last of his drink.

"Fellas, I see the bottom of my glass. I believe we should fill these up again . . . courtesy of Mr. Thomas Edison."

Chapter 21

Breakfast at the boardinghouse had been excellent. I suspect it was designed to keep Edison's staff happy in this isolated miniature village. The cook offered to make me anything, but I wolfed down a bowl of mush, a couple of biscuits, and coffee so I could hurry over to see Virginia.

She answered my knock at the Edison home. I nodded toward the porch, and she stepped out with me. She confirmed that she wanted to stay with the Edisons a few days. I told her to be careful. I didn't tell her what we had discovered, because McAllen insisted on controlling all disclosures about the case. I explained that we'd be gone for a day or two and felt deflated when she told me I needn't hurry back. My face must have shown my feelings, because she assured me that if she wanted to leave, she was fully capable of getting back to our hotel.

Sharp, McAllen, and I left Menlo Park on the morning's second train. It was still too crowded for McAllen, but he got through the short ride without shooting anyone. When we reached Cortlandt Street dock, Sharp went off on his own in search of the foreman he had spoken to earlier. McAllen didn't speak until we caught a cab and were well clear of the bustle on the dock.

He slid the glass partition open. "Take us to District 1," he ordered.

"Where 'bouts, sir?"

"Drop us at the Western Union station on Wall." He slid the partition closed and turned to me. "Send a telegram to Thomas Doolittle. Get an appointment for tomorrow. While you wait for the return message, I'll go over to the Pinkerton office. It's a short walk. When I return, we'll look at this subway."

There was no more discussion. McAllen was as talkative in a cab as he was on horseback. That was fine with me. I was more interested in becoming reacquainted with my city. What I saw didn't please me. Electricity had become a mania, wires strung every which way. I spotted three work crews hanging more wires from newly installed poles. Edison had the right idea. One supplier for a district meant a monopoly, but it also meant safe streets and a clear sky.

New York City generated energy and wealth, but after the West, I was disappointed by its seedier aspects. Everywhere I looked, there were hustlers, ragpickers, beggars, prostitutes, and children hunting for anything to steal. If this was going on in the streets, what was happening in the alleyways?

The coachman opened the glass panel. "I'm going up Broadway. Edison has Nassau torn up."

"No . . . go up Nassau," McAllen ordered. "I

want to see what this supposed genius is doin'."

"It'll take forever, mate." He leaned his head almost into the hole. "I'll have to charge you extra."

"If it's an honest charge, I'll pay." McAllen slammed the window closed to emphasize his condition of payment.

"I guess we'll get an early look at the subway," I said.

"Yep. Keep your eye on the sightseers. Look for someone who appears indifferent to the work, but watchful. Maybe we'll get lucky."

"Man or woman?"

McAllen looked out of the window for so long, I thought he was ignoring my question. When he spoke, he sounded as if he were musing. "If this were my operation, I'd pay a flower girl to keep an eye on things. She'd look natural. Flower girls are always lookin' for a crowd. Nobody would think it odd for her to be there day after day."

Then I heard a yell from another driver.

"Damn it, man, hold yer horses!"

Our cab pulled up so quickly, I was thrown forward. McAllen and I stuck our heads out of opposite windows. The street ahead was dug up on the right side, with workmen everywhere. Carriages, buggies, and cabs lined up single file tried to squeeze their way through the turmoil by keeping to the left. Adding to the disorder, traffic was trying to merge from a cross street. Our driver had evidently tried to sneak in before his turn, which got him a curse and a challenge from a teamster driving a beer wagon. The teamster was beefy, and our driver wisely pulled up to let him enter the street.

I settled back in my seat. "Joseph, we can't see anything from inside this carriage, and we're going to look odd with our heads sticking out these windows. Let's pay the driver and walk."

McAllen slid the glass panel open. "We're gettin' out. How much?"

"Oh no ya don't. I'm stuck in this mess now. Ya stay put until I clear Nassau. There's a copper on the corner. He'll stop ya if I yell at 'im."

"How much to the end of Nassau?" McAllen asked.

"Five dollars . . . at least."

I saw McAllen's face go red, so I interjected before he could jump out and jerk the driver down into the street. "You mean three dollars, I believe, sir. Otherwise, we'll be the ones requiring the services of that policeman."

"Plus a fifty-cent tip, mate."

I handed him three silver dollars. "We'll get out here . . . and that includes your tip."

Without waiting for a reply, we both jumped out of the cab into ordered chaos. Dust flew everywhere as workers threw shovel after shovel of dirt onto mounds that ran along the trench. Three foremen paced back and forth along separate sections of the footway, constantly urging their team to dig faster than the scalawags on the other two teams.

Edison's crew seemed to have dug up only a single block. I surmised that Tammany would let them disrupt only one block at a time. We tried to take a closer look at the work, but the policeman held his baton against McAllen's chest to stop our progress. He told us to cross over to the left sidewalk. McAllen stopped, looked at the baton blocking his path, and then looked up until he held the policeman's eyes. Neither blinked for a moment. The policeman lowered the baton.

"Sir, please move to the sidewalk on the other side of the street."

Without taking his eyes off the policeman, McAllen said, "Steve, do we have any document that shows we work for Mr. Edison?"

I started to say no but remembered I still had the telegram Edison had sent, bidding us to Menlo Park. I handed it to the policeman.

He handed it back. "This is signed with an E. That doesn't tell me anything."

"Hey!" McAllen yelled. "This policeman wants to speak to a foreman."

Several men looked up and then yelled further up the street. Soon a big, gruff-looking man sauntered over.

"What's the problem?" he asked.

Before the policeman could speak, McAllen

asked, "How does Edison sign his correspondence?"

"With an E," the foreman said immediately.

McAllen showed the telegram to the foreman. "I'm with the Pinkerton Agency, and we've been engaged to protect the materials at this work site. I want to talk to my man. Where is he?"

He scowled and pointed up the street. "Hell, we work around the clock here. Who do ya think's gonna challenge my crew to steal something?"

McAllen leaned almost imperceptibly closer to the foreman. "Most materials are stolen by workmen . . . usually with a payoff to the foreman."

For a moment, I thought the foreman was going to take a swing at McAllen, but in the end he just turned and walked back to the line of swinging picks and shovels. Any hope of a good relationship with the crew was gone. I could have objected or tried to smooth out the situation, but in my experience, everything McAllen did had a purpose. I trusted him.

We followed directly on the heels of the foreman. Without looking back, he said in a loud voice, "Watch those picks. They hurt like hell when they hit ya."

McAllen grabbed him by the scruff of the neck and flipped him around. "No threats," he said in his quiet tone that really meant business. "If even a shovel of dirt gets dumped on our feet, I'll see

160

you fired. Let's get this straight: I don't like you and you don't like me. That's the nature of things." McAllen let him go. "Now take me to my agent."

The foreman made a quick sweep of the workmen with his eyes. Everyone pretended not to notice, but they did. He threw McAllen an angry look but barked orders to be careful with guests in the area. With no more delay, we marched single file down the line of workmen.

At the intersection of the next street, we found copper wire wound around huge wood spools and stacks of iron pipes held in place with four-foot steel spikes. Other building materials were thrown wherever room could be found. I looked back at the workmen. There had been no letup in their rhythmic swings, and I saw not one pair of eyes looking up in curiosity. I found that odd, especially since McAllen had demeaned their foreman.

I had no trouble identifying the Pinkerton agent. He was the only person in the work area wearing a dark suit. He had positioned himself so he could watch the entire street and the staged materials. And at the moment, he was appraising us.

"Wait here," McAllen said. "I need a moment."

McAllen showed the agent his identification, and they walked a few paces up the street to talk in private. I watched the work until I remembered that McAllen had told me to keep an eye on the crowd of onlookers. The first thing that caught my attention was a flower girl. She was pretty in a light pink dress, pushing a cart full of colorful flowers. Without a doubt, she was the sunniest object on this harsh gray and brown street. If her brightness didn't cause her to stand out, her immodestly untied neckline certainly drew attention. Was that the way to observe without being noticed? I watched her for several minutes, and her sales were brisk. As she moved along the street, she sold flowers not only to the men on the opposite footpath, but also to those in carriages stalled in traffic. As she bent low to show off her wares, her eyes would flit across the street to the grunting men laboring on the subway. They were intelligent eyes. She impressed me as far too sharp and pretty to be earning her keep as a flower girl. Damn. McAllen was uncanny.

Marveling at McAllen's detective skills, I saw something far more startling on the other side of the street. Hugo Kelly. What the hell was he doing here? He must have returned to New York City after we had chased him out of Leadville, but what were the chances I would run into him on the street? I got my answer when he tipped his bowler hat to me. This was no accident. The man had somehow found me. Without a second thought, I hurried to the corner and raced across the street. I lost him in the crush of people but then spotted him ducking down an alley. I raced after him. As soon as I entered the alley, I stopped. What was I doing? I had reverted to my old city habits and was not carrying a gun. Kelly had obviously lured me into this alley, and I had been a fool to pursue him. Just as I made up my mind to retreat and talk this over with McAllen, I felt a searing pain just above my neck.

Then everything was blackness.

Chapter 22

I woke to pain. I tried to move my head and realized that was a horrible idea. Pain seared through my legs, my neck, my head—even my eyes throbbed. The ceiling told me I was in my room at the Fifth Avenue Hotel, but any further thought was too painful. I passed out.

The next time I woke, the pain had been replaced by an unremitting ache. I could move my head a bit without feeling like I would faint again. I spotted Sharp asleep in an easy chair that he had pulled up alongside the bed.

"How long was I out?" I asked.

He didn't respond at first, but my words must have penetrated his sleep. He slowly opened his eyes and said, "How're ya feelin'?"

"Like I've been beat up."

"Ya have. Worked over pretty good by a couple of toughs with blackjacks. Ya got bruises all over, includin' yer legs, but no broken bones, an' the doc doesn't think yer concussed."

"Good to know, because I feel broken and crushed. My head hurts . . . well, everything hurts."

"Blackjacks'll do that. Nasty weapon. The good news is they hit you in the back of the neck to put ya to the ground. Never banged yer head around once ya were down. Nice professional beatin'. Lots of pain, but no permanent damage."

"How long?"

"How long what?"

"How long was I out?"

"A day."

"Sure could use some water."

"Now that's a problem. When ya were out, we lifted ya into a sitting position to pour water down yer throat. Now yer gonna need to sit up while awake . . . and it's gonna hurt."

I moved one leg to get leverage and pushed myself up with a grunt. Sharp immediately shoved two pillows behind my back. The good news was that I could move, but the exertion caused the aching to worsen. I had been thrown from my horse when I was fifteen. I had suffered lots of bruises, but they were only on my shoulder and buttocks. This was much worse. Whoever worked me over had managed to hit every muscle in my body.

Sharp handed me a cool glass of water that I drank as fast as I could swallow. It was wonderful—better than any beer I could remember. When I finished, I tested my limbs and confirmed for myself that nothing was broken. If my recovery was similar to that when I was fifteen, I would be moving around in a day or two and fairly fit in about a week.

"Where's Virginia?"

"Still at Edison's. We didn't want to disturb her

until you woke. Nothin' she could do here but worry."

I didn't speak because I was angry. I knew it would be hard to raise my voice without putting stress on my battered body. My guess was McAllen didn't send her a telegram because he didn't want to interrupt her spying. Her being set up in the Edison house was just too good an opportunity to discard. I had experienced his single-mindedness before. He let nothing interfere with pursuing a case. I took a breath to calm myself and decided to deal with this later.

After a moment, Sharp asked, "What caused ya to charge into that alley?"

"Stupidity." I answered too aggressively and winced.

"You got that right."

It was McAllen's voice. He had either been in the room the whole time, or I hadn't heard the door. I turned my head slowly to get sight of him. He was standing in the passageway to the sitting room of my suite.

"If I hadn't followed you, the beating would have been worse."

"You stopped it?"

"I noticed you weren't fightin' back."

"Did you catch them?"

"One. The other ran while I was corrallin' the first. He's already out on bail. Told the police you insulted his girl and he lost his temper."

166

"Did the police know him?"

"Yep. Street thug for hire. No known address, no regular associates. Probably gone now. His bail was a pittance." McAllen left the passageway and walked over to my bed. "Steve, what drew you into that alley?"

"Hugo Kelly."

"What?" This came from Sharp, but McAllen's expression also showed rare surprise.

"I saw him across the street and chased him. It was dumb. This is my hometown. I'm not supposed to be a tenderfoot here."

McAllen chewed on what I'd told him. Eventually, he asked, "Do you think it was a chance meetin'?"

"Doubtful. He tipped his hat to me and looked smug. In hindsight, it was a trap. He might always have men around to protect him, but they would be members of his gang. From what you told me, those men were hired for the day. Also, they were positioned to jump me from behind, not to protect Kelly."

"He used himself as bait to get you into that alley," McAllen said, almost to himself. "That raises two questions. How did he know where to find you, and is he involved with this Edison business?"

"Ya know the answer to either of those questions?" Sharp asked.

"No." He paced back and forth at the foot of the

bed. "You embarrassed him, so he had reason to get even. Someone in his employ must have followed us . . . but all the way from Leadville? It's been almost two months since we chased him out of town. I'm sure I would have spotted someone in that amount of time. Also, whoever it was would have had to lie in waitin' at the ferry dock, because a stranger would have been spotted in Menlo Park. And how would Kelly find out we were on Nassau Street in time for him to get there with his hired thugs?"

Sharp rubbed his chin. "A telegram from the New Jersey side could have alerted him that we had boarded the ferry. Then he could have met us at the Cortlandt Street dock an' followed our cab." He looked directly at McAllen. "It could be done."

"If it's revenge, Kelly might not be involved with Edison's problems," McAllen said, continuing to pace.

"Joseph, if Kelly is part of this Edison business, he would have bided his time with Steve," Sharp said. "He wouldn't want to draw attention to himself . . . or his gang. Besides, yer the one with the entire Pinkerton organization behind ya. If he was protectin' a saboteur, it'd make more sense for him to come after the man with a detective badge, not an investor. He just wanted to teach Steve a lesson."

McAllen shook his head. "What you say sounds

right, but I don't believe in coincidence. He might be part of this and decided he could settle a score on the side." He stopped pacing and suddenly turned toward Sharp. "Did either of you mention Edison or Menlo Park to anyone in Leadville?"

"No one outside of us," he answered.

I nodded agreement.

He resumed his pacing. Finally, he stopped at the foot of the bed. "Here's my thinkin'. Kelly left a few men in Leadville. They kept an eye on the three of you. Kelly's not a man to let a public slight go unanswered. When you left Leadville, someone followed . . . possibly all the way to New York, but probably just to Denver, where he saw you buy tickets to New York. He had us followed after we arrived in the city. Then he picked us up at the dock, like Jeff said. When we separated at the work site, he saw his chance and lured you into the alley, where his men tried to beat you to death."

For the last few minutes, I had only been listening, because talking made my head throb. However, McAllen's comment prompted me to speak.

"I don't think they meant to kill me, just hurt me bad."

"Not accordin' to the doc," McAllen said. "This is a ritualistic murder used by New York gangs. They bruise you so bad with saps and blackjacks that eventually a deep clot in a muscle breaks free and travels to the lungs. The victim is in agony for days and then suddenly dies. It's slow and very painful. A revenge killin'."

Damn. It looked like McAllen had saved my life again. And in New York, of all places. This was going to take some thinking, but my head hurt too much at the moment. I simply said, "Thanks, Joseph."

McAllen looked a bit exasperated. "I know you won't heed my advice, but think before you act next time." He came around the side of the bed and spoke in a tone that let me know he wasn't really angry. "How are you feelin'?"

I proceeded to test each arm and leg. Then I ran my hand lightly along my ribs. There was severe soreness, but no real pain. "Better than when I first woke. Good enough to see Virginia." I hoped he saw I was angry. "I'd appreciate it if you'd send her a telegram . . . today, if it wouldn't be too big of a bother."

"I'll send it." In typical McAllen fashion, he offered no further explanation.

Still irritated, I said, "I'm hungry. And is there coffee around?"

Sharp stood and pulled a cord hanging on the wall to call a room attendant. "What do ya intend to do about all this, Steve?"

"Heal first." I paused. "Then think before I act."

Two people in the room laughed. I hurt too much.

McAllen said, "Steve, take the time to heal proper. My Pinkerton contract with Edison must be my priority, but after we clear this up, I'll give you a hand in dealin' with Kelly and his men. Not as an engagement, but as a friend."

For McAllen, this constituted an explanation and an apology. I sipped some more water and kept my voice even. "I suspect we'll be dealing with Kelly and his crew at the same time as the Edison sabotage."

McAllen cocked his head disapprovingly. I explained.

"Listen, Joseph, Kelly's a swindler and an extortionist. He can sniff out a racket from miles away. He wouldn't just follow us. He'd figure out why we were here. He came to town hungry, and my guess is that if he wasn't involved before, he is now."

I could tell from McAllen's expression that what I said made sense to him.

Sharp put into words what McAllen was probably thinking.

"Damn. Kelly probably shouldered his way into our business."

Chapter 23

A gentle shake woke me. It was Virginia's hand on my shoulder, and I was happy to see Sharp's cragginess replaced by a pretty face. She was a welcome sight, but I didn't care for her expression. She looked worried.

"What time is it?" I asked.

"Ten thirty."

Light was leaking from behind the curtain. "Morning?"

"Yes. You slept through the night. The doctor said that was good."

"Sharp plied me with whiskey last evening, so I'm not sure I wasn't just passed out." I moved a bit to test how much I still hurt. It was better, but I was probably not going to ride around in a bouncy carriage today. "Can you help me sit up?"

Virginia moved me into a sitting position and fluffed up the pillows behind my back. A hearty breakfast sat waiting on a tray, but I wanted water first. My mouth felt like it hadn't experienced the slightest moisture for a month. After drinking a full glass and part of a second, I swung my legs over the side of the bed. I was in a short dressing gown and saw my legs for the first time. They looked discolored, but not as bad as I expected.

As I studied them, Virginia said, "The doctor

says your bruises are already receding. He wanted you to try to walk today."

"No time like the present." I slid my feet to the floor and then allowed my legs to gradually support my full weight. So far, so good. Virginia offered me her arm, and after a moment of stupid hesitation, I took it. Without prompting, she helped me to the chamber pot, which I used standing. After washing my face and hands, I began to feel more normal. Then I tried a step alone and quickly grabbed Virginia's arm for support. Luckily, it was only three steps further to a stuffed chair. I fell into it with relief. She handed me the breakfast tray. I was suddenly famished and ate faster than usual.

"How do you feel?" she asked.

"Sore, but better than yesterday," I said while chewing. "Thankfully, that damn throbbing in my head is gone." I wolfed down a couple more bites. "When did you get here?"

"Last night. I caught the last ferry. You were already out, so I let you sleep."

I looked at the double bed and saw that she had slept beside me. I must have known at some level, because I had slept peacefully.

"Virginia, I'm glad you're here. I missed you."

"You shouldn't have had to miss me at all. I gave Captain Joseph McAllen a stern scolding. I don't believe he'll again delay telling me when you're in trouble."

I just kept eating, but her remarks made me happy. Not the part about getting in trouble again, but her insisting that McAllen tell her next time. I think I loved this self-assured, intelligent woman, but I constantly fretted that she didn't feel the same about me. If I'd had more guts, I would straight out ask her. I normally had no problem being direct, but I feared her answer more than I feared the upcoming confrontation with Hugo Kelly.

She watched me eat for a few minutes and then assumed a determined expression.

"Steve, I know I haven't told you this before, but I love you. I didn't realize how much until I read the telegram saying you were hurt." She shook her head as if amused by something. Then she forced a smile. "I think we ought to get married."

I almost choked. "Damn . . . that's a surprise."

Her smile vanished.

"A good one," I hurriedly added. "A very good one. I love you too." I was relieved to see her smile again, if somewhat hesitantly. I had blundered, so I made a lame excuse. "I just thought the man was supposed to ask."

She crossed her arms. "You'd never ask. You're a coward."

"Some might disagree."

"I'm not talking about a fight. I'm talking about love. Two different fields of combat. In one,

174

you're brave to the point of foolishness . . . in the other, you're just a fool."

"That's an odd argument for marriage."

She looked taken aback. "You're right." Uncrossing her arms, she held my attention with a sudden seriousness. "Let me try again. You ran to the frontier at least in part to get away from society women. Women like me. I was born to that life, but I ran away from it as well. We're kindred spirits—neither of us completely fits in the West or the East. To a large extent, we're strangers in both worlds, especially now. The point is, we're alike. We shun pretentiousness, resist wrong-doing, crave adventure, and above all, we want to make it on our own . . . following our own rules." She laid a hand on my forearm. "Steve, we shouldn't let fear of our past lives frighten us from living our future lives." She picked up my finished tray and set it aside. "I think we should marry—but not here. Out west. A wedding in the West will wed us to each other and our new home."

"You don't want family to attend our wedding?"

"Do you?"

"No. It would give my mother too much satisfaction to see me marry a socialite from Philadelphia. With my father gone, I don't intend to make my family part of my life again."

"Me either. So . . . we get married . . . and we marry out west?"

I had wanted reassurance, but marriage? Was I ready for that? Then I could feel a big smile on my face as I remembered the last two months with Virginia. Now those were two months I could repeat forever.

"I do."

"I do?"

I laughed. "Sorry . . . I mean yes. Let's get married."

I was happy. Very happy. My grin must have looked pretty silly. Thankfully, Virginia looked just as foolish, especially when she bent toward and then away from me a couple of times. She obviously wanted to embrace me but didn't know how much I still hurt.

"Can I hug you?" she asked.

"Tell you what, put your arms gently around me, and I'll hug you."

She did and I did. It felt natural. I had been with other women, but I felt like I'd only been marking time. I had gone west searching for something and found it. But if someone had asked before I left New York, I would never have said I was looking for a woman. Now I realized I was looking to fill a void in my life, a void caused, or at least exposed, by the death of my father. Virginia filled it nicely. I did need to clear up one thing, however.

I whispered in her ear, "When you say west, are you talking about Leadville?"

She laughed and broke our embrace. Leaning

back, she smiled with what looked like self-satisfied pleasure. "No . . . I suppose we're done with that town." She seemed to think through alternatives. "Steve, I don't need a permanent home . . . or at least one I live in all the time. You've been to Nevada, Arizona, and all over Colorado. I want to see this new land before there's a telegraph pole on every corner of it."

"You sound like my kind of woman."

"I'd better be. I take marriage seriously. And don't die on me like my first husband. You'd better start being careful. Think before you jump into a fight. I want you to hang around for a long time."

"I'm getting that advice a lot lately. The repetition is beginning to scare me."

"Because we're all worried." The expression she'd worn when I woke returned. "You're going after Kelly, aren't you?"

"Kelly's after me. There's no reason to think he'll give up because his last attack failed. Unless I'm ready to run, I think the smart thing to do is to find our friend and make sure he is no longer a threat to me or my family."

"Your family?"

"You, Virginia. You're my family now. If memory serves, you were on that dusty street as well. In fact, you were the one who got all the women fired up to face down Kelly and his crew. You're on his list. I also want you to hang around a long time, so that means putting Kelly behind bars . . . or underground."

She looked like she was about to argue, but then I could tell by her face that she realized I was right. It was Kelly or us.

Chapter 24

For supper, I wanted to go downstairs to the hotel restaurant. I needed to get out, or I'd start to feel like an invalid. During the afternoon, I had taken several walks around my room. Each had been less painful, so I felt like I could handle a longer jaunt, as long as I remained inside the hotel.

The hardest part was getting dressed. I was surprised how much I moved my limbs to put on clothes. Something I had done daily without a thought suddenly became a horrific chore. Despite my initial protestations, Virginia helped me dress. Secretly, I was grateful. I needed the help. Everything was fine until I grabbed the shoulder holster I used to carry my Remington .38.

"Steve, you don't need that," she said.

I managed to get an arm through one of the straps. "How would you know?"

"Joseph has assigned you a bodyguard. He's outside the door."

"Good." I struggled until I got my other arm through the leather strap. "I don't think I can draw quickly, but I feel more comfortable with my gun."

"We'll be safe inside the hotel."

"I thought I was safe on the street in front of hordes of onlookers. I'm not going unarmed. Not until this feud is settled."

Virginia sighed in exasperation. "McAllen also has someone outside the hotel and another agent in the lobby. They can handle any threat. If a fight starts, you're in no shape to be a part of it. You need to get down at the first sign of trouble. Wait until you can move freely. Listen, you can't even put on your shirt."

I was angry. "And where's your Colt?"

She returned my angry glare before stating, "I was not beaten to a purple pulp."

"So you'll pull your gun to protect my backside as I scurry away?"

"Fine. Wear your gun. Get in a shooting match. You're the big man. I'm just a soft woman."

I suddenly wilted. "You're not a soft woman. Not by any means. My fear is that you may be too brave." I saw her anger fade as quickly as mine. "Listen, we're both Kelly's targets. He won't relent. Let's agree to protect each other."

"We need to trust McAllen's team."

"I trust them. I'm sure he picked the best in the New York office. But I won't rely solely on them. And neither should you. Kelly may find a way around them. Remember, someone followed us all the way across the country." I hugged her. "We're the only team we can completely trust."

She put her head on my shoulder and whispered in my ear, "Even if I can't shoot worth a damn?"

"Now that's something we can work on. In a day

or two, we'll practice again. In the meantime, just remember to squeeze the trigger."

"And don't point my gun at you."

"And please don't point your gun at me."

We laughed and the awkward moment passed. During my first trip to Leadville, I had given Virginia her first shooting lesson. She had been both an atrocious shot and careless in pointing her pistol. After the showdown on State Street, I had given her a few more practice sessions, and her aim had improved a bit. She had also developed safe gun-handling routines.

"Virginia, I think it's time for you to get a different pistol."

"Why?"

"The Lightning's single action has a long, hard trigger pull. That makes it difficult to aim. Your husband bought it for you because he thought you mishandled guns. He wanted you to have something difficult to shoot accidentally. Now you deserve something easier to aim and fire. The next time out, I want you to try my Remington."

"When?" She looked excited.

"As soon as I can leave the hotel. Maybe tomorrow."

"I want to try your Colt too."

"One step at a time. Right now, let's go downstairs and order supper."

She adjusted a twisted shoulder strap on my holster and I tucked in my .38. Then she held my jacket in a way that made it easy to get my arms down the sleeves. After checking my appearance in the mirror, I touched my hand to the small of her back and led her to the door. When I opened it, I was startled by the largest man I had ever seen. He stood nearly seven feet and was thick as a bull. He made Tree seem small.

"Damn, you're big," I blurted.

He nodded. "Mr. Dancy, Mrs. Baker. My name is Mathew and I work for Pinkerton. May I ask where you're heading?"

"Downstairs to supper." I made a show of looking him up and down. "Do you have a brother living in Leadville?"

"No, sir. I have only sisters." He did not smile. "Please allow me to proceed in front of you to the lift." He smoothly walked down the hotel hallway, with unusual grace for a man of his size.

In the lift, I asked, "Play any school sports?"

He looked confused by the question and then answered briskly, "Yale Bulldogs . . . football."

I looked up at him. "When they won the championship?"

"We won the championship three of my four years."

It took me a second to figure out the dates. "That fourth year must have been 1875 . . . when Columbia won . . . my alma mater."

"I think you mean when Columbia tied with Harvard and Princeton."

"I don't believe Harvard and Princeton are serious about the game."

The man's expression remained placid. "Sir, we're not friends. Our conversation should be restricted to my assignment. When the gate opens, I will precede you and Mrs. Baker. I will block the lift for a few seconds as I survey the lobby. Remain behind me until I step forward. Understood?"

"Yes," I answered.

McAllen had indeed picked the best from the Pinkerton New York City office. When the lift gate opened, Virginia and I were both able to use Mathew's body as a shield. He was huge, and he looked even larger in the openness of the lobby, where he towered over other men. A Yale football player . . . possibly a Yale graduate working for the Pinkerton National Detective Agency. He might be smarter than the average agent, but his profession indicated that he used his body rather than his head to acquire what society had to offer. As we followed him into the dining room, I noticed his suit had been nicely tailored, but I detected bulges under both arms. Two guns? I wanted to ask, but my limp hampered me as his athletic stride put a good deal of distance between us. I thought that was unprofessional until I realized that he made it look as if we were strangers who shared nothing but a ride on the lift.

With only a nod, our guardian was seated at a table by the door. He took a chair with his back to the wall, which allowed him to inspect everyone who entered the room. We were directed to a table in the middle, providing our guardian angel with an unobstructed sight line to watch us. I almost laughed out loud at the thought. It seemed unlikely that angels came from Brobdingnag, Jonathan Swift's mythical land of giants.

We were on our second glass of wine, waiting for our main course, when someone in the doorway caught my attention. Damn. It was my mother. She marched straight toward us.

"Stephen, dear, I'm hurt I had to learn you were in town from my friend, the police commissioner." She gave me a reproachful look, one I had seen many times. "He told me you had been severely beaten by street ruffians. Are you all right? I was so worried."

"It happened two days ago, Mother, and as you can see, I'm up and about."

Without asking permission, she sat at our table. My bodyguard seemed unconcerned, so I guessed he knew who she was from her previous attempts to see me.

She used two fingers to beckon a steward over. "It was cruel to hide your return."

"When I left, you told me I was impolite, ignoble, and unworthy of the Dancy name."

"Dear, that was years ago. A gentleman does not

carry a grudge . . . especially against his own mother."

"Why are you here?"

"To see you, of course." She smiled with what appeared to be genuine motherly love. "What are we drinking this evening?"

"A white Sauvignon from the Loire Valley," I answered automatically.

"Oh, dear. The Loire Valley has not fully recovered from the blight. I'll order a bottle of Château Lafite Rothschild. It will be much better. You'll see."

"We ordered fish."

"They make a decent white, my dear." She turned in her seat and acknowledged Virginia for the first time. "And who is this lovely creature, Stephen? You must learn to introduce your guests."

Virginia answered for herself. "Virginia Baker. I believe you must be Mrs. Agatha Dancy."

My mother looked pleased. "So, my son has told you his mother's name. My, things may be looking up." She cocked her head. "Virginia Baker? Do I know your family?"

"You do," Virginia answered without a hint of sarcasm. "He's sitting at this table."

She looked between us with a horrified expression. "You're married?" Her look of shock threw me into a fit of muffled laughter. She squeezed my wrist as she used to do when I misbehaved in public as a child. "That's enough, Stephen." She looked sternly between us. "Well, I suppose that makes adjoining rooms more acceptable, but I'm—"

"How do you know our arrangements?" I demanded, suddenly angry.

"These things can be learned quite easily," she answered. She turned her attention to Virginia. "Do you have family beyond this table, my dear? I certainly hope you're not ashamed of them." She winked and reached out to take her hand. "We all have a few skeletons."

"Mother, quit prying. We're not married."

"Oh." She looked between us. "Oh, dear."

She was suddenly at a loss for words. She contemplated the situation for a few moments and then called the steward over again. I was disappointed to see her peruse the menu. That meant she would be with us throughout the meal. Despite studying it as if she had never dined here previously, she ordered her standard fare: a piece of grilled sole with no sauce, green beans boiled until limp, and precisely three new potatoes without butter. Her secret to remaining thin was to eat boring food.

After she dismissed the steward, she said, "Stephen, dear, we must talk. I don't know what happened to you out there on that ghastly frontier, but you are no longer in the backcountry, where morals and women are loose. You are back in society. My society." She looked around as if she owned the place. "Especially when you stay at the Fifth Avenue Hotel."

She had been studiously ignoring Virginia. "Your recreation is no concern of mine, but you must at least book rooms without a common door. Appearances are important . . . far more important than what goes on behind closed doors. Remember what I taught you; always close doors gently so you never draw attention to moments that can embarrass you in the light of day."

"Mother, I'm not embarrassed." But I was angry.

"My dear Stephen, this—" She stopped and gave me a queer look, glanced at Virginia, and then shrugged her tiny shoulders. "Very well. Live your life as you choose. You always have . . . with little regard for my feelings, I might add. I only suggested more discreet arrangements because I want your book publishing party to be about your book. Now, I suppose, there will be nothing but whispered gossip about you and this Miss . . . Barker." She said this last with a flip of her wrist aimed at Virginia that both pointed her out and dismissed her simultaneously.

I stammered a second and then closed my mouth. I remembered why I feared my mother. She could reduce me to being tongue-tied with anger.

Seeing a wounded animal, she pounced. "Is it

the money, dear? Heavens knows, the rooms here are very expensive. I can certainly help until your royalties come in."

I was about to storm out when Virginia spoke in a calm voice that had taken on an eastern boarding-school intonation.

"Mrs. Dancy, perhaps with your advancing age, your hearing is not as good as it once was. Anyway, my name is Virginia Baker, not Barker. And it is not Miss. I am Mrs. Baker. Thank you for your gracious offer, but I prefer our current arrangements. It is so much more convenient. Perhaps you can tell people I'm your son's nurse, staying in servant's quarters so I can care for his wounds . . . if that meets your need to gently close the door." She smiled benignly. "I promise, neither Steve nor I will spoil your little fib."

I was flabbergasted, and so was my mother, but for different reasons. I had never won an argument with my mother. We fought differently. While I prepared for a frontal assault, she darted in from the flank to prick me. I strove to deliver a blistering blow that would win me final victory. She deftly slid to the side and watched me attack empty air. Virginia was different. She engaged my mother on her own turf to skewer her with stiletto-like precision. My mother knew it too, as I could read from her startled expression. She looked as stunned as I felt.

Recovering quickly, she asked evenly, "Do you

intend to marry? Are there, ah . . . encumbrances?"

"Does that make a difference?" Virginia responded in an innocent tone, ignoring her roundabout way of asking if she was still married.

"People are more tolerant of engaged couples."

Virginia raised her hand to display an empty ring finger. "No engagement ring. I doubt that story will carry water." She again smiled benignly. "But it pleases me that you do not object if we choose to marry."

"I never said that!" Now she was in a huff, a rarity for my mother. "I would need to learn much more about you and your family. You speak with educated erudition. Where were you schooled?"

Virginia laughed lightly. "Actresses speak with many different accents," she said, reverting to the western drawl she had always used in my company.

I admired Virginia's wit. She hadn't actually lied to escape this trap. If my mother knew Virginia's married surname and the name of a private girl's school, she might uncover Virginia's identity. Now she looked perplexed. My mother may have met her match.

"Were you an actress? I find the theater so fascinating. How did you meet?"

"In a store. It was a chance meeting. Your son put me in business on the most disreputable street in a notorious town." She winked. "We had great fun and made some money as well."

"How—" Instead of finishing, she looked at me in disbelief.

It was time to change the subject.

"Mother, what did you mean when you mentioned a book publishing party? Is there something I should know about?"

"Ah, yes, of course, dear. It's why I came to see you." She patted my hand possessively. "I've arranged a book party right here at the Fifth Avenue Hotel. A literary career is a respectable pursuit for you. It will enhance our family reputation in many circles, especially compared to shop keeping. And don't worry about the expense; I charmed your publisher into covering the entire event. It will be splendid."

"How did you find out about my book? I've already agreed to a book party, but I haven't even met with my publisher yet. Damn it, Mother, there's a reason I never told you I was writing a book. This is mine."

"Of course it is, dear. I have no idea why you're upset. And please do not use profanity in my presence, especially in public." She punctuated this last with a finger poked at the tabletop. "As for finding out about your book, did you really believe a Dancy could publish a book without my learning about it? Have you forgotten how small fashionable society is in New York? And after all, Mr. Benson is a cousin, distant, but still part of the family. He's very put out with you for not visiting him to set up the arrangements." She patted my hand again. "Don't fret; Mother has taken care of everything. But you really should pay more attention to your affairs. What have you been doing? I mean, before this unfortunate incident, of course."

As I was counseling myself to learn from Virginia and parry with false-hearted banter, my mother said something that destroyed my composure.

"I must say, you have an active imagination. That book is filled with outrageous episodes. Those parts will most certainly make it popular, but they are embarrassing in the extreme. I've told my friends that none of it is true, and you were using this unsavoriness to insure good sales. Thankfully, none will read it before the night of the party. By the way, Mr. Benson and I have set up a series of newspaper interviews directly after the formal events; you can use the interviews to put those awful aspects of your little story in perspective." She patted my hand once again. "Always remind everyone it is a work of fiction, dear. And tell the reporters that your next book will be a much more serious endeavor."

I was about to shove my chair away from the table and yell something inappropriate, when stewards arrived with our main courses. I took three slow breaths as my mother watched me with a satisfied expression.

I addressed the steward who was holding my mother's plate.

"I'm sorry; my mother will not be able to eat her meal. Our apologies, but she has a sudden attack of diarrhea. She must leave immediately before she ruins all of your customers' meals." I turned to face my red-faced mother. "Should I call you a carriage, or did you arrive in your own?"

She didn't hesitate a second. She bounded from her chair without a word and was gone. The steward was standing there agape, so I said, "Return that meal to the kitchen, but you have my permission to put it on my bill."

Once we were alone, Virginia and I looked at each other and burst out laughing.

"Thank you," I finally said. "That's the first time I won an argument with my mother, and you showed me how. You were wonderful."

"You're welcome. I can certainly see why you left New York. Although she's not really that different from my parents."

"She ran away," I exclaimed, still impressed with myself. "Maybe she'll leave me alone now."

"You know better than that."

I looked toward the door. Our bull-like guardian looked amused. I wondered how much he had heard but decided that our body movements were enough to clue him in. Just then, Captain McAllen stepped into the doorway. He nodded at his employee and walked over to our table as he surveyed the restaurant.

"Supper?" I asked.

"Already ate."

"Whiskey?"

He nodded agreement. After exchanging friendly greetings with Virginia, he asked, "What'd you do to make your mother scurry away like a startled rabbit?"

"I embarrassed her."

"Yep. That always works with her kind." That seemed enough of an explanation for him, and he ordered a bottle of Jameson's. He had made a good start on it by the time we were finished eating.

"You must be feelin' better," he said as I nudged my plate away from me.

"Not fit, but better."

"Good. We need to talk about this Edison affair."

"I want to ask about something else first." McAllen looked at me with a blank face, so I went ahead. "I want you to make some inquires and find out who my mother has hired to spy on me."

"I already know, but I wouldn't call it spyin'. More like keepin' tabs on you from a distance."

"Who?"

"The Pinkerton National Detective Agency."

Chapter 25

"Can you terminate the engagement?"

"No. Your family has been a steady client. The New York office would never throw that away. She also has many friends who contract our services." He glanced toward Mathew. "I can get you copies of the reports. She's not payin' to follow you around the country but has us keep track of any publicity about you. She's been sent stories about a couple of your exploits that were reprinted in bigger newspapers, but she's not payin' for us to check every rag in the country. She dismissed many of the stories because she doesn't believe you're a killer. She assumes they're about someone else with the same name. Steve, I'll keep you abreast, but right now we need to talk about the Edison case."

He was avoiding the subject I was most interested in. "Joseph, first you're going to tell me about Kelly."

He rolled his whiskey glass back and forth between his palms. "No sign of him since the beatin'. He seems to have disappeared. Maybe he left New York again. The first time he left because he got too big for his britches, and other gang lords were ready to put him away for good. He's clever and before they could nail him, he ran off to Leadville with a few trusted followers. Since his return, he's made no attempt to take back his old turf. The other gangs are watchin', but nobody's huntin' him . . . not yet, anyway."

I had a thought. "Would you tell me if you found him?"

"I would."

That was good enough. McAllen had never lied to me. "Okay, what have you discovered about the Edison problem?"

"The Edison delays *were* caused by teamsters. Jeff has been hired by the express company chartered by Doolittle Copper Wire Company, and tomorrow he'll drive a wagon between Naugatuck Valley and New York City. His idea. The other drivers told him he'll be offered a bonus to pull his wagon off the road and put his horses out to graze. Nobody's namin' names. With you in bed, I sent my agents to the supplier offices in Connecticut and New Jersey. They confirmed that shipments were made on or close to schedule. The superintendents for the express company won't admit anything. Say it was probably just normal delays, and the Edison dispatchers should have accounted for uncontrollable circumstances."

"So we know how, but we don't know who bribed the express superintendents."

"Findin' out has become more difficult. I just returned from Bridgeport. The Connecticut super-intendent was choked to death with six Pinkerton broadsides jammed down his throat. It seems someone sent a message. Now no one's talkin' . . . about anything."

I was surprised at this news. "That doesn't sound like ordinary sabotage. Crooked businessmen cheat, they seldom kill."

McAllen shrugged. "The stakes are high. Remember I asked you to estimate how much money is involved?"

I nodded.

"Again, with you in bed, I talked to a Pinkerton bookkeeper. He said whoever wins will get tens of millions in business . . . each year. Even more when electricity goes national. Edison has a great reputation for inventions, but a lousy reputation for construction. Important people think he's too much of a perfectionist. He always has to do things his way . . . like buryin' these wires instead of hangin' them on poles. Whoever is behind this wants to prove he can't get his creations out of his laboratory."

"Murder still seems extreme."

He sipped whiskey and seemed to think. "Killin' may be rare, but not unknown. This might be more money than even railroads or telegraph. No tellin', once it goes national. The point is, everyone's scared, and no one is gonna squeal." He drained the last of the whiskey from his glass. "Any ideas?"

"This appears to be a gangland killing, not

teamsters. Crooked businessmen hide their dirty work; gangs hang a lantern on it for everyone to see. Pinkerton broadsides? That's something Kelly would do. It's his style."

"Steve, that's just plain stupid. You want him involved so you can go after him. I can't tell you what to do, but you're barkin' up the wrong tree. Gangs don't have anything to do with this . . . except possibly as the hired hands of a competitor. My client is Edison and your money is bet on Edison." He gave me that stare that caused most bad men to back down. "I don't have time for games. Are we workin' together or not?"

"Yes . . . but Virginia and I are in danger from this man, and if I get a bead on him, nothing else matters. I'll chase that man until I catch him."

"Fair enough."

"Did you talk to that flower girl?" I asked to show my mind was back on the case.

McAllen shook his head. "I saw her when I was talkin' to my man, but she disappeared when I ran to help you in that alley."

"Who's watching the work on Nassau Street now?" This smart question came from Virginia.

"No one we've spotted. Shipments arrived on schedule the last two days. Everybody knows we're watchin', so things are workin' the way they're supposed to."

"Is Edison satisfied?" she asked.

"No." He handed her a telegram, which she passed on to me.

It read, "Find culprit. More delay will ruin."

"Well, I guess he's still nervous. What does your New York office have on Edison's competitors?"

"I checked the files. We had very little on Brush, Maxim, Jablochkoff, Lewis, Sawyer, or Fuller. None of them have hired the agency and none have been investigated by us. All we have are news clippin's."

I poured myself a drink and took a shallow sip of the whiskey. Finally, I asked, "Didn't some workers fail to show up at critical points?"

"Yep. All gone. No longer on the crews."

"Fired or just disappear?"

"Disappeared . . . like the flower girl. Everyone involved in this case seems to have disappeared."

"We've got to find one of those workers."

"The foreman doesn't have a record of their names. Says he picked 'em from a line of men that responded to flyers."

"Do you believe him?"

McAllen looked down at his empty glass and then shoved it away, evidently deciding he had had enough. He examined the ceiling for a moment. "If the workers who didn't show up used picks and shovels, I'd believe him, but the ones that caused delays were the engineers who connected electrical gear in the trenches. Can't be many men with those kinds of skills." He succumbed to temptation and poured himself another half inch of whiskey. After a sip, he said with finality, "He's lyin'."

"Edison will know their names," Virginia said. "He's at the work site often, and he knows everybody in electricity."

"He'll be in the city tomorrow. I'll ask. If he doesn't know, I'll figure out a way to get it out of the foreman. Seems we have a path to investigate tomorrow."

"Might be difficult to get that foreman talking," I said. "You humiliated him in front of his men."

"Foremen are often bullies. I wanted the workers to see there was someone who could stand up to him. If they were fed up, they might seek me out to squeal on him. Nothin' yet, but another demonstration won't hurt. Like all bullies, he'll back down easy enough." He looked at Virginia. "What did you learn in the Edison house?"

Virginia looked conflicted. "I don't feel comfortable tattling on my hosts."

"I don't want gossip," McAllen said abruptly. "Did you observe anything that might help this case?"

"No." She answered without hesitation. "Listen, it's true Edison doesn't treat his wife as an equal. But it's not because he doesn't like her, it's because she's not an engineer. He's an obsessed man. People think single-minded individuals are unhappy. They're wrong. Obsessed people are happy, but only when they get to work on their obsession. Mary is not part of his world, so she bores him."

"That might give her motive."

"You don't really think she could be behind this? It will ruin her husband, and I'll tell you one thing, she likes the life money buys."

"Women are not rational," McAllen said. "If she feels spurned by her husband, no tellin' what she might do for revenge."

"She doesn't feel spurned, she feels ignored." She snapped her wineglass on the table. "And I can't believe a good detective would throw all women together in the same emotional stew."

For some reason, McAllen seemed amused at her outburst. He swallowed the last remains of his glass and stood.

"I'm going to bed."

Chapter 26

I was up very early the next morning. Given all of the time I had spent in bed, I was certainly not short of sleep. I dressed myself because when I rolled out of bed, Virginia remained still and peaceful. I moved easier and realized I was recovering fast. Another day or two, and I would be as good as new. Or at least, that was my hope.

I opened the door and saw that Mathew had been replaced by a being of normal size.

He raised a hand to stop my progress. "Sorry, sir, my instructions are that you and the lady must remain together. I cannot protect you both if you separate."

"That's all right, Steve," I heard Virginia say behind me. "I'm awake and can be ready for breakfast in a few minutes."

The curious guard glanced back with me, and we both saw Virginia standing in her nightgown and bare feet. I had pulled the curtains open in the sitting room so I'd have enough light to dress. With a double window directly behind her, Virginia's body was perfectly silhouetted, and it was obvious she was not wearing undergarments.

"We'll be a few minutes." Before I could complete this sentence, I had already slammed the door.

She looked behind her, and when she faced me again, she seemed unembarrassed and indifferent. "How are you feeling?"

"Better. I dressed myself."

"I gathered."

I looked down at my clothes. "Yes, I suppose you would."

For some reason, a slow, wicked grin came over her face.

"Did I miss something?" I asked, confused.

She laughed. "I presume you missed nothing. But if you feel up to it, how about showing me if you can undress yourself?"

In one smooth motion, she lifted her nightgown up and over her head and dumped it at her feet. Without a thought that I can recall, I found myself following her into the bedroom.

Chapter 27

During breakfast, Mathew switched places with the night guard. I was glad to see him because the other man couldn't quit staring at Virginia. I didn't want to know what was on his mind. I thought about waving Mathew over to dine with us but realized he wanted his back against the entrance wall so he could surprise anyone who entered the room with ill intent.

I returned my attention to Virginia. "I believe I'm ready to venture beyond the hotel."

"You're ready," she said, without the slightest hint of coyness.

"McAllen said Edison is coming to town today. I think we should find him . . . either at the dig or his office."

"The missing engineers?"

"Do you have another idea?"

"That *was* my idea. He'll know the names and then we can find them."

"It's a big city."

"When I was staying with the Edisons, I saw the way these men live. They're a separate breed. They work all day on electrical gear and talk all night about electricity. They're tighter than any club you ever saw. I bet they stay at the same boardinghouses, patronize the same pubs, and eat at the same cafés."

"What if they're gone? Left New York?"

"Electricity is a rage. It's more popular with the public than train travel, steamships, phonographs, or the telegraph. All those are expensive for most people. But electricity comes right into your home to make life better and it's inexpensive. The public is fascinated with each and every development. They're spellbound with the contest. It's in the newspapers every day. Who will win? But engineers go beyond fascination. At night, they drink and drink and talk and talk . . . and they talk about nothing but electricity. And New York is the hub of everything that's happening in the world of electricity." She looked sure of herself. "So what do you think?"

"I think our engineers are still in New York, and if not, they probably blabbed to someone during one of those drinking sessions."

"Exactly."

"You're a very bright lady." I stood slowly, feeling sore. "I bet Edison goes to the dig first, so let's start there."

She threw her napkin on the table and stood as well, and then walked directly over to Mathew.

"We're on our way to the dig on Pearl Street."

"Wait at your table until I check with my outside man."

He returned in a few moments and sat beside us. "He's calling a carriage. When it's positioned right outside the door, I'll let you know. I'll ride up top with the driver. My partner will follow on horseback. It'll take a few minutes to get everything arranged."

"You don't seem surprised."

"Captain McAllen warned us you would be leaving the hotel today."

"How would he know?" Virginia asked.

"It's his job to know, ma'am."

"Do you know what he's pursuing today?" I asked.

"No, sir. The captain does not confide in me."

A thought occurred to me. "What about the man in the lobby?"

"I'm sure he doesn't know either, sir."

"No. I mean, is he coming with us to Pearl Street?"

"Excuse me, I misunderstood. No, he'll wait here and watch to make sure no one sets up an ambush for our return."

"So, two of you to protect two of us."

"Yes, so stay together. No matter what happens. I know you have used a gun before in deadly situations, but rely on us. We know how to protect you." He looked at the door and waved acknowledgment. "We're ready. Follow me, and when we get to the door, step directly into the carriage. Understood?"

"Yes."

I put my left hand in the small of Virginia's back, and we headed out. The carriage was closed with curtains drawn. This was going to be a dreary way to get around the city. As soon as the door snapped shut, I felt the carriage rock like a bear was trying to shove it over. The rocking movement startled me until I realized Mathew had pulled himself up to sit next to the driver. Almost immediately, a whip cracked above the horses' heads, and we were trotting down the street.

In less than ten minutes, the carriage pulled up alongside the trenching crew, and we stepped out, our bodyguards on either side. I was surprised to see the crew working in the same part of the street as the last time I had visited the site. I had assumed they would have moved forward another block by now. The crowd watching the excavation was still large, but I didn't see a flower girl or anyone else looking out of place. A Pinkerton agent still guarded the materials stacked at the corner.

Virginia immediately spotted Edison and waved. He urgently beckoned us over, as if we were far more important than what he was doing. Mathew went over to talk to the Pinkerton watching the supplies, but the other bodyguard remained with us. When we reached Edison, he grabbed our arms and led us out of the earshot of the workers and their bosses.

Without preamble, he said, "This is not over."

"Do you have an inkling of what they'll try next?" I asked.

He looked back to make sure we were far

enough away not to be heard. "I already know. I discovered connections installed in reverse sequence. If we had applied electricity, it would have shorted the entire system."

I thought about that a moment, then nodded toward the work crews. "Does that mean these engineers purposely did it wrong?"

He looked worried. "Not necessarily. This work could have been done days ago . . . by the missing engineers. I haven't inspected the work in nearly a week. But . . . you could be right. I just don't believe it. I've sent men here from Menlo Park to inspect. Men I trust. It doesn't make sense. How is this happening? Everyone can't be bought."

"Is the skill to do the connecting work rare or difficult?"

"No. It's simple. I could teach anyone of moderate intelligence in an hour."

"Then a shift supervisor or inspector ought to be able to spot shoddy work. Why did it take you to notice?"

"Someone buried it. I told them to leave the trench open until I had personally inspected the work, but despite my orders, they filled the subway with dirt. I made them dig it up again."

"Can I talk to the supervisor?"

"I should do that," Mathew said. He had returned a few minutes previously and had been listening to the conversation.

"Together?"

He stared at me, but when I wouldn't blink, he finally said, "Don't interfere with my line of questions. You may not understand what I'm after or how I'm going about getting it."

I looked at Edison. He nodded.

"Very well," I said.

As we started off, Virginia stayed at my side. "No," Mathew said. "She should stay here with Mr. Edison."

"I want her to come along. She knows more about engineering than I do."

"This could be salacious," Mathew said.

The comment was puzzling, but before I could frame my thoughts, Virginia chimed in. "I ran a general store in the brothel neighborhood of a mining town. Could this line of questioning be more salacious than that?"

"No, ma'am, but—"

"Let her accompany you," Edison said. "Mr. Dancy is correct. She knows engineering, and I would like to hear her opinions after the questioning."

"Very well, sir."

Our guards walked in front and behind us on the narrow walkway. The supervisor had been watching our exchange with Edison and seemed to expect us to approach him.

"Are you a Pinkerton?" he asked Mathew.

"I am. Mr. Edison would like us to ask you a few questions."

"Figured. Who are these two?"

"Investors," I answered.

"What do you want to know?"

"Who buried the trenches?"

"We call them subways. It was done last night. I was surprised to find them buried when I arrived this morning. They're supposed to be left open until Mr. Edison gives the order to bury them."

"Did you ask the night supervisor about it?" Mathew asked.

"He was nowhere to be found."

"Is that unusual?"

"Not really. He often leaves before I arrive. Not supposed to, but I'm frequently late because I start at the Fifth Avenue headquarters. I come over after I finish with telegrams and meetings. It's never been a problem before. He's a good man."

"Did any of the night shift work over into days?" Mathew asked.

"Three. We're short a few men."

"Did you ask any of them why they buried the subway?"

He looked uncomfortable. "They said a foreman shook a bag of silver dollars and offered one to every workman if they could get the subway buried before daybreak."

"A foreman?"

"They thought he was a foreman. The supervisor was gone, and this man acted like he was in charge. Foremen have been changing a lot since the project got in trouble. He said they were behind schedule—which they knew—and he would give each of them a dollar bonus if they helped catch up. A silver dollar can keep a man in brew for a week."

"Where was the supervisor?"

"Ask him."

"I'm asking you." Mathew loomed over the man like a huge apparition. "You know where he was. Where he probably still is."

"Oh hell." He shook his head. "If you knew, why didn't your man stop him?"

"Not his job. He was told to protect the supplies and report what he saw. Now, tell me what he saw."

The day supervisor looked up at a window about three floors up. "He's up there. Probably sleeping . . . beside her. She's not a whore. Her husband was killed last year, and she just gets lonely."

"Who could have reversed the connections?"

"I was told that this supposed foreman was down in the subway before he started shaking his bag of silver. My guess is he did it."

Mathew looked at me and then back at the supervisor. "I'll be back with a few more questions."

"Thought you might." He returned to directing the men in their work.

"Are you sure you want to go upstairs?" Mathew asked Virginia.

I answered. "No. You can handle that. We want to talk to Mr. Edison. We'll leave as soon as we're finished, so hurry."

Mathew took a step in my direction so he could look down at me. "Do not leave without me."

"Then don't dawdle," Virginia answered. "There's nothing to find out up there anyway."

"She was hired," he responded, assuming she would be surprised.

"Of course, but she won't lead you anywhere useful."

Mathew looked annoyed. "I'll be quick."

As he charged into the building, we walked back to Edison. Our other bodyguard immediately took station between us and the street. Now that Edison had corrected the connections, workers feverishly shoveled dirt back into the trench. It looked like they would be shifting to the next block by afternoon.

Edison looked dour. "Well?"

"You're right, sir," I said. "This is not over."

Chapter 28

The plain brick buildings looked identical. The monotony was partially broken up by pubs on every corner and an occasional food store with fruit stands outside. I saw no restaurants, general stores, or individual row houses. For the most part, the four-story buildings formed a brick wall that ran down both sides of the street. The whole area looked as bleak as the mining shanties in Leadville. I wondered how long it would be until electricity was brought into this neighborhood. Then I had a new thought: probably not long. The buildings might look boring, but this was a working-class district, which meant they were already spending money for gas lighting. This was the great mother lode. Eventually, the middle class would dwarf the rich in demand for electricity.

Edison had given us the names of the engineers who had quit without notice, but more important, he knew the haunts of men who worked in electricity. We had decided to investigate the neighborhood in daylight. Driving through the district once, we had parked the carriage around the block and gotten out to get a closer look on foot. The main living quarters for electrical engineers were concentrated in this area. Most of the occupants were single, sharing an apartment with one or more coworkers, but some rooms were available for married couples. We needed a plan. Our first problem was that most of the night shift would be asleep. The second problem was Mathew and our second bodyguard. No one was going to talk to us with those two hanging around. They looked like unsympathetic private cops, which was exactly what they were. I was about to suggest we return in the evening, when I spotted a man leaving a pub on the corner, staggering in our direction.

"Virginia?" I asked, hesitantly.

Without responding, she headed in his direction. I put a hand on Mathew's chest to stop him from following her. "She can handle this. Let's pretend we don't know her."

Mathew reluctantly relented when it became obvious that the two of them would meet only about fifteen feet away from where we stood. I hoped Virginia realized she was dressed too well for the neighborhood and would think to concoct some explanation. I shouldn't have worried. She had learned on State Street how to lure working-men into conversations that served her purpose.

Virginia and the drunk talked for nearly half an hour. Her back was to me, so I didn't see her face, but I heard her laugh softly several times. When they parted, they acted like they had known each other for years. Instead of walking toward us, she crossed the street and wandered up the block. We followed on our side, but I could tell Mathew wanted to barrel across the street. His dilemma was that Virginia was obviously pretending not to know us, and he didn't want to expose her deceit—but he wanted to protect her. When she turned the next corner, we crossed to her side of the street and hurried our pace. Hearing our footfall, she said, "Stay back until we round the next corner."

We did as we were told. When we turned the corner, I realized that Virginia was leading us to where we had left our carriage and the other agent's horse. Virginia and I clambered aboard, and this time, instead of climbing up with the driver, Mathew followed us inside the carriage.

"Where to?" he asked Virginia.

"The hotel," she answered.

Mathew gave the order, and we waited for Virginia to tell us what she had learned. She sat quiet for several moments and then looked directly at me. "Steve, I want you to stay calm and listen to everything before you make any rash decisions."

I waited for her to continue, but she evidently was not going to say anything further until I responded.

"I'll hear you out . . . all the way."

"Good." She folded her hands in her lap. "I pretended to be involved with one of the engineers who disappeared. That drunk—his name was

Hank—knew him. He's gone . . . to parts unknown. He told me that disappearing is not unusual for Edison men. He believes they leave the city after making a grubstake. He says most of them think they're going to build their own little electric empire in a town too small for the big boys. He wants to get on the Edison crew because he hears that if you don't mind soiled hands, there's extra money to be had. He winked when he said that."

"Did he tell you who paid for those soiled hands?" Mathew asked.

"No. At least not directly. From what he did say, my guess is that it's George Lewis, his current employer."

"If that were true, why wouldn't his boss sneak him onto the Edison crew?" Mathew asked.

"Because he's a blathering drunk." Her tone was exasperated.

He ignored her belittling tone and simply said, "Go on."

"I told him I came from a decent family but wanted to marry someone with a future in electricity. I told him I was desperate to find my man because I was in the family way." She laughed. "He told me he was a great electrical engineer and offered to take care of me. I suspect it was a temporary offer. Anyway, he suggested I talk to his boss, a superintendent at the Lewis Electric Company. He might know where my man had gone off to because rumor has it that the Lewis company hires Edison men and helps them set up shop in far-off cities."

"Lewis?" I asked, and then remembered. "That's the company that illuminated the Hamilton Hotel."

"That's the one. Before electricity, his main business was gas lamps. He was—in fact, still is—the largest gas lamp supplier in New York. I believe he's the biggest business threat to Edison."

"Why?" Mathew asked.

"Edison has big-money men behind him, but Lewis has established connections with most of the city businesses and Tammany, he has a large sales staff, and his installation crews are first-rate. He figures he owns the illumination business, whether it's gas or electricity. To his way of thinking, Edison's an interloper . . . and a blowhard. He doesn't believe Edison deserves all the publicity he gets."

"How would this Hank know so much?" Mathew asked.

"Gossip mostly. The word in his shop is that Edison needs to be taken down a peg. He told me a lot. He was trying to impress me . . . for obvious reasons."

"How far will Lewis go to protect his business?" I asked, as the carriage hit a pothole and jarred the last word out of me like a belch.

"Unclear, but Hank bragged about the Lewis family connections with Tammany."

"Why would he tell you all of this?" Mathew asked doubtfully.

"Why do you think? He wanted me to go upstairs with him." She leaned forward and put her elbows on her knees, her hands fisted beneath her chin. "Mathew, Pinkerton must have files on Lewis."

"Captain McAllen said there was nothing more than clipping files on any of Edison's competitors," Mathew answered.

"He probably looked for the Lewis Electric Company," she said. "Try Lewis & Sons Gaslight Company. And check on Charles Lewis. He's one of the sons. Most people call him Chuck. Hank told me he's rowdy as hell. Hank and Chuck are occasional drinking partners . . . or perhaps he was trying to impress me by lying about a friendship with an heir to the business."

"Does Lewis have crime connections?" I believed I already knew the answer to my question.

She gave me her don't-fly-off-the-handle look.

"He claimed Hugo Kelly started joining him and Chuck for drinks about two weeks ago."

Chapter 29

Virginia and I ate dinner at the hotel with McAllen and Sharp. At first they weren't going to let Sharp into the dining room because he was wearing filthy garments fit for a teamster, but they had to seat him once he proved he was a hotel guest. Sharp enjoyed the whole episode.

Sharp had driven a load of copper wire from Connecticut to Pearl Street. He had proceeded directly, and nobody had asked him to dally or otherwise obstruct his delivery. He had succeeded in getting friendly with a couple of other teamsters who lamented that the extra cash had dried up, but they had not been forthcoming about where it had come from or what they had done to earn it.

Sharp volunteered to drive another load. He liked teamstering because it reminded him of his youth, got him out of the city, and he could bring his Winchester along. I kidded him that he was really after the two dollars a day. McAllen thought it was a bad idea. Since the bribes had stopped, there was nothing to learn from drivers. The money had probably been passed to them by the express company superintendent. One was dead and the other mute. He thought Sharp should stay with us. Sharp's face registered his disappointment.

Virginia and I related our morning's discoveries. McAllen was displeased that, contrary to orders, his man had not stopped the sabotage of the wiring connections. He didn't get over his annoyance despite my pointing out that nothing would have appeared unusual about a foreman jumping into the trench or a crew burying the subway. He said a good agent would have made a point of remembering the men on the job and raised an alarm when he saw someone who didn't belong at the site. I knew McAllen well enough not to argue further.

McAllen got downright angry when he discovered that we had allowed Virginia to put herself in danger. He interrupted her halfway through her story. How much she'd learned didn't seem to matter. McAllen might have to wait to reprimand the agent at the work site, but he practiced no such constraint with us. He lectured me again about going off half-cocked and then immediately marched over and had a whispered conversation with Mathew. Despite being almost a foot taller and weighing at least fifty pounds more than McAllen, Mathew looked like a small boy browbeaten by a stern father.

After McAllen sat down again, Virginia finished telling him what she had discovered. The import of the information did not mollify him.

"I can't believe Kelly is tied in with this Lewis son," I said. "It's too much of a coincidence."

"There's nothin' coincidental about it," McAllen snapped. "I received your telegram at our office about the Lewis & Sons Gaslight Company and checked them out. We had an extensive file on the gaslight company. The old man is a hard business-man. Very hard . . . but he hasn't used violence to get his way. Instead of comin' at you with a knife or gun in his hand, he comes at you with a bribe or a politician in his pocket. He uses Tammany Hall to knock down competitors. Do you remember when I told you Kelly had gotten too big for his britches and angered the other gang lords?"

I nodded.

"His ambitions grew because he had success-fully brought his violent ways to big business operators. At first, he made money by extortin' small shopkeepers, but he discovered he could make more by providin' thugs to large businesses. His specialty was arson. If you wanted your competitor burned out, he was the man you called. It was natural for him, because he had used arson to get his shopkeepers in line. Once a business-man engaged him, Kelly stuck to him forever, threatenin' to expose illegalities if dismissed. First, he charged a fee for his services, then he extorted big cash payments to stay quiet. His men were also experts in a certain type of beatin's, like the type you've personally experienced."

"Joseph, I don't believe that a man we ran out of a remote mining town would end up in New York

City where he found and beat me, and then is revealed to be the criminal element behind the problems I came here to sort out. That's too much. We have something wrong."

"No, we don't," McAllen said. "You're confusin' what came before and after."

That stopped me.

"What are you talking about?"

"Kelly never worked for Lewis. He took care of rough stuff for other businessmen, but never Lewis . . . at least not as far as we can tell."

McAllen shifted his attention to two men who had entered the dining room. He waited until they were seated before he continued speaking. "Before Kelly ran away from New York, he was makin' loads of money sellin' thuggery and blackmailin' his clients, but his mountin' violence was threatenin' the other gang lords' prostitution and gamblin' operations. Kelly had angered men with enough juice to send police into the tawdry neighborhoods. Raids were goin' on every night."

"Let me guess," Sharp said. "Tammany sent a message: If ya want to be left alone again, get rid of Kelly."

"Yep. They meant permanent, but the clever rat scurried out of town just before they got to him," McAllen said with admiration.

"Are you saying Kelly has nothing to do with this Edison case?" I asked.

"He does now. Not because Lewis used him, but

because he discovered that Edison is the reason you came to New York. He's after you. Lewis Electric Company and the son are just a pathway."

"Damn," was all I could say.

"Does Kelly work for Lewis or the son?" Virginia asked.

"I don't know if he's workin' for either of them or just buttin' in. He probably killed that express company superintendent. That work has his brand." McAllen paused, as if thinking. "If he did, somebody may have paid him, but it doesn't sound like the way Lewis goes about things. Perhaps he did it on his own to prove his worth to Chuck Lewis . . . or maybe the younger Lewis hired him. I don't know."

"From what I was told, hired murder might not be beyond Chuck Lewis," Virginia said. "He's a black sheep . . . a drunk."

McAllen leaned back in his chair until his weight was supported by the back legs only. "Kelly's a clever bastard, isn't he?" he again said with admiration. "Worked his way into the family through the weak son. This makes sense. Everythin' says the father would never hire a killer. But an inebriated son might if he was playin' the big man with his new buddy. Drunk, he might have thought it would impress his father. Show he can handle things. The father finds out and is furious. He stops delayin' shipments and sends those who know or could guess out of town."

"But the father didn't give up trying to ruin Edison," I interjected. "He messed with the connections."

"Stubborn son of a bitch," Sharp said. "He wants Edison's head on a platter. Betcha this feud goes back years. Also bet the father has a history of cleanin' up his son's messes."

McAllen rocked slightly, using the heel of his boot to push the chair back and forth on the rear legs. "The old man is as smart as the son is stupid. He only needed a whore and a man who can pretend to be a foreman. The whore wouldn't need to know anything, and the foreman was probably someone he trusted. Tidy."

"Desperate too," Virginia said. "It didn't work, because Edison would never allow electricity to run down those wires without personally checking every connection. Lewis should have known that."

"Probably did," Sharp said. "He probably hoped Edison felt so far behind that he wouldn't order completed work undone."

"Jeff's right," McAllen said. "The press has been ruthless toward Edison lately. He's no longer the shinin' knight of electricity."

I tried to lean back in my own chair. When I felt precarious, McAllen smiled with closed lips and leaned even further back. How had this become a contest? I let my chair settle back on all four legs.

"So Lewis looks like our saboteur, with Kelly

elbowing in from the side to get at Virginia and me. What now?"

"That's the client's decision."

"Do ya got an inklin' what Edison wants?" Sharp asked.

"I do."

"Well, let's hear it, Captain," Sharp said.

McAllen looked at me for some reason. Then he said slowly, "He wants us to scare the crap out of the old man. Threaten to sue him until he's down to his last pair of socks. Threaten to send his son to prison. The coup de grâce will be Tammany Hall. The bosses will let Lewis know that if he doesn't stop, he can no longer call on their services. He'll be an outcast. That oughta shut down the sabotage. Then we can deal with Hugo Kelly the ol'-fashioned way."

I had a bad feeling. "How do you propose to get Tammany to shut the door on Lewis?"

"By using someone with an even stronger voice at Tammany . . . your family."

"No."

"Steve, I know you have problems with your mother, but swallow your pride. Let's get this case closed and put our attention on Kelly. He's the real threat."

"Not no to my mother. No to all of it. I left New York because my family practiced business like Lewis. That kind of behavior needs to be punished. I want to see Lewis and his son in court. I want the whole ugly affair aired in public. There are three types of businessmen. The hardworking, honest ones who run small businesses and stay within the law. They struggle to earn an honest living despite criminals like Kelly demanding a piece. The second type is visionaries like Commodore Vanderbilt. I knew him before he died. He had made transportation over land and water cheap, fast, and safe. Visionaries sometimes use corrupt politicians, but they see government as part of the terrain, something to get around. Lewis is representative of the third type—men who have no vision and can't succeed by competing fairly. Crooked politicians cater to this type. The visionaries ignore or go around politicians unless they have no other choice, but the Lewis breed always feeds the hogs." I shook my head. "No, Joseph, I won't look the other way. I did that by running out west, but no more." I was angry as hell and stared at McAllen. "I'm going to see Lewis convicted in court."

McAllen leaned forward, the front legs of his chair banging against the floor. "No, Steve, you won't. Courts require evidence. We have none. My client is Edison, and he believes completin' this project is the best revenge against his cheatin' competitors."

I pointed at Mathew by the door. "Who's paying for those guards?"

The question confused him for a moment.

"You are." He hesitated. "Aren't you?"

"We never discussed it."

"You were out cold. I knew even if you didn't want protection, you'd want my men to guard Virginia. You do, don't you?"

"I do." I leaned back and tried to appear calmer. "Thank you for acting quickly, but my point is that I'm your client too."

He appeared perplexed. "That has nothin' to do with the Edison affair."

"It does . . . and you know it."

"Meanin' what?"

"Meaning I'm your client and I'm unwilling to accept your resolution. Find me a couple of those runaway engineers and convince them to testify against Lewis. Make the superintendent at the express company in Pennsylvania more scared of you than he is of getting handbills stuffed down his throat. Find the person inside Edison's company and convince him to testify against Lewis. And let's catch Kelly and force him to testify against Chuck Lewis."

"You know that'll never happen. He would have to admit to killin' that express superintendent."

I noticed McAllen's anger was gone. He was disagreeing, but with a tone that said he was making a plan, not knocking me down.

"You're right. Let's just kill him, hide the body, and bluff Lewis that he's still alive and wants to put a noose around his son's neck."

McAllen's head jerked back. "Are you serious?"

"Hell no. It might be what I'd like to do, but if we kill Kelly without provocation, we'd be just like him." I smiled. "A beating, however, is another matter."

"I agree with Steve," Sharp said.

"About what?" McAllen asked sharply.

"Hell, I tried to get away from these pretend businessmen too—my former partner, among others. He destroyed my reputation in the worst possible way. Said I stole young girls from their homes in South America, brought them here, an' sold them to men who like that sort of thing. I agree with Steve. Let's put the son of a bitch behind bars. Maybe the next gent will think twice before playin' crooked."

"You're willin' to pay for this?" McAllen asked me.

"I am."

"We are," Sharp added.

McAllen looked between us and settled on me. "What if this criminal activity had been done by a member of your family?"

"I'd like to believe I'd do the same thing . . . instead of running away again. When I left, I thought they'd rot in their own stew, but I was wrong. Absent a conscience, you can sleep quite well after stealing from others. In fact, that type of person sleeps better knowing they rest on expensive linens others can't afford. It makes them feel special, not soiled."

McAllen scratched his head. "How can we go after Lewis if Edison doesn't want us to?"

"Ya gotta convince him that Lewis'll never give up," Sharp said. "When his son went too far an' hired a killer, Lewis shut down one operation but started another. Tell Edison that tyin' him up in criminal court is the only way he can finish illuminatin' the first district."

"Sharp's right," Virginia said. "Edison sees competitors as gnats. Instead of swatting at them, he wants to throw netting over his head and plow ahead. Joseph, you're the netting. He just wants to get on with his business . . . with his vision. You need to convince him that Lewis will never relent."

"That shouldn't be hard."

"Why not?" I asked.

"Because of what I found in the Lewis file."

None of us asked the obvious question. We just waited for McAllen to continue. After a moment, he said, "He has a habit of puttin' people inside his opponents' companies. That's how he destroyed his gaslight competitors." He looked at each of us in turn. "He's got someone in Menlo Park."

This didn't seem like a grand revelation. We had suspected someone inside from the start. It took Virginia to figure it out.

"You said *people* and *someone*. Male or female?"

"In the past, he's always used women."

"Damn it, you suspect Mary Edison. Why do you dislike her so?"

"I don't. In fact, I don't know her." For the first time in my experience, McAllen seemed defensive. "Listen, I don't think she knows what goes on in the laboratory or at the work sites in the city. That would make her a poor inside person. It's more likely a woman in the kitchen or one of the supply cribs. All the same, I can't eliminate her . . . no matter how much you like her."

"Edison suspects her, doesn't he?"

"He's concerned about her use of morphine."

"She has headaches. Severe headaches."

"I understand, but it makes her vulnerable."

"You're wrong," Virginia said. "Edison's wrong. It's not her. I know who it is. It's one of the servers in the mess hall."

"Why would you say that with such certainty?" McAllen asked.

"For the same reason you knew a flower girl was watching the dig. Who would look so ordinary that nobody would even take notice of her as they discussed work?"

"You might be right. If you are, I know how to find out which girl," McAllen said.

"How?" I asked.

"He uses women willin' to go to bed with men for information. We find out which mess gal is sleepin' with one or more of Edison's key men."

Chapter 30

After supper, we devised a plan for the next couple of days that included a return to Menlo Park the next afternoon. In the morning, Virginia and I went with McAllen to the Pinkerton office. Sharp slept in to catch up on his sleep after driving a freight wagon straight from Bridgeport to New York City.

The Pinkerton New York headquarters looked like any other office building in the Wall Street district. McAllen sent a few telegrams and then led us to the basement. The underground room included a gymnasium, a shooting range, and a weapons stores locker. We started on the range.

Virginia proved much more accurate with my pistol. With a target ten feet away, she repeatedly shot patterns the size of a dinner plate. Not great shooting, but better than she did with her double-action pistol. McAllen reemphasized gun safety, and she never once pointed her gun in the wrong direction. I'm not sure whether it was our life-threatening situation or our admonitions, but she took the lesson seriously.

After Virginia tired of shooting, McAllen and I made small bets on our respective ability. We bet on accuracy after a draw, but not on speed. We shot together, and although the gunshots sounded close, I believed I had an edge in firing quicker. I won all the bets, until we went beyond thirty feet. At that distance, his Smith and Wesson .44 was more accurate than my Remington .38. That confirmed my decision to give my Remington to Virginia and start carrying my trusty Colt .45. Since I used a short-barrel Colt, McAllen would still have an advantage at a distance, but I would probably retain an edge for another ten feet. We had bet two bits on each round, and in the end, I won two dollars from McAllen.

He waved at me to follow him over to the mats in the gymnasium. Along the way, he picked up a policeman's nightstick with a leather strap. I wondered what he was going to do but guessed that it had something to do with winning back his two dollars. McAllen did not lose gracefully.

McAllen twirled the baton so fast it looked like a blur. I had seen cops on the beat use the leather strap to flip a nightstick in one direction, catch it as it came around, and then effortlessly flip it in the opposite direction to be caught once again. Beat cops could do this endlessly. I supposed it gave them something to do and impressed women and children. McAllen made the typical beat cop look ham-fisted. His baton went in so many directions, the blur looked like a circle surrounding his fist. All of a sudden, the blur stopped and the baton was lying casually in his palm. He extended it to me.

"Go ahead, take it."

"I've never used a nightstick."

"It's time you learned. In the city, it's often more useful than a gun."

"I've never seen a civilian carry one. When I was beaten, they used saps, which can be hidden in a pocket. Why not teach me how to use one of those?"

"A nightstick is twenty-six inches long. If you know how to use it, you can break an attacker's arm before he can get his sap anywhere close to you." He pushed it slightly forward to encourage me to take it. "If you can touch me with this stick, I'll pay double on our bets."

"And if I fail to touch you?"

"We're even."

I nodded. I was probably going to lose, but I didn't really want McAllen's money. Besides, I might learn something useful. I took hold of the nightstick. As soon as it was in my hand, McAllen grabbed my wrist and spun until the back of his head was in my face. My arm hurt as he twisted it, and I dropped the baton.

"Damn it, Joseph. I'm not letting you off the hook on our bets. Let's do it right. This time, we start five feet apart. And remember, I'm still healing from a rough beating."

He backed up a few feet, his open palms facing me. His expression concerned me. Instead of looking playful, he looked like he wanted to tear me apart. I had a feeling this lesson was not going to be easy.

When he was out of arm's reach, I warily leaned down and picked up the baton. He didn't rush me or try any other tricks. Now what? I had no idea how to use this thing, but I had taken fencing in school, so I tried a lunge. McAllen twisted to his right and grabbed the baton as it passed harmlessly in front of his chest. He bent my wrist, and again I dropped the baton with a short squeal of pain.

"If you had hit me like that, it wouldn't hurt much," McAllen said. "Not unless you were real close so you could jab it hard into my chest. A nightstick is a club, not a foil." He picked it up off the floor and held it up. "A sap is flat. As you discovered, it's designed to bruise. Billy clubs and batons are round. They're meant to break bones, crack skulls." Staying well away from me, he made a jabbing thrust with the club. "You can poke with it, but do it in close, use an under-handed thrust, and aim for the upper gut. He'll bend at the middle and you follow with a roundhouse to the back of the skull. Fight's over."

He held out the club to me again. I took it, wondering how to surprise him. He was quicker than he looked and always moved to the side. To hell with it. I raised the club and charged McAllen. I veered left, but he went in the other direction. The next thing I knew, I was flat on my face on the mat. That might have been bad enough, but I heard Virginia stifle a laugh.

I rolled over onto my back. I hurt like hell because of my bruises, but I tried to make light of it by smiling. "Figure I had half a chance to catch you moving to the side."

"You had *no* chance. You signaled which way you were attackin'." He offered me a hand and helped me to my feet. "Are you okay?"

"Yep, except for my ego." I rubbed my front shoulder, which had taken most of my weight in the fall. It was sore, and I didn't think banging it against these mats was going to help my recovery. "Perhaps we should wait a day or two before we continue this lesson."

"That part of the lesson is over. Now I'll show you how to use that thing. We'll do it slow . . . no falls. That is, as long as you agree the bet is even."

"We're even. Otherwise, I suspect next time I hit this mat, it will be even more painful."

He took the nightstick from my hand and walked a couple of feet away. His lack of response told me I was right about the consequences of demanding my two dollars. He held the club up and then swung it slowly until his arm pointed straight.

"See the length of—"

"Joseph, why are we doing this? I can't walk around this city carrying that thing, and it's too long to hide under my coat."

"Steve, you were beaten to a pulp. You appear to heal faster than most men, but others don't know the extent of your recovery. From now on, you will grimace when you walk or take a seat. You will always move slowly . . . and with a limp." He quickly pointed at Virginia and then himself. "We'll show impatience having to wait for you. You're infirm. You will carry a cane to help you move around. Do you see? If you play it right, you'll have an advantage when you're attacked again. Assailants will underestimate you."

"Can't I just shoot them?"

"No. If you want Lewis convicted, we want your attackers alive." McAllen used his closed-mouth smile. "But if I remember correctly, you said knockin' them about was a different matter."

"If my weapon is going to be a cane, why am I working with a nightstick?"

"We don't have canes here. This nightstick is twenty-six inches long, so it will work for now. We'll practice with a cane after you buy one."

"What about Virginia? Is she depending on her pistol?"

That caught McAllen by surprise. He looked at her appraisingly and then walked toward the door.

"Where are you going?" I asked.

"To find one of our female agents who can show Virginia how to knock a man silly with her purse."

Chapter 31

I leaned one hand on my cane and clutched the ferry railing with the other. The Hudson River looked as smooth as glass, with nary a ripple except for the wake spreading out behind our steamship. The day was perfect. No wind, warm, but not hot. Sunny, with sparkles of light dancing on the water. Virginia, Sharp, and I enjoyed the scenery without conversation.

McAllen had decided we should all go to Menlo Park. It was fine with me, because the day was so nice. I had been cooped up in my hotel room for days and had spent the morning in the basement of a Wall Street building. Fresh air and sunshine felt invigorating. It was especially pleasant because McAllen was off talking to the ferry captain.

Two of our bodyguards had accompanied us, but neither were Mathew. I presumed McAllen thought Mathew's size made him too obvious. The two Pinkertons pretended not to be part of our group. They separated and took positions at either end of the ship's deck.

Discovering that Edison would remain in the city, McAllen recognized our advantage of being able to pry without having to engage in pleasantries or be prompted to watch endless technical demonstrations.

We had stayed in the gymnasium most of the morning. After I'd improved somewhat with the nightstick, McAllen had sent me out to buy a cane. I thought he'd want me to buy one with a metal handle, but he insisted on a standard one made out of mahogany with a curved wood handle. I had left Virginia in the capable hands of a woman who was having more luck teaching her how to wield a purse than I had had teaching her to shoot.

When I returned from my short shopping trip, McAllen had me practice three maneuvers. The first was the jab to the gut and then a crushing blow behind the head. This was the same maneuver we had practiced with the nightstick. I found the forty-two-inch cane easier to jab, but more difficult to use for the back of the head blow. McAllen pointed out that I had to move, getting a half step further away and a bit to the side. The next maneuver was for close quarters. He taught me to lift the cane up behind the assailant, hook the handle around his neck, and pull. The first maneuver required some open space, while this one worked only when I was chest to chest with my attacker. We practiced the first two maneuvers with one hand on the cane. The third maneuver could only be done with two hands. He had me hold the cane parallel to the ground with my hands spread far apart, then ram the portion of the cane between my hands into the attacker's neck. He made me practice shoving the cane forward as I stepped into the attacker and snapped my arms to full length. After we finished, I realized he had taught me maneuvers that would work at a distance, in close quarters, or in between. He told me to practice the motions whenever I was alone.

Virginia relished her newly developed skill. In fact, back at the hotel, I could hardly get her to quit swinging her purse around our sitting room. The Pinkerton woman had given her a beaded purse that looked like the ones most women used for casual dress, except that it was constructed of reinforced canvass under the hundreds of beads that covered the entire surface. Inside the purse was another canvass sack of lead shot. It was heavy to carry but lethal. McAllen instructed her not to put her pistol in the handbag. Her purse and gun should remain separate so she could use either one without making the other weapon unavailable. He suggested that she carry the gun in her waistband and wear a jacket to conceal it. Later, she should have a heavy-duty pocket sewn into all of her dresses.

The fresh air and sunshine made me feel good. So good, I had to remind myself to move as if I were infirm. When I forgot, Virginia pinched my arm. I think she enjoyed making me wince. The four of us were highly competitive individuals. I decided I liked that. I liked my friends, and I loved Virginia, and I trusted them all. I was happy, and I had not always been happy. They also kept me sharp. Why was I attracted to this sort of person, and why did I feel comfortable only in their presence? I thought about what I had run away from, and I knew. I ran away from corruption, and these people were honest . . . and true to each other.

Virginia and I had been engaged in some sort of contest since I had first met her in an exclusive haberdashery in Leadville. I pushed her and she pushed right back. She handled herself so well that Sharp and I had hired her to run our general store so we could gallivant around the West. She did a terrific job, adapting easily from rich clientele to the roughest sort of men. In fact, these hard, uncouth men were not a threat to her; they ended up being her protectors. She could take care of herself with ruffians, comport herself like a lady when the need arose, and even joust with my mother.

I gazed at her.

"What?" she asked.

"I was thinking how much I love you."

"Normally, Steve, I'd want to hear that, but right now I'm worried about a gang leader who wants to kill us."

"Don't make him stop with the sweet talk," Sharp said. "I enjoy listenin' to a man woo a woman. Might pick up a thing or two."

"You don't need lessons from Steve," she said.

"I'll bet you've used that sentence quite a bit yourself."

"I love you?" He laughed. "Yep, I've been known to toss that one about."

"Ever mean it?" she asked.

"Every damn time." No laugh. "Couple times I felt the same way at breakfast. Those women broke my heart."

"Should I believe you?" she asked.

"Yep."

Sharp looked out over the river. He seemed absorbed, so we left him alone. I turned and leaned my buttocks against the ship rail. Virginia turned toward the crowded ship deck as well, but she didn't lean against the rail.

"Do you see him?" she asked.

"No."

We suspected someone was watching us, but I had glanced around occasionally and never spotted anyone who seemed interested in us. There were some scoundrels working the passengers. This was normal. Swindlers loved the ferry, especially on the return to New York. They liked to swindle rubes excited to be on their way to see the big city. Cardsharps also plied the ferries. What I didn't see were any thugs or obvious gang members.

I leaned my head in toward Virginia and whispered, "Do you think Kelly would use someone normal looking to keep an eye on us?"

She thought that over. "I don't think so. Kelly's not subtle."

"Then why can't we spot our watcher?"

"Maybe he's a member of the crew . . . or he hasn't got anyone following us today."

Sharp turned from the river. "No, he's right in front of your eyes."

"You've spotted him," I asked.

"Before we left the dock." Sharp wore a smug grin.

"We can do this one of two ways." Virginia sounded exasperated. "Steve and I can sweep the deck with our eyes over and over until we find this guy—which would probably alert him—or you can just tell us."

"He's the cardsharp in the middle of the deck."

I stole a glance. The gambler didn't appear interested in us. "How did you pick him out?"

"He waited to board until we climbed the gangway. That was odd. A cardsharp would never let a ship shove off without him. An' at the last minute, he gave some kind of a message to a stevedore."

"He seems normal . . . like he belongs. Are you saying Kelly's as savvy as Lewis about surveillance?"

"No." Sharp turned back to face the river, so we followed suit. "The gambler has a prime piece of real estate, right smack dab in the center of the passenger deck. That means he's payin' whatever gang controls gamblin' on this steamship line. That man's already connected to the gangs, so he's a natural for our Mr. Kelly."

Virginia asked, "Do you think he'll sail on the return to Manhattan or disembark to wait for us?"

Sharp waited to answer. "My guess is he's gotta stay on board. That seat's too valuable to let another gamester grab his spot. Probably got an accomplice that will go ashore with us."

I turned around to look. Without turning back, I said, "I believe he's that young man standing at his shoulder. Probably an understudy. He's protecting anyone else from crowding in to get a look at his cards." I returned to face the railing. "So what will Kelly do? He'll soon know we're in New Jersey. Does he take the next ferry to ambush us?"

"Possibly," Sharp said.

"That's enlightening," Virginia responded.

No one spoke for a few moments, and then Sharp said, "If they watched us board, they know McAllen's with us. Might even have spotted our two guards. My guess is he doesn't want Pinkertons after him, so he'll wait for us to return an' watch for a better opportunity."

"You're right." It was McAllen who had come up behind us. "And we need to give him that opportunity."

"Give it to him?" Virginia asked. "Why?"

"So we can set a trap."

Chapter 32

"Why were ya talkin' to the ferry captain?" Sharp asked.

We were on the train to Menlo Park. The four of us sat across the aisle from each other, and our guards had taken seats at either end of the car to watch the doors. The cardsharp's accomplice had indeed followed us but had stayed at a table outside a tavern with a view of the ferry dock.

"What you already figured out. I wanted to know who controlled gamblin' on his boat. The cardsharps are not actually gang members; they just pay juice for exclusive use of the territory. Kelly probably paid them only to telegraph him if they spotted us."

I knew McAllen was telling the truth, but I bet he had also liked the lack of crowds in the pilothouse. The top deck of the ferry had been teeming with people, but our railcar was almost empty. McAllen already seemed less anxious.

"How do we proceed when we get to Menlo Park?" Virginia asked.

"Our theory about kitchen help is only a guess. It could be anyone, so don't get sloppy. Steve, you can't forget you're an invalid." He thought a moment. "I'll talk to the head cook. Virginia, you talk to Mrs. Edison. See if she's heard any gossip about any of the men gettin' together with the kitchen help. Jeff, get friendly with the clerks. See if you can find out which are married, betrothed, or whatever."

"What about me?" I asked when he appeared to have finished.

Evidently, he hadn't thought of an assignment for me. "Why don't you go upstairs and get friendly with the engineers," McAllen said without conviction. "You shouldn't be climbin' stairs, so do it slowly."

"May I offer an alternative?" Virginia said.

"Of course," McAllen said flatly.

"I'm the one who married an engineer. I'm the one who spent countless hours talking electricity with Tom. And if you want to find out who is sleeping with a Lewis agent, well, I'm a bit prettier than Steve."

"You're suggestin' you go upstairs?"

"You are perceptive, Captain."

"What about questionin' Mrs. Edison?"

"She likes Steve."

McAllen didn't like his plans questioned, but he was making this up as he went along, and Virginia had made sense. It solved the problem of my supposed diminished physical ability, because the Edison home was the first building encountered and the shortest walk from the train platform.

"Steve, it's time for your boyish charm," he said.

Damn. She had handled my mother and now

McAllen. I wondered how much she had been handling me. I decided that was a path better not traveled.

"Cap, how do we set this trap for Kelly?" Sharp asked.

McAllen turned his cold stare on Sharp. "Do not call me Cap. It's Captain, Mr. McAllen, or Joseph. Never Cap. Understood . . . Jeffery?"

"Understood, Captain."

I smothered a laugh. Not because Sharp hated to be called Jeffery, but because these two hardened men were so concerned about how they were addressed. Then I remembered that I didn't like to be called Stephen because that's what my mother called me. It was funny how we remained touchy over things we should be eager to forget. Why couldn't we leave past hurts behind us? Human nature, I supposed.

"I don't have the trap fully figured out, but it's probably goin' to be dangerous." McAllen looked at Virginia and me. "Dangerous for both of you."

"Why?" I asked, not at all pleased with the idea of putting Virginia in danger.

"Because a trap needs bait."

I thought about what he meant. "So Virginia and I need to appear alone somewhere where Kelly can get at us without being observed. And he needs to be sure we're without protection. You and your men will be too far away to thwart the first blows."

"I'm sorry, Steve."

"Where?" I asked.

"I have a couple of places I need to think through. Give me a day or two. I assume Kelly won't be the assailant, but he'll want to watch from a safe distance . . . like he did when you were beaten in that alley."

"So ya need a place where Steve an' Virginia appear vulnerable, but Kelly'll be the one really exposed," Sharp said.

"A difficult puzzle," I said.

"Yep," McAllen said. "But we won't spring anything until we find a good answer, one we're all comfortable with. In the meantime, your guards will remain obvious, and you'll stay away from locations where you're vulnerable."

"And our lessons at the gymnasium continue," Virginia stated as if already confirmed.

She was smiling. She had never liked guns, but I had a feeling she would enjoy swinging a leaded handbag into the face of Hugo Kelly. Her next words confirmed my suspicion.

"It appears that under your plan, we get to swing the first blows."

She was still smiling.

Chapter 33

I limped up the front steps to the Edison porch. Before I could knock, Mary Edison opened the door.

"Mr. Dancy, a pleasure. Is your lovely fiancée with you?"

"Fiancée?"

"Oh my goodness, you said no?"

"I said yes, but how did you know?"

"When she got word of your injuries, she ran out of here declaring that she was going to ask you to marry her. She muttered something about you being an oblivious moron."

This was the first time I had heard Virginia referred to as my fiancée. I liked it, but it made me think I probably ought to buy her a ring to make it official. My mother shopped at Tiffany & Company near Union Square, so the store had to be the best jeweler in the city.

"Virginia is in the laboratory. She has a few more questions for your husband's engineers, but she'll stop by as soon as she's finished."

"You aren't accompanying her?"

"Mrs. Edison, Virginia knows far more about electricity than I ever will. I invest in your husband, not his inventions." I tapped my leg with the cane. "Besides, I can't keep up with her at the moment."

"I believe you may always find it difficult to keep up." She made a welcoming wave and stood aside. "Please, come in. I was just about to sit down for tea and cakes."

"That would be a pleasure, ma'am."

As we walked to the parlor, she said, "If you bet on my husband, you will do very well. His will is certain and firm. He thinks of nothing except his creations."

I didn't know how to respond, so I just followed her. Menlo Park seemed distant from the hubbub and glamour of New York, but her home was tastefully furnished in the popular Victorian style. The walls were light blue with white crown molding and door frames. A recessed white ceiling displayed a sophisticated floral relief pattern. The centerpiece of the room was an elaborately carved wooden mantel that extended above the fireplace to surround an expansive beveled mirror.

I followed her into the parlor and across a lavish woven rug that covered all but the edges of the hardwood floor. She led me past the main seating area of upholstered chairs and a settee to a small table by the window. The table had been set for tea for one. Heavy brown drapes had been drawn wide open to fill the room with sunlight. I looked around. The electric lights were off. Was this some type of petty rebellion by a neglected wife?

"Would you move over one of those chairs?" she asked.

Along the wall opposite the fireplace were several cushioned wooden chairs. I picked up one and placed it across from her at the round table. As I sat, I noticed she could watch everybody's comings and goings along the single Menlo Park road. She rang a small bell, and a servant immediately appeared.

"Sara, dear, could you please bring another setting for my guest?"

"Right away, ma'am." She disappeared after an abbreviated curtsy.

Mary Edison gazed out the window.

"It's a beautiful day," I offered.

"Indeed." She returned her attention to the service and shook out a napkin to let it float to her lap. "Are you here to investigate my husband's troubles in District 1?"

"We are."

"How can I help?"

"We believe the saboteur of your husband's work has someone working here at Menlo Park. Do you have any idea who that might be?"

"I don't believe anyone here is disloyal to my husband. He's a hard taskmaster, but he's respected by the people who work for him. This is the center of the world for electricity, telegraph development, phonographs, ticker tapes, and now even telephones. If you're an engineer, this is where you want to be. No one working in the laboratory would put that at risk."

"Perhaps not," I responded. "I'm certain your husband feels as comfortable as you in the loyalty of the people here at Menlo Park, but we must consider all possibilities. There are others at Menlo Park who may not have the same motivation for loyalty. Cooks, servants, crib attendants, grooms, kitchen help, and probably others I know nothing about."

Sara returned with a tray holding a teacup, saucer, spoon, and small plate. As soon as she arranged them in front of me, Mrs. Edison poured cream into both cups and then filled them with steaming tea. She offered me a silver sugar bowl, but I shook my head. I waited for her to sweeten her tea before taking a sip.

"Irish breakfast tea?" I asked.

"Yes. You have discerning taste."

"No, you have the same taste in tea as my mother. I grew up drinking this tea, but I've been drinking coffee since I went west." I felt myself smile. "This brings back my childhood."

"Your mother is the matriarch of the Dancy family, is she not?"

"She is."

"Well, I hope to receive an invitation to your wedding."

Requesting an invitation was impolite, but the Wizard of Menlo Park and his wife were probably not subject to the rules of others. Celebrities seemed to be able to do whatever they wanted without the petty restrictions of social norms.

"I'll be sure to send you an invitation, although the ceremony may not be in New York."

"Oh, I know. But we travel to Philadelphia quite frequently." She leaned back in her chair, holding her cup by the saucer just below her chin. "I suppose we must return to this awful traitor discussion. So you think it's one of the servants or tradesmen. Interesting. Have you discovered who might be employing this turncoat?"

"We have suspicions, ma'am, but no confirmation." I wasn't sure how to proceed, so I just blurted, "Our prime suspect has a tendency to hire women to spy on his competitors."

"Women?" She glanced at the door. "You don't suspect Sara. Oh my goodness, certainly not."

"No. We don't suspect anyone in this household."

"I should hope not. There is only Sara, a nanny, and myself. Despite whatever my husband may have told you, it was none of us . . . none of us."

She sounded far more agitated than she should have been by my vague comments.

"Ma'am, I choose my words poorly. There is no suspicion of you or your staff. I never meant to indicate there was."

"Then why are you in my home? I don't go into that laboratory except as a decoration for important guests."

I tried to look contrite, but I was no actor. "This

is embarrassing, but I was hoping to ask you about gossip you may have heard, gossip about the women who serve food to the men in the dining hall."

She looked relieved. "Mr. Dancy, people do not share gossip with the wife of Thomas Edison."

I looked out the window for a moment. "You have a grand view of the road. Have you ever noticed any peculiar comings and goings?"

"What would be peculiar?"

"I don't know. Perhaps one of the women leaving the village with a man."

"This is not a garrison. People may come and go as they please."

"Of course, but train and ferry fares are not cheap."

She sipped tea and looked at me with what I thought were frightened eyes. Finally, she said, "Marsha White leaves the village several nights a week. Ten minutes later, a man goes down the road. The men . . . vary." She looked embarrassed.

"Who is Marsha White?"

"She . . . she serves food, chops vegetables, cleans, washes dishes, and whatever else needs doing."

We had been right about the flower girl and now the spy at Menlo Park. Actually, McAllen had been right about one and Virginia the other. Was this too easy? And why did Mary Edison look frightened?

"Do you have any idea where she goes on these evenings?"

"Sara told me she goes to the tavern down by the ferry dock. She has a room upstairs. I presume you have an idea what goes on there."

"I do." And I knew the tavern. That was the same establishment our watcher was at right now, drinking beer until we returned. "I'm sorry to have to ask this, but do you know if she charges?"

She glanced toward the door to insure that Sara had not entered the room. "You said you invest in the man. That man is my husband. You don't intend to get him in trouble, do you?"

"Trouble? What kind of trouble?"

"That kind of activity is illegal in New Jersey."

"I don't understand. Mr. Edison has—"

I did understand. Edison had a village of men with few distractions after grueling days of work. He knew what White was doing. The only question remaining was, had he instigated it, or was he merely turning his head away and pretending not to see.

"Mrs. Edison, I have no intention of harming your husband . . . nor do I have any incentive to do so. Quite the contrary, I can assure you." I sipped my tea and crossed my legs in a relaxed pose. "It must be difficult for you. A woman of your upbringing must find this distasteful."

"Distasteful? That's an odd expression, Mr. Dancy. I find it reprehensible. I've argued about it many times with Tom. He says it's best to ignore the shortcomings in others. Shortcomings? Hah. Sin is more like it. And how does he suppose I am to ignore depravity? They parade right in front of me . . . almost nightly. Sometimes more than one man leaves the village before she returns."

My first thought was that she could move away from the window, but I suspected that despite her protestations, she got some kind of secondhand thrill out of the illicit spectacle.

"Do you know how this started?" I asked.

"If you're asking if my husband hired her for this purpose, he did not. She ventured into this realm wholly on her own. My husband, however, has chosen to turn a blind eye to these nightly trysts."

She blushed at her own words.

"Do you know her employment prior to coming here?"

"No. She showed up one day and begged for a job . . . any job. We had a cruel cook at the time, and all of our food help had quit after one of his tirades. She was hired on the spot. I know, because Tom fired the cook, and I had to help with food preparation for almost a week."

"Does that mean you know Miss White?"

"Mrs. White." Mary Edison squared her shoulders. "The harlot has a husband in Quincy, Massachusetts. She ran away because of his temper. At first, I was sympathetic and took her under my wing. She seemed such a sweet girl. Pretty too. But I've shunned her since she found a way to supplement her wages . . . which are quite decent, I might add."

"Did she have letters of reference?"

"No. It was all part of her sad story. She'd never held any kind of position and ran away without thinking about character references." She shrugged. "We needed help and she worked hard."

This fit the way swindlers worked. They overcame normal caution with a story designed to produce sympathy. A small town would make it hard to check her story without an expensive visit by a detective. My bet was that George Lewis also employed Marsha White. As a kitchen servant, she had a perfect opportunity to overhear conversations about developments in the laboratory, and her nightly forays would fill any holes in her knowledge. Lewis probably paid well for her information. That thought made me wonder how much money she made from Edison's wages, Lewis's money, and fees for service.

Then I had another thought. Prostitution was part of every town and camp in the West. It was so prevalent that I thought of it as normal. When females were as rare as chilled beer, women found a husband, a schoolhouse, or a brothel. Many men married women of ill repute, and only the self-righteous gave it a second thought. Now I was back east again, and I found myself thinking of prostitution as illicit and disreputable. Was morality determined by geography? I didn't think so, but it was easy to dismiss immorality when it was widespread.

Mary Edison interrupted my musings by saying, "I want you to get Mrs. White out of Menlo Park."

That surprised me because she had seemed skeptical about a traitor on the premises.

"Why?" I asked.

"Last week, she made advances toward my husband."

Chapter 34

Virginia had spent an hour with Mrs. Edison, and both women seemed to enjoy the visit. While they talked, I had limped up to the boardinghouse to find Sharp. He was in the kitchen eating a pork chop with the cook. They acted like they were old friends who hadn't seen each other in ages. When McAllen joined us, we went back to the Edison home, gathered up Virginia, and started toward the platform.

The four of us walked as a group, everyone moving slowly as I continued to pretend infirmity. The cane and limp now felt more natural, and I enjoyed having a weapon always at hand.

When we were out of earshot, McAllen simply said, "Marsha White?"

All three of us answered yes at about the same time.

After a moment, Virginia asked, "Does that remove Mary Edison from your suspect list?"

"She was never on my suspect list," McAllen answered.

"Then would you please inform anyone who had her on a list that we have found the real spy?"

"I will," was all McAllen said.

We walked on, waiting for McAllen to lead the conversation. We were approaching the platform before he spoke again. "I think I know how to drag Lewis into court."

"Tell us," I said.

"I'll have White arrested the next time she takes a man to her room at that tavern. They'll lock her up and forget about her for a few days. After she has some time to stew, I think she'll testify against Lewis to escape prosecution for prostitution."

"Put her in a separate cell," Virginia said. "Keep her all alone. Then, when you talk to her, promise to shield her from any mention of prostitution. She only has to testify that she was paid for information. The jury and newspapers don't need to know how she acquired it."

"Ya think she's embarrassed by her work?" Sharp seemed skeptical.

"I don't know. I don't know her. But I know she's a swindler, and Joseph can tell her that pretty young girls accused of prostitution get their picture in the paper. If she's going to pursue her profession, she needs anonymity. Promise her no police record . . . and no notoriety."

McAllen quit walking and looked at Virginia. "Clever. If you ever get tired of Steve, see me about employment." He started walking again. "I'll promise her no police record, but that doesn't mean no Pinkerton file."

"That surely ain't enough for a judge?" Sharp said.

"No. But we'll have the Adams Express

Company superintendent in Pennsylvania, as well."

"How ya gonna make him testify?" Sharp asked.

"Anyone who would hire himself out to Lewis is not honest. We investigated other shippin' consignments, and our Philadelphia office is puttin' together a case against him for smugglin' rum. Not payin' the excise tax makes it a federal crime. He'll cooperate when we threaten to put him in a federal penitentiary, especially after we tell him we're gonna put the word out that his sentence will be light because he informed. Suddenly, a throat full of Pinkerton flyers will seem a humane way to die."

"Is that enough for conviction?" I asked.

"Perhaps not, but it's enough for a civil case for tortious interference. That should take care of old man Lewis. We'll need more against the son."

"Torture?" Virginia asked. "Are you talking about Steve's beating?"

"Not torture," McAllen said. "*Tortious interference* is a legal term for interferin' with a contract between two other parties. Lewis interfered with the delivery contracts between Edison and the express company. Put a spy in his operation. Probably a civil case, but it'll put George Lewis in the docket. Is that enough for you, Steve?"

"If we can't get more, it will do. The publicity will harm his business . . . but I want the son as well. If the whole family gets dragged into court, the Lewises will be ostracized from society, and probably ruined financially. So how do we get the son?"

"First off, we need proof Kelly killed that superintendent in Connecticut, then we need to tie Chuck Lewis to Kelly. We have nothin' yet . . . except a tavern keeper who'll testify to Kelly drinkin' with the younger Lewis." McAllen started descending the final incline to the train platform. "Steve, you may need to make a choice: Hugo Kelly or Chuck Lewis. It looks like one will need to testify against the other, so one will get amnesty."

"That's easy," Virginia answered for me. "Hugo Kelly's the one threatening our lives."

I wasn't comfortable with that, but I let it go. No matter what else happened, I would never allow Kelly to continue threatening Virginia. I didn't believe I needed to let Chuck Lewis go free to accomplish that.

McAllen climbed the three wooden steps leading to the platform. It was late evening, and we were the only four people waiting for the train. The waning light made the world look soft and safe.

McAllen turned to me. "Steve, I haven't figured out a safe way to entrap Kelly. Not yet, anyway."

"I have," I responded.

I enjoyed the surprised look on his face.

"Tell me."

"I won't tell you the exact location yet, but what if I could make sure Kelly knew where Virginia and I would be on a particular day at a specific time? It's in Manhattan, and there's a busy park across the street. I know it's not very much information, but if you were Kelly, how would you ambush us?"

"You expect me to come up with a scenario based on that? Damn, Steve." He walked to the end of the platform and looked around to make sure we were alone. "How would you get there?"

"Cab."

He returned to where we were standing. "I'd position a cab to pick you up afterwards and take you to a quiet alley. Put a gun to your heads through the windows on either side, disarm you . . . and then do the worst."

I shook my head. "A carriage is too tight of a space for us to maneuver. You may not be able to follow, and you can't pick the right alley to pre-position your men. We need to avoid that trap."

"Then go for a walk in the park. Did you say the park was busy?"

"We can do it any time—when it's busy or uncrowded. Which is better?"

McAllen paced the platform. "Busy," he said. "It'll make Kelly feel comfortable. Busy means an easier escape. Murder in the open is not hard, but he doesn't want you just dead. He wants you both to suffer . . . be humiliated. A slow death, that's the difficult part when the assailant needs to get out of there fast."

"Gut 'em," Sharp said immediately.

McAllen wheeled around. "Yep. Killers walk to either side of you lovebirds and slice each of you across the belly. An agonizin' death in public with Kelly watchin' from a distance. You'll both be wailin' and watchin' each other die. Perfect revenge."

"I don't find that so perfect," Virginia said in a shaky voice. "I can't imagine anything worse."

"That's why he'll go that way," Sharp said.

Now I was the one to pace the platform. Suddenly, I turned. "I can do it."

"Do what?" McAllen demanded.

"Set it up so Kelly plans it just that way."

"Steve!" Virginia exclaimed.

"Don't worry. We can make it safe."

"Safe? How? My God, dying in awful pain while watching you die in agony? I'm scared. Please, Steve, find another way."

I stood directly in front of her. I gently grabbed her shoulders and looked her in the eye. "Virginia, any way we deal with Kelly will be dangerous. I can't control the situation if he makes his own plan. We need to guide him. I can't protect us if he decides to shoot us in the head, but if he goes for a gutting, I can."

"How?" Sharp asked.

"By wearing bamboo shields under our clothing. Bamboo is stronger than you think. A knife can't cut through it with a single swipe."

"Bamboo?" Virginia said, puzzled.

A slow smile grew on Sharp's face. "That'll work. Ya can shape bamboo with steam. When it dries, it holds its shape an' turns sinewy. Lightweight. We could line it with felt too."

McAllen looked interested. "Tell me the whole scheme," he demanded.

I did.

Chapter 35

I was nervous. I fidgeted with my napkin, my cuffs, my hair, all the while taking far too many sips of whiskey. I was waiting in the hotel restaurant for my mother and Mr. Benson, my publisher. My mother still unnerved me, but I felt reassured that Virginia sat directly to my left. As I reached for my whiskey glass, Virginia covered my hand and simply shook her head. She was right. Handling my mother was difficult enough sober.

Mother arrived with my harried-looking publisher chasing along behind her. I glanced at our oversized guardian sitting in his usual place by the door and nodded to let him know these people were not a threat. He smiled indulgently, like I was a slightly befuddled old uncle. He certainly remembered my mother from her last visit to this dining room, and he was probably hoping for another argument to relieve his boredom.

We both stood.

"Mother, I'm glad to see you."

We kissed the air in the general proximity of our respective cheeks. I extended my hand to my publisher. "Mr. Benson, it's been far too many years."

He shook limply.

"Mr. Dancy, it's my—"

"Stephen, dear, you didn't mention that this woman would be joining us."

My mother had not even bothered to look at Virginia.

"I'm sorry, I assumed you wanted to see me. If you do, Virginia will be at my side." I watched her glance quickly at Virginia. "Well . . . are you going to sit or leave?"

"That doesn't sound like a gracious invitation."

"I'm afraid the frontier has scrubbed away my faux politeness."

My mother looked as if she might explode, but only for the briefest of moments. Then her face lit up with what appeared to be a genuine smile. "Mr. Benson, may I introduce Mrs. Baker, a friend of my son's."

He walked around the table and actually kissed her hand. "The pleasure is mine, I'm sure."

Benson hadn't noticed the tension. I had known Benson, a distant cousin, for years. He had always been oblivious to the tones of social interaction. He might miss mockery or sarcasm in real life, but he could spot a misplaced comma three pages away. Although we hadn't seen each other since I left New York City, we had traded telegrams and letters all through the planning and writing of my book. Despite my mother's misgivings, Benson liked the book. His judgment mattered to me because he never lied. I suspect he was incapable of telling falsehoods, which amplified his praise . . . or intensified his criticisms.

"Steve has talked so much about you, I feel I already know you," Virginia said to Benson.

"How unfortunate. I shall endeavor not to be myself this evening."

We all laughed politely, but I wasn't entirely sure he intended humor. After we'd taken our seats, I poured wine for everyone. I saw my mother sneak a peek at the label. It was Château Lafite Rothschild. I didn't want to give her another opening to posture as a connoisseur.

"I love your book," Benson said. "It should sell well. Your characters are fascinating creatures. If only we had such brave and stalwart men in the real world. But that's what makes fiction popular . . . heroes and heroics, no matter how illusory. At least your book doesn't idealize heroes like those dime novels. Your characters appear as genuine human beings."

"Which character did you like the most?" Virginia teased, knowing that for the most part, the book enlarged on the exploits of Sharp, McAllen, and myself.

"Oh, the men were valiant, but that female shopkeeper was intriguing—smart, independent, poised. She'll appeal to women and make the book much more popular."

I stifled a laugh. Virginia shot me a dirty look. Benson and my mother looked baffled at our response. Little did they know that the female shopkeeper sat beside me.

Benson appeared miffed at our levity. "Mr. Dancy, my comment was not frivolous. Women buy books, and they are not attracted to these Wild West tales cranked out by scribblers who have never ventured beyond the Hudson River. You may not have intended it, but you've created an attractive and engaging female character who will appeal to women and, if I may say, men as well . . . at least men who desire a woman for more than producing children."

"Thank you, Mr. Benson," I said. "I appreciate the compliment. To be truthful, I didn't initially appreciate this woman's attributes, but I can assure you, I do now. Perhaps I'll make her the heroine in my next novel."

Now it was Virginia's turn to smother a giggle with her napkin. Our tomfoolery had gone far enough. My mother was not stupid and already looked suspicious. I changed the subject.

"Mark Twain said something along the lines that we hero-worship men with qualities we lack. Heroes are men who do things we can't or won't do. He said we privately want to be like somebody else."

"Mark Twain is full of himself," Benson

declared, as he brushed his napkin wrinkle free over his lap.

"You know him?" I asked.

"Of course. He's a ruffian westerner with pretentions of fitting into eastern society. He married well, but his supposed refinement is belied by his writing."

"I admire his writing," I said, surprised.

"Well, you shouldn't. It's coarse and uncivil. Your writing shows your education and standing in society."

"I'd prefer it showed Twain's brilliance."

"Overestimated by all. His novelty will wear off, and he'll soon be forgotten."

"Is he that redheaded man from Hartford?" Mother asked. "The one who married into the Langdon family?"

"The same," Benson answered.

"Oh, dear," Mother said. "Stephen, you write beautifully. You need only to find a more appropriate subject. Don't emulate that social climber. He does not belong in our circle. Listen to Mr. Benson, dear. You will be the toast of the New York literary set if you follow his advice. I'm sure this book is just a beginning."

Virginia and I traded guarded glances. Before they arrived, she had cautioned me to concentrate on setting our trap for Kelly. She was right. I had the rest of her life to argue with my mother.

After we ordered our meal, I opened up the subject of the book event. "Shall we discuss the reading?" I said. "How many people are you expecting?"

"At least two hundred. All the right people will attend, and select journalists have committed to the evening. I've promised five one-on-one interviews after the reading, each for fifteen minutes." Benson appeared to sip his wine but merely wet his lips. "Your book is generating enormous excitement. People want to experience the frontier from the safety of their parlor. You have everything necessary for a popular book: danger, excitement, bad men, damsels in need of rescuing, and larger-than-life heroes. It will do splendidly and build an audience for a second book with a more literary theme."

"And what would a more literary theme be?" I asked, a bit miffed myself.

"Oh, struggles of conscience, man's predilection for violence, the circle of life, hanging on to sanity, dealing with inevitable death . . . whatever you choose."

"How about man's inborn need to elevate himself above others through pretense and artifice?"

"Excellent." He straightened his posture in response, ignorant of the intended slight. "A great theme. Are you working on it now?"

"No. At the moment I'm considering a book

about a man's quest for true independence—complete freedom from the judgment of others."

"Another excellent theme. You must begin work on one of these."

My mother's expression was reproachful. Nothing escaped her, especially sarcasm delivered in a conversational tone. After all, she was the master, I the mere pupil.

I used the service of our meal to direct the conversation back to the reading.

"Let's talk about my book debut. After the reading, I'll have an announcement. I want all the newspapermen present."

"What announcement?" Mother asked.

"It's a surprise."

"I'm your mother. Surprise others."

"This is my book, my event, my surprise." She was about to argue, so I added quickly, "I'd like to invite you to a celebratory banquet at one o'clock next Tuesday afternoon at this hotel, two days after my book debut party. You as well, Mr. Benson."

"Celebratory?" Mother leaned slightly toward me. "Then this is a good surprise?"

"The very best. Can you make it?"

"Is this a business or a personal surprise?" She glanced at Virginia.

"If I answer that, you will only pose another question. Let me just say, you should be pleased." Should, but probably not.

"Then in that case, of course. I shall wait with bated breath."

"Please don't, Mother. It's nearly a week away. You may continue to sniff dismissively in the meantime."

She bristled noticeably. "I certainly hope the East will reacquaint you with your manners. You have become quite snippy."

"I had a good instructor."

"Do I need to storm out of my favorite restaurant once again?"

"No, Mother. Let's eat and pretend to enjoy each other's company."

Benson and Virginia looked at each other, both seemingly embarrassed by our bickering. I assumed to alleviate tension, Virginia said, "Mr. Benson, what was the theme of *Little Women*, by Louisa May Alcott?"

"*Little Women?*" He wet his lips with his wine again. "That book was about an unremarkable family. My, my." He picked up his wineglass, then set it back down. "I suppose you might say it's about how a young lady can rise above her station in life. I understand that it is highly autobiographical."

"That seems a narrow interpretation," Virginia said. "I think it's about striving to fulfill one's dreams . . . and how healthy family relationships help a person attain those dreams. Alcott's celebrity status was a mere by-product of writing novels people wanted to read. Readers were her dream, not fame."

Benson looked annoyed at her "narrow interpretation" slight. "Concord was a hotbed of literary figures. She probably received help from Ralph Waldo Emerson, Nathaniel Hawthorne, Henry David Thoreau, and maybe even Margaret Fuller. These authors were far more important than family to her success."

"Then you must have read a different book," Virginia said.

"Shall we discuss the schedule?" I wanted to get the discussion back on my book debut party. "Do you have suggestions on the selection I should use? How long do you expect me to read?"

For the remainder of the meal, we discussed schedules and logistics. When the check arrived, Benson made a show of telling me his publishing house would pick up the expenses for the party. I took the hint and signed our meals to my room.

Finally, we were sitting at the table, with only our wineglasses and a centerpiece of flowers low enough to see over. Benson's wine was less than half gone, despite my never having refilled his glass. I emptied our second bottle by pouring equally small portions in the other three glasses.

"Mrs. Baker, what are your intentions for the coming social season?" Mother asked.

The so-called social season ran from after Christmas to the start of summer. It didn't have the same panache as London's, but the New York elite still aped British high society. The social season remained many months away, so my mother's question was subterfuge. She was nosing around to find out if our liaison was temporary.

"Oh, I hope to be home by then," Virginia said nonchalantly.

"Home? And where might that be, dear?"

"I suppose Denver at the moment. At least that's where I left my belongings."

"You have no home? My, that must be distressing for you." Mother took a sip that drained her glass while appraising Virginia over the rim. She set it back on the table, the stem in both hands. "I know this is indelicate, but I must ask. Is your husband in Denver with your other belongings?"

"My husband is dead," Virginia said in as flat a voice as I had ever heard her use. I had a sense she was coiling like a threatened rattlesnake.

"Oh, dear, I'm sorry to hear that." Mother twirled her empty wineglass. "Was he fixed well enough to leave you some money . . . or is my son paying your keep?"

"Mrs. Dancy, that's none of your business and quite rude. Far too rude for a person with genuine class."

Now I heard a tail rattle meant to warn predators to go away.

"That answered my question, dear." She turned

toward me. "Stephen, I hope you are getting your money's worth."

Before I exploded, Virginia placed her hand on mine.

"I'm disappointed in you, Mrs. Dancy. You're unworthy of respect from me or your peers. Your son is thirty-one years old. I can assure you, he no longer needs your protection. I'm twenty-eight. I do not need your insults, condescension, or permission. But I do demand your civility."

"Young lady, you may demand nothing from me. You're a common tart, an actress of ill breeding who lost her husband and fastened onto my son for his money. Make no mistake; I can have you arrested for illicit behavior. You will not threaten me, and you may never question my standing in this community. These are things you do not understand . . . will never understand. You should immediately return to your belongings in that godforsaken Denver. You don't belong here, nor do you belong with my son."

When I started to respond, Virginia squeezed my hand so hard it hurt. Benson was literally cowering in the face of my mother's wrath. I wanted to tell Virginia not to defend herself by telling my mother about her family, but she spoke before I could figure out a way to say it without spilling the beans.

"Madam, in the West, we don't allow anyone to insult us. Everyone is polite because everyone is armed. Men still duel in the West. Armed women have been known to stand down men in the street."

I was almost afraid she would pull her pistol, but instead she engaged in a staring contest that she finally won when my mother dropped her eyes to her wineglass.

"Now, for your information, this is not your decision, it's your son's decision. If he tells me to leave, I'll be on the next train, but not before."

Silence followed. I glanced around at the other diners, who were pretending not to watch us. Mathew, on the edge of his seat, remained still, looking confused about what he ought to do.

"My God, you're a barbarian."

"Yes, ma'am. I am." Virginia looked around. "We have nice rooms in the West, but we don't have this elaborate social order that separates people into different groups. People—men and women—are judged by their self-reliance, courage, fair play, and honor. You would not survive. Not because you're a gentlewoman, but because you lack courage, decency, and common sense. You hide behind your society to disguise that you are really nothing: a frail woman who is incapable of even dressing herself."

Virginia stood defiantly. "Steve, do *you* want me to stay?"

"Yes."

I stood as well, grabbing my cane for support before addressing my mother.

"The other reason you wouldn't survive the frontier is that you don't know how to pick your fights."

We left.

Chapter 36

Sweat made my shirt cling to my chest. McAllen had a new instructor teaching me how to use a cane for defense. He was young and wiry, and possessed unbelievable endurance. We had been working strenuously for over an hour without a rest. He told me the work would improve my skill and help me recover full mobility. When he finally gave me a break, I had no mobility whatsoever.

As I sat panting on a bench, he paced back and forth in front of me, giving additional verbal instructions. Most had to do with readiness for trouble. He was obsessed with remaining alert. I had learned that lesson in the West but saw no need to tell him about my previous fights. Then he said something that caught my attention.

"Did you say you can practice seeing behind you? That's silly."

"Get up," he commanded me.

"I just sat down."

"Get up!"

I got up.

He turned his back on me and walked about five feet away. Then he said, "Attack me from behind. Just try to put your arm around my neck. Take your time and don't make a sound."

I waited and waited. He never flinched. I slid as

quietly as possible to my left until my attack would be at about forty-five degrees. I had no intention of sneaking up. I held still a few more moments and then leaped at him. The next thing I knew, my head was locked in his arm.

"You were noisy, so it's hard to say I proved my point. That was smart, though, moving to the side."

I wasn't grateful for the small compliment. "You really believe you can see behind you?"

"Maybe not see exactly, but you can train yourself to sense what's going on all around you."

"All right, let's work on it."

An hour later, I wasn't convinced, but I saw some merit to what he was saying. Maybe one time in three, I anticipated the attack's timing and correctly guessed the direction the strike was coming from. When I asked how long it would take to get three out of three correct, he said it would take months, perhaps years. He promised to give me another lesson the next afternoon.

Afterwards, I washed as best I could with a cloth and a bowl of fresh water. When I put my shirt back on, it was clammy. Damn. Tomorrow I would bring a change of clothes.

I found Virginia upstairs in the lobby waiting for me. She had finished swinging her purse at a punching bag an hour earlier and then had spent a half hour shooting.

"We're becoming a dangerous pair," I said.

"You mean more dangerous." She looked concerned. "I can't imagine how we escaped Leadville knowing so little."

"We knew something, or we wouldn't be spending our afternoons in a basement gymnasium."

"Sometimes I think we should have killed Kelly in that street."

I sat beside her and put my arm around her shoulder. "We'll settle it for good this time."

She let her head rest on my shoulder. "I know. I just want us to be the ones who survive."

"We will. It's a good plan." I touched her cheek. "Don't worry."

In a matter-of-fact voice, she said, "I couldn't shoot worth a damn today."

"How'd you do with the leaded purse?"

"Broke skulls. I can handle that. At least, against a mannequin."

"Then quit worrying. We're not likely to get in a gunfight in the middle of the city. It'll be close quarters, close enough for you to break skulls. Besides, everyone has good and bad days shooting."

"Not you."

"Years of practice since I was a little boy. My dad had me shooting a varmint rifle when I was six. We shot every day at the gun shop."

She raised her head off my shoulder. "McAllen has Marsha White upstairs."

I nearly jumped to my feet. "When did they bring her in?"

"About fifteen minutes ago. He said we should go. He'll let us know if there's any news."

"Why is she here instead of a police station? Or a lawyer's office giving a deposition? What are they planning?"

"I don't know. She looked angry as hell. Completely out of sorts. I don't think she's been convinced to testify against Lewis."

"Let's go up."

McAllen had a temporary office on the third floor. After we climbed the two flights, we found his office empty. A secretary told us he was on the fourth floor. When we got to the stairwell, a guard held up the flat of his hand.

"Pass, please."

"I'm a client of the agency," I said.

"I'm sorry, sir, clients are not allowed on restricted floors without a pass. The top two floors house confidential records. As a client, you wouldn't want someone snooping through your files. You must afford the same courtesy to others."

"Captain McAllen is on the fourth floor with Marsha White, whom we helped identify as a criminal. We have no interest in the records. We only want to see them. You may escort us if you like."

"Captain McAllen is head of field operations in

Denver. He has use of this facility as a courtesy, but he does not have the authority to change our rules. I'm sorry, sir."

I was getting very irritated. "How do I find the head of this office?"

"Sir, I—"

Virginia grabbed my elbow and tugged. "Steve, please, come over here for just a moment."

I wanted to argue further with this underling but let her pull me to the side. Perhaps she had a clever way around him.

"Don't you trust McAllen?"

"What?"

"Why are you trying to interfere? He knows how to convince her to testify against Lewis. You're trying to throw your weight around. For what reason?"

"I'm paying for this. It's our lives at stake. I have a right to get in there and see what's going on."

"Edison is paying for this part. Lewis has nothing to do with the threat to our lives. McAllen has the same goal as you, and he's good at his job. You just want to go up those stairs because someone told you no. Now you're about to barge in on the head of this office and make a scene. Again, for what reason? You're acting like your mother."

I was stunned. I hated the way my mother intimidated people with her money and influence.

Yet Virginia was right. I was about to storm into the head of this office and demand that he break the rules for me for no other reason than that I had paid for services that had been worth every penny. McAllen was fully capable of getting what we needed from Marsha White. Why was I adopting behaviors I found abhorrent? Virginia had accused me of behaving like my mother. Damn. It was true. My father would never have acted this way. He might have used his power to get something done, but always for a moral purpose, never to satisfy ego. I walked back to the guard.

"Sir, I apologize. Your rules obviously have an appropriate purpose. It was wrong of me to threaten to go to your boss."

He looked relieved, and I realized that this posting would be for a newly hired agent.

"No problem, sir."

"Is there a place to get a drink nearby that's suitable for a lady?"

"Yes, indeed. The Wall Street traders often take their wives to the Bowling Green Tavern."

"If you could do me a favor, would you please tell Captain McAllen that Steve Dancy left about this time to have a drink at that tavern? If he's delayed, we'll meet him back at the hotel."

"I will tell him, sir."

When Virginia and I were in the empty stairwell, she said, "Mr. Dancy, I love you all the more for that."

"Well, it appears if I'm going to keep your love, we need to get away from corrupting influences."

"I agree. Let's finish this business and get the hell out of here."

Chapter 37

McAllen never showed up for a drink at the Bowling Green Tavern, nor later at the hotel. In fact, we didn't see McAllen until the next afternoon. He walked in and leaned against the wall as we finished our lessons in the gymnasium. He looked tired.

As we approached, he said, "Let's go for that drink you mentioned yesterday afternoon."

I changed into dry clothes before we walked over to the tavern. It was an expensive establishment that catered to the rich bankers and traders on Wall Street. It was dark and quiet: dark wood, dark upholstery, and dark carpet. The tavern's hushed tones catered to rich men conducting private affairs. In contrast, western saloons were bright and boisterous. The cold beer was the same, and it tasted very refreshing, especially after the lesson.

"We've been pretty good at guessin' on this case, but we messed up badly," McAllen said. "Chuck Lewis, the son, had nothin' to do with killin' that express superintendent."

"Are you sure?" I was startled by this news. "It looked like Kelly's work, and Kelly had no motivation to kill the man unless hired by Lewis."

"He was hired by Lewis, all right. The father, not the son. Our files were wrong, or rather incomplete.

The father wasn't above violence after all. He just hadn't been sloppy enough to raise suspicions. It seems George Lewis has a long history with Kelly. Kelly had done some arson work for him in the past . . . before he left New York for Leadville. They were considered accidents at the time. It was assumed his gaslight competitors had been careless. In one case, a couple of workers were killed."

"Then the son was a go-between?" I asked.

"No. He had separated himself from his father. He found out about the deaths, left the business, and started drinkin' heavy. Kelly was sent by the father to entice Chuck back into the family and the business. It didn't work. Chuck Lewis had become too distrustful to be taken in by his father's deceptions. He sent Kelly away after he guessed the reason he had sidled up to him."

"What about Marsha White?" Virginia asked. "Can you get her to testify against Lewis?"

"No. She's a smart girl." He finished his beer and signaled the tavern keeper to send over another round. "We picked her up, but there was no evidence of a crime, only an illicit encounter. There was absolutely no money in the room, so there was no evidence of prostitution. My guess is she was paid before they left Menlo Park, and she instructed the men to bring nothin' with them. Remember how we were gonna leave her locked up alone for several days to soften her up? Well, her lawyer got her out in hours."

"How'd you get her to agree to come to your office?" I asked.

"A bluff. We told her two men were willin' to testify against her, but I would get it all dismissed if she'd come to our office to answer a few questions. I tried to sway her to help us, but she's too savvy. We let her go after tellin' her she was fired from Edison's and her belongin's had been transported from her room to our building. She was told never to return to Menlo Park."

"Damn it, then we're nowhere?" I banged the table with the flat of my hand.

"Steve, relax. I'm not done. Tomorrow, George Lewis'll be arrested as an accomplice to murder. Just not for the murder of the superintendent. We haven't gotten any evidence on that one yet. He'll be arrested for two explosions and the resultin' fires that killed employees of his competitors. Hugo Kelly will also be indicted. We have an ironclad case against the old man."

"How?"

"Chuck Lewis has agreed to testify against his father. He gave us the name of the person who negotiated with Kelly to set those gas accidents. He's George Lewis's second nephew, and he's in safekeepin' on the fourth floor of our office. I've seldom seen anyone more frightened. We searched his home and found a can of faulty valves that would create a gas leak and a formula for a sulfuric acid ignition device that would take several minutes to set off the gas. This nephew would take a job with a Lewis competitor and tell Kelly when the timing was right to set an explosion. We have people who'll testify that the nephew worked for them just prior to the fires." McAllen took a long swallow of beer. "Accidents aren't uncommon in the gas business, and these were originally written off as accidents. George Lewis didn't want any deaths, but you know what happens when you play with fire."

"Does this mean George Lewis goes to prison?" I asked.

"Yep. George Lewis will go to prison. We have the nephew dead to rights, so he won't be a problem, and the son seems sincere."

"Why would Lewis's nephew have the valves and formula?" Virginia asked. "Kelly wouldn't share them with him."

"It was the other way around. Kelly learned the tricks of his arson trade from this guy. He was an engineer."

"What about Kelly?" I asked.

McAllen studied his beer.

"Tell me," I prodded.

"Neither Chuck Lewis nor the nephew will testify against Kelly unless he's in custody, and a judge has ruled against bail so he can't get out. At least, that's what they say now. They're afraid members of his gang will kill them even if he's put away. They insist on police protection. I talked to the precinct captain, and he said they'll provide protection only if they live in the station."

"What do you think?" I asked. "Will either of them ever testify against Kelly?"

McAllen shook his head. "When it comes down to it, they'll back down. Neither of them are what I would call brave men."

"It all makes sense, doesn't it?" Virginia said. "The connection between Kelly and Lewis going back years. The pattern of spying and sabotage. The sullen son turning to alcohol."

It made sense, but I didn't like it. It struck too close to home. Instead of running to a pub, I ran west. Of course, my mother's side of the family had never resorted to violent tactics, but they were not above using political power or graft to put undue pressure on an opponent. I was suddenly sympathetic toward Chuck Lewis.

"Edison?" I asked, but I knew the answer.

"Just returned from seeing him. I have a few ends to tie up, and then we're done. Lewis will no longer hinder his progress, and his wife is pleased that Marsha White's gone."

"What about the civil case?" Virginia asked.

"He won't touch it. Says any Lewis money will go to lawyers or his ruined competitors. He'd be last in line, and he'd rather apply his energies to new inventions."

"Then we're left with our little trap for Kelly," I said.

"Yep."

Chapter 38

The hotel ballroom beyond the curtain was buzzing with conversation, but Benson kept me in an anteroom separated from the main area by a heavy drape. Earlier, I had peeked from behind the curtain, and the only thing I could ascertain was that wine and refreshments were popular. I could see only people's backs as they congested around the food table and bar situated at the rear of the room. I had decided to keep Virginia with me on the off chance that Kelly decided to strike during the party. Virginia kept giving me reassuring smiles, but I was nervous. My anxiousness didn't come from speaking in front of people. It came from Hugo Kelly.

Every time I thought about Kelly, I got angry. I took a long look at my book, which I held in my hand for the upcoming reading. I had worked on it for over a year and had looked forward to this day—daydreamed about it. It was supposed to be a gala event with me as the center of attention. Kelly spoiled it. Even if he didn't show up, which was likely, his menace hovered over the event like a flock of vultures waiting for someone to die.

Although I doubted he would show up, I had arranged for him to hear about what I said here. It was all part of my trap. With nothing to do, I went over my plan again. Was I acting stupidly? Did my trap make sense or was I deceiving myself? I had doubts, and they seemed bigger in this closed-in room. Did we have enough protection? I peeked again and was reassured to see Mathew by the door. His size alone should scare off any would-be attacker. McAllen was wandering around the room. He had a man in the lobby and another outside. If I was wrong, and Kelly attacked here, would we react quickly enough? Would we both survive? Damn. I couldn't imagine carrying on my life without Virginia.

Somebody placed a hand on my shoulder and gently shook me out of my reverie. It was Benson. He pointed toward the curtain, signaling that it was time for my grand entrance. I stood a second, trying to shake off my anger. I needed to emerge from behind this curtain with a smile and a happy outlook. Kelly was a temporary problem in our lives, but with any luck, my writing would go on for decades. That meant I needed to introduce my novel with all the fanfare I could muster. I took Virginia's hand, and we burst through the curtain together.

The room exploded with motion and noise as people stood and applauded. What for? Very few of these people had read my book. We had sent galley proofs to newspapers for reviews, and several of them had been glowing, but general sales wouldn't start until after my remarks. I held up the copy of my book, and people applauded even louder. The attendees were relatives, friends of my mother, people employed by my publisher, a few book enthusiasts, and newspapermen. Generally, a stacked deck meant to build an impression of huge popularity for the book. Everyone present would get one free copy, which, along with free food and drink, made for a happy audience. This event was merely a grand exhibition for the newspapers, not a gathering of admirers. What had I expected? Ardent fans of Steve Dancy? I shouldn't be cynical. I wanted the book to be a success, and this debut would surely give it a major boost. Then I spotted Thomas Edison in the front row. I was honored he would come but worried that his celebrity would divert attention away from my book. I shook away the selfish thought and nodded a thank you to him.

With a jolt, I noticed Hugo Kelly in the middle of a row toward the back. He was dressed as well as any of the other guests and applauded as if bored with the whole spectacle. When everyone took a seat, he remained standing just long enough to insure that I would notice him. When our eyes met, he smiled creepily and sat down. I looked at Virginia, who had taken a seat in the front row. She hadn't noticed. My mother sat beside her, and others in her vicinity were my relatives. Next, I checked Mathew. He sat in his place by the door, but I couldn't catch his eye because he was looking over the crowd. I visually checked the rest of the people, but saw no one the least bit threatening. Back to Kelly. He had been watching me look around, and his creepy smile had been replaced by a genuine grin. He wasn't here to harm us, just rattle us. To hell with him. Then I saw something that made me feel better. The man next to him leaned over and whispered in his ear. The grin vanished. McAllen straightened and looked forward, caught my eye, and held it for just a second. I instantly relaxed.

"Thank you, everyone," I said as people settled into comfortable positions. *The Devil's Play-ground: Tales of the Wild West* has been a big part of my life for over a year. Now I'm pleased to share it with you."

More applause, and then I read a selection Benson had previously approved. It took no more than fifteen minutes. When I placed the book back on the podium, the applause started anew, only this time, it was more reserved. Evidently, the anticipation exceeded the reality. I answered questions for another half hour, mostly about how much of the story was true. I told them it was all true . . . and some of it was even accurate.

As the questions wound down, I raised my voice and declared, "I have a major announcement, but first I would like to introduce the greatest inventor of our time . . . Mr. Thomas Edison."

Edison stood and received an ovation that made

the applause at my initial introduction seem paltry. He turned a full circle, waving with one hand. After the applause died down, I added, "Mr. Edison's latest endeavor is to fully illuminate District 1. This means the streets and every office and home. There will be no unruly wires strung from wobbly poles. Everything will be underground, where it will be safe for your children and reliable for decades to come. New York City District 1 will soon be the eighth wonder of the world!"

The audience started clapping vigorously, and some even stomped their feet.

Before the applause completely died away, I yelled, "People will come from all over to see light, heat, and motors running without the danger of explosion, noxious fumes, smoke, or eyestrain from unnatural light. There will be no need to individually light each lamp. The simple flip of a switch will instantly bring light as natural as day." I realized I had done a better job of selling Edison than my book, so I added, "What all this means, ladies and gentlemen, is that your days can be as long as you like . . . and to fill that extra time, may I suggest *The Devil's Playground* by Steve Dancy."

I held up the book again and took a half step away from the podium. The room exploded with applause, and then people began to stand until the entire room was on their feet. I congratulated myself with how clever I had been. Although the applause was mostly for Edison, mentioning my book just before it began made it appear that the demonstration was for my book. At least, that's the way I hoped it would play out in the newspaper articles. Besides, I was heavily invested in the Edison Electric Light Company, so I would benefit from any slant the newspaper writers chose.

I let the applause ebb slightly before I set the book on the podium and raised both hands, palms out. Everyone soon sat quietly in their seats. I glanced at Edison and he winked. I wasn't sure if it was a thank you for promoting his work or acknowledgment that he knew I had used his fame for personal advantage.

I held out my hand, and Virginia rose from her seat and joined me on the short dais. "Ladies and gentlemen, may I introduce Virginia Baker."

There was only a smattering of applause, because no one really understood why I was introducing her.

"This has been a great day for me, and I'd like to make it my best day yet." I hesitated slightly for dramatic effect and then bellowed, "I would like to announce my engagement to the most wonderful woman I have ever encountered!"

I relished the gasp that came from my mother's mouth just before the room burst into applause again. Now the audience was a sea of smiling faces. Women delighted in a budding romance, and men enjoyed gazing at a beautiful, radiant woman. I stole a glance at my mother and knew she would set my relatives straight at the earliest possible moment. She would make sure they understood that this engagement did not meet her approval and that they should withhold their congratulations.

When things quieted down a bit, I said, "Tomorrow we'll visit Tiffany's at eleven in the morning to purchase an engagement ring."

Virginia looked appropriately surprised and hugged me. When she pulled away, she wore a genuine smile and then kissed me on the cheek.

Someone yelled, "And what are your plans for later in the day?"

Most people laughed at the ribald insinuation. I pretended amusement, even though the question had been prearranged and came from a Pinkerton agent.

"Well, sir, if it's any of your business, we'll walk hand-in-hand through Union Square back to this hotel for an engagement luncheon in the dining room." I laughed again. "I apologize, but we cannot accommodate all of you fine people. In fact, it will be a small affair. I hope those of you not invited remain in your sitting rooms enthralled by *The Devil's Playground*. Which brings us to book sales." I waved Benson onto the dais. "My publisher has arranged enough copies for everyone here, one per person. If you would like additional copies, you may buy them, and I will be happy to sign all copies. So . . . pick up your copy and start a queue. I'll sign books until they're all gone."

Three hours later, the room was empty of guests. I had signed hundreds of books and done fifteen-minute individual interviews with five reporters. Same questions, same answers. McAllen had escorted Virginia to our room after commenting that we needed to talk after the party was over. My mother had disappeared when the signing started, but she reappeared as soon as the last guest departed. Before she could accost me, Benson came bubbling over.

"Stephen, we sold nearly as many copies as we gave away."

"Is that good?"

"Very good . . . and don't think the newspaper-men didn't notice. We're going to get a lot of good publicity. This has been an exceptional book debut." He patted me on the arm. "We'll meet later in the week to discuss events in Boston, Philadelphia, Baltimore, and Washington . . . maybe even Savannah."

"Are all of these events really necessary?" I asked.

He looked taken aback. "Of course . . . we've discussed this before. You already agreed to Boston."

"I did, but I have not agreed to the other cities. We'll meet . . . but I believe you are being narrow-minded."

"Narrow-minded? What on earth do you mean?"

"What do all those cities have in common?"

"Book buyers."

"You suppose only people who live on the Atlantic coast buy books? What about St. Louis, Chicago, Cincinnati, Denver, or even San Francisco?"

"I don't travel west," he said with a sniff.

"I do. We'll talk later, but if I agree to any of those cities, you'll need to agree to some of mine."

"Stephen, the romance of the West is on the East Coast. The people who live on the frontier have the real thing. They know the truth of the so-called Wild West: the dreary sameness, the hardship, the loneliness. Believe me, you'll sell more books to people afraid to venture beyond paved streets than to men and women struggling to survive on the edge of civilization."

"You're right. You don't travel west." I was annoyed and showed it. "If you did, you'd discover a vibrant economy. Doctors, lawyers, bookkeepers, and bankers work alongside ranchers, farmers, and miners. You'd even find politicians intent on bringing to the West the very things people fled when they left home. And by the way, I seldom ran into anyone completely uneducated. Most people read and like a good story."

I spotted my mother looking very impatient. "Please excuse me, Mr. Benson; I need to talk to Mother." I left before he could respond to my outburst.

"Should we find someplace private?" I asked Mother. She looked furious.

"Well, that certainly wouldn't be your room. I presume *that* woman is making herself at home there."

"*That* woman will soon be your daughter-in-law. If you want to see me or any of our future children, you'll learn to be civil."

"Oh my . . . are you saying she is in the family way?"

"No, Mother, but we do plan on having a family of our own."

"And you would withhold my grandchildren unless I approve your choice in a wife? That seems heartless."

"Heartless would be inflicting your scruples on my children."

"Since you have chosen to be blunt, I will be as well. Listen carefully. Do not lecture me on being civil when you make a public announcement of the greatest consequence without informing me first. I can't imagine a son being more disrespectful of his mother."

I started to respond, but she held up two fingers and after years of training, I closed my mouth.

"The Dancy name doesn't retain its privileged

place in society without my determined effort. Who is this woman and why does she deserve a place at the Dancy table? You have told me nothing of her . . . or her background. What little you have said would lead me to believe she has an immoral past. That is not good enough for my son. Not at all. I insist you break this engagement immediately."

It surprised me how calm I felt. I didn't care about her opinion. I was not the person she thought I was. My adventures in the West had tested my mettle, and my love for Virginia gave me all the family I needed. Ever since my father's death, I had been unmoored, but now I felt secure. My mother would never understand, so I didn't try to make her understand.

"And if I don't?"

"You will be disinherited . . . publicly."

"I see. Both barrels, as Father would say. No claim on the family fortune and the shame of being ostracized by the venerated Dancy family."

"We understand each other."

"Not really."

I turned and walked out of the hotel ballroom.

Chapter 39

When I returned to my suite, McAllen was alone in the sitting room. "What did you say to Kelly to scrub that smile off his face?" I asked as I came in the door.

"I whispered I should have shot him dead on that street in Leadville. Then I told him I correct my mistakes."

McAllen's face remained passive, so I couldn't tell if he had been playing with Kelly or was serious. With McAllen, it could be either way.

"When did he leave?" I asked.

"As soon as people stood up to get in line for books. Don't worry; he heard where you'll be tomorrow at eleven."

"I'm not worried. If he's serious about coming after us, he'll read the newspaper accounts of the party. They'd never miss an opportunity to spice up a dry article with a love story."

"Kelly was there?" The question came from Virginia as she emerged from the bedroom. I heard the anxiety in her voice and saw the worry in her expression. I immediately walked over to her.

"Yes, he was there, but Joseph sat beside him. We were safe, just like we'll be tomorrow."

I tried to lay a reassuring hand on her shoulder,

but she walked past me to pour herself a whiskey from the liquor cart. She didn't drink often, so the action made me uneasy. She took a good swallow and turned toward me.

"I know I'm supposed to be brave, but I'm not."

"You *are* brave. You've shown bravery countless times. This isn't a matter of bravery, but of uncertainty. I'm unsettled as well. Will he take the bait? Are we protected enough? Can we end this for sure?"

"Steve, think about it, Kelly won't be the one to attack us. What if we succeed, but only in arresting two of his lackeys? I'm scared this will never end. A lifetime vendetta." She took another good swallow. "I don't want a tranquil life, but I don't want to fear what might be around every corner."

After the book debut, I wanted a whiskey myself, but I didn't want to give Virginia the impression I was worried as well. Her concern was real. If this didn't ensnare Kelly, we were in for another chapter. I wanted a drink for the same reason she did—to settle my nerves.

As usual, McAllen read the situation correctly. He sauntered over to the liquor cart and poured two large drinks. He gave Virginia his closed-mouth smile as he walked past her to hand one of the glasses to me.

"My job is to think like a criminal in order to capture them." He motioned us to sit, which we did on a settee opposite him. "Kelly will send a couple of his gang members to kill you, but he'll need to watch . . . I guarantee it. So that only leaves figurin' out where he will position himself so we can capture him. Union Square will be crowded with people, and trees make sight lines tricky." McAllen took a sip of his drink and nodded in approval at the quality. He looked between us and said, "He'll be on a roof lookin' down on the square."

"How can you be certain? He could be inside a building." Virginia said.

"The buildings around the square are commercial and cater to the carriage trade. We couldn't find easy access to upper floors except in one, and it provided a poor vantage point due to the angle and trees. So that leaves the ground or a roof. When the square is crowded, it's hard to see over all the hatted heads, so he'll go for a roof."

"Wouldn't that make his escape difficult?" I asked.

"It could, but that's how we narrowed it down to one of two buildings where a plank would make it easy to get to another building on the block behind . . . same number of stories with no intervening alleyway. A pre-positioned plank would give him a clean escape path. Even if he's spotted, which is unlikely, by the time the police figure out how to get up to the roof, Kelly will be long gone."

Virginia thought for a moment and then asked, "What about a second attack?"

"What?" we both said in unison.

"Say we're attacked the way you expect, and we fight them off. What if he has a second team in the square? Perhaps someone with a gun. Someone to make sure we're at least killed."

"Oh hell," McAllen said.

"That doesn't sound reassuring." Virginia drained her whiskey glass in a single swallow.

"Let me think a minute." McAllen stood up and paced the room. "The square will be full of people, especially after the newspapers tout your visit to Tiffany's. So if there's a second assassin, he'll need to be close, or you'll be shielded by people after the first attack." He sat back down, resting his forearms on his knees, his glass in his hands. He rolled it back and forth in his palms. "The second assassin will come from behind. He'll follow you from the store, maybe even have been inside with you, which means he'll be well turned out. His job will be to act only if necessary. He'll probably use a derringer because it's easy to conceal in a palm. He'll need to be close. Very close." He settled back into the cushions. "I'll use two more men to cover your back."

"You seem sure," she said.

"It's how I'd do it. It's how any smart criminal would do it."

"Kelly's smart," I said. "Smart enough to think

up several ways to get to us. One of the men protecting our rear should come inside the store with us."

"Yep." This was all McAllen said, because he was thinking.

After a moment, he added, "Kelly wants you more than dead, he wants you humiliated. Like he was in Leadville. On second thought, if the first attack fails, I'm not sure he'll send another assassin at you. He'll more likely bide his time until he can make the way you die more important than your death."

"You're wrong," I said immediately. "Kelly wants his reputation back. His gang and other gang leaders will be told what he's going to do. If it goes awry, he has to fix it right there on the spot. I'm sorry, Joseph, this time Virginia has it right. He'll be prepared for a second attack. It's perfect. If the first attack fails, our guard will be down. The second assassin can kill us and get away in the confusion."

McAllen didn't like being told he was wrong. He rose and started pacing again. When he sat down again, he said, "You're right. He can't afford failure. He'll lose his status with his peers. It may be a criminal culture, but status is no less important than in your mother's highfalutin society. I'll have Mathew and another man at your back."

"Thank you," Virginia said.

I had mixed feelings about Mathew. His size would make it difficult for a second assassin team to get around him and into position, but he was inexperienced. I decided to bring up my reservations indirectly.

"How long has Mathew been out of college?"

McAllen looked at me, immediately knowing where I was going with the question. "Oh, I don't know, maybe six, eight weeks."

"Six, eight weeks? Didn't he graduate back when he played football at Yale?"

"Sure, but he went on to graduate school. Finished Columbia this past June." McAllen seemed amused. "He's due to transfer to the law department, but he's available tomorrow."

"Okay, he's smart, but can he be dangerous if the need arises?"

McAllen laughed, a rarity. "We've used him mostly for guard work because he's so intimidatin'. No one has ever attacked one of his charges. To my way of thinkin', that's better than havin' to fight off hoards of bad men because they think you can't handle yourself. And Mathew can handle himself. I've watched him in the gymnasium. He's quicker than any man I've ever encountered. He was an all-star not because of his size, but because of his speed. He was the enforcer at Yale. Someone once hit his teammate after he was down. After the next play, that opponent was out of the game with a dislocated shoulder. Clean hit." McAllen looked between us. "If it was my life, I'd want Mathew at my back."

"How do you know all this?" Virginia asked.

"He's a Pinkerton." McAllen said, as if that fact explained it all. "Listen, if you're that concerned, I'll make sure the second man is highly experienced."

I nodded okay, but I had another concern, and that had to do with the entire purpose of this little trap. "What about Kelly? If you catch him, what crime will he have committed?"

"You mean what proof will we have?" He leaned forward again, his forearms on his knees. "In the unfortunate event he chooses not to fight, we'll get one of the attackers to talk."

"How?" Virginia asked. "They'll be more afraid of the gangs in prison than of you."

"We have ways to make them talk."

"How? I want to know."

McAllen again rolled his glass between both palms. "Whoever we capture alive will be given a choice between goin' to prison as a stool pigeon or freedom in New Orleans."

"What if they don't blab?" she asked.

"Doesn't matter. We'll tell gang members that they did." McAllen got up to refill his glass. Over his shoulder he added, "They'll talk. Just don't kill them."

Chapter 40

Tiffany's sparkled. Dark wood cabinets with glass-topped cases displayed sparkling silver, sparkling diamonds, sparkling gold, and sparkling porcelain. Illumination came from high windows running the entire length of the store, augmented by gaslights hanging in a line from the ceiling. My first thought was that Edison's light bulb would render Tiffany's sparkle even more magical.

The staff had evidently read the newspaper stories of our planned visit. The manager and someone I assumed was his best salesman greeted us. Newspapermen jammed up against the door trying to get in, but two policemen held them at bay. Mathew remained outside in the crowd of onlookers. As the manager made solicitous introductions, I glanced around the showroom and spotted a Pinkerton. We had met that morning before we departed for the store. He was so sophisticated that my mother would have welcomed him into her parlor.

When the manager stopped talking long enough to take a breath, I asked, "Excuse me, sir, but can customers gain access to your store?"

"No additional customers will be allowed in until you depart." He motioned toward the crowd trying to peek through the window. "Your dramatic announcement has created quite a stir."

"I apologize," I said. "We had no intention of disrupting your business."

"No apologies necessary. The publicity is phenomenal. Tiffany's strives to identify itself with romance. You have done us a great service. Thank you." He waved around the store. "Besides, as you can see, the store is already crowded. Now, how may we help you?"

"Tell me about the diamond discoveries in South Africa."

"They're extensive but pose no risk to the value of diamonds."

"Why not?"

"These discoveries are always exaggerated. If you select a high-quality stone, your investment will be secure."

"Nevertheless, let's start with emerald rings. Green will match Virginia's eyes. Besides, her birthday is in May."

"No." Virginia's voice was firm. "I want a simple gold band. No precious stones."

"Virginia, you know I can afford whatever you want, and I want you to have something special."

She faced me, arms akimbo. "Did you listen to that stupid sentence?"

We had not discussed what type of engagement ring we would buy before coming into the store. Now, she was angry at me for not listening to her, her strong feelings made apparent by her harsh words, heated tone, rigid body language, and unblinking stare. Unless I wanted a row in the finest jewelry store in the country, I needed to surrender quickly.

"Dumb thing to say, of course. If you want a simple gold band, then that's what I want."

"It is. I left my jewels in Philadelphia . . . along with other debris. I do not intend to start another collection." Suddenly she was struck by a new thought. "I presume we are still heading west. If not, I want to know now."

"We are. Soon, I suspect."

"Then I don't want to wear an emerald, diamond, or any other stone. I prefer my finger attached to my hand."

"Oh, dear," the manager exclaimed.

"She exaggerates," I added quickly. "The people in the West are not savages, but her point is valid. Why tempt criminals . . . whether in the West or here in the city?"

The manager looked perplexed. "The Dancys don't normally encounter the rougher elements."

"This Dancy has on occasion. Please show us your gold bands."

"Of course." He tried to hide his obvious disappointment.

In less than an hour, we had selected a gold band with a crosshatch design that actually made the ring appear duller. It only remained to have the ring sized and engraved. After the salesman measured her finger, I pulled a piece of paper from my pocket and handed it to Virginia.

"Is this okay for an inscription on the inside?" I asked.

She took one quick glance, then threw her arms around my neck and kissed me. When she pulled away, every feature of her face reflected happiness.

"That's perfect, Steve." She handed the salesman the piece of paper.

Chapter 41

When we stepped outside, the throng of news-papermen practically attacked us. We answered questions for about five minutes. When they asked to see the ring, we told them it wouldn't be sized for another week. One of the newspapers had set up a camera to take our picture in front of the store, but we firmly declined, promising another opportunity when we were dressed properly for an engagement photograph. The real reason we refused was fear that Virginia's family might see her photograph in the newspaper.

Eventually, we broke free and meandered across the street to Union Square. A few reporters followed, but most were returning to their offices to file their stories. The square was busy, people walking in every direction. I hoped that many of the men worked for the Pinkerton National Detective Agency.

Virginia leaned her head toward me and whispered, "I'm sorry."

"For what?" I asked.

"For speaking sharply to you in Tiffany's. It wasn't about the ring. I was scared. I feel better now that we are out here doing it."

McAllen and our teachers in the Pinkerton basement had rehearsed us over and over again for this walk. We had done everything to prompt an attack against us. If Hugo Kelly wanted revenge for Leadville, we were to appear as sitting ducks for an assault. I walked to Virginia's left, and she gently swung her purse by its beaded strap in her right hand. We were separated from each other only by my cane. Our teachers had suggested that we keep a little space between us, so we took up the entire pathway. They had trained us to walk slowly and appear unconcerned about the people in front who stepped off the path to pass us on either side. We had spent several hours practicing the appearance of looking at each other as we chatted but actually keeping our attention on the people approaching. Mathew and Sharp followed our footsteps and talked with animated arm movements to make it difficult for an assassin to pass and get behind us. McAllen had promised to find an experienced partner for Mathew, and he thought I would be amused that he had picked Sharp. Actually, I found it reassuring.

Looking around, I spotted the Pinkerton who had been inside Tiffany's on the periphery of the square. When I looked forward again, I spotted them.

Two men approached, wearing clothing meant to make them presentable in the better part of the city, but instead they stood out like poor relations at a wealthy family celebration. Their poorly tied cravats were out of fashion, their shirts thin from too many washings. Scuffed shoes and poorly fitting suits were another giveaway. These were our assassins—gang members attired in clothing from a secondhand shop.

We had prearranged to use the code words *Union Square* if either of us spotted the attackers. We said the words simultaneously, laughing at what should have been a tense moment. Our sudden gaiety fit our masquerade as strolling lovers and seemed to put our assailants at ease. They came directly at us. As I waited for the right moment, I hoped Sharp's idea that they would try to gut us was correct. A gunshot from a distance would ruin our budding engagement.

Our luck held. I spotted the glint of a knife blade as the men separated to walk on either side of us. Damn. I wished I could be on both sides at once. How stupid to expose Virginia like this. But I had no time for regrets.

Just as I had practiced, I kept my eyes averted while giving my cane a little extra swing, grabbed it in the middle with my left hand, and jammed it into my assailant's chest before he reached me with his knife. I made eye contact as I heard the knife clatter to the gravel pathway. His eyes were wide. I slipped my left hand to the end of the cane, raised it parallel to the ground, and drove it into his neck. As he fell to his knees clutching his throat, I turned to help Virginia. She didn't need my help. Her man was lying on the ground, apparently out cold.

"I love this purse," she said, a bit breathlessly. "Can I keep it?"

Sharp was immediately at our side, trying to shield us as he looked in every direction. Where was Mathew? Sharp yelled, "Stop!" and pointed at a man backing away from the scene. When he heard the shout, the assassin drew a pistol from beneath his coat and turned to run. He didn't get far. Mathew had maneuvered behind him, and when he turned his head to search for an escape route, hit him so hard he flew backwards off his feet. When he hit the ground, he was knocked out as surely as if John L. Sullivan had landed the punch.

Without prompting, all of the innocent strollers ran from the square. Soon, Pinkertons and the police had cordoned off the park. I looked up at the rooftops but saw no activity. Returning my attention to the two men on the ground, I saw Sharp examining the man I had hit with my cane. He was on his knees, making an awful gurgling sound.

Sharp looked up and said, "He's dyin' . . . suffocatin'."

"What? How?" I asked.

"Crushed trachea." This came from Mathew, who had come up to cover our backs.

He knelt to examine the second assailant, so I

again looked at the surrounding building tops. I still saw no one. Lowering my gaze, I examined the people surrounding the square. No sign of Kelly. I noticed Sharp was looking for further trouble as well, turning in a tight circle while holding a big Smith & Wesson .44 like the one McAllen preferred. Sharp's preference was a Winchester, but a rifle looked out of place in a city park. I wished he were carrying one in case someone took a shot at us from a rooftop.

Mathew stood and said, "Concussed."

"Will he die?" Virginia asked.

"No," Mathew said. "But he'll have one hell of a headache."

She looked down at the still unconscious man. "Too bad. He wanted to kill Steve and me in the most painful way imaginable. I would have preferred him dead."

The choking man on his knees keeled over. "You got your wish with this one," Sharp said evenly. He rapped me on the stomach to hear a solid thump. "Glad ya didn't need to find out if these worked."

We had tested the bamboo shields, and I was confident they would protect us from a slicing knife, but we had also learned that they provided little protection against a stab to the stomach. Of course, they provided no protection if the assassins went after another part of our bodies or just shot us. We had been lucky.

I turned from Sharp to Mathew. "Go see if they captured Kelly."

"I was told to stay with you."

I pointed at the policemen running around blowing whistles. "We're safe. I need to know about Kelly."

Mathew hesitated. "Those police could be on the gang payrolls."

"Probably are," I said. "But we have hundreds of witnesses now."

He looked at the crowd surging around the periphery, vying to get a look at the cause of the commotion, and made a decision. He sprinted off toward the building McAllen had said was the most likely vantage point from which Kelly could watch our murder.

The police came over, examined the three men on the ground, and demanded to know what had happened. Sharp pretended to be an innocent onlooker and claimed we had defended ourselves from attack. One of the policemen started to slip one of the knives inside his tunic.

Sharp put a cautioning hand on his arm and loudly said, "Be careful with that unsheathed knife, officer. It's very sharp an' could cut you if you're not careful how you put it inside your blouse."

The policeman looked irritated, then taken aback when he noticed the big gun in Sharp's hand. He laid the knife carefully back on the ground.

"Put that pistol away, sir. We have the situation in hand."

Sharp holstered his gun and said, "When I saw the attack, I wasn't sure these were the only three."

"You should leave this work to the police."

"Yes. I noticed your whistle scared the other marauders away. I'll have to get me one of those."

"Sir, please step back." The officer looked at his partner. "Hank, get these citizens' names, especially this gruff one with the sharp tongue."

Sharp laughed. "Seems you're way ahead of me."

The policeman looked uncertain, then more perplexed when Mathew busted into our circle, breathing heavily. "Kelly got away."

"What? How the hell did that happen?" I yelled.

"McAllen said he was inside an office they had thought was inaccessible. Whole different building."

"Damn it. This whole charade was meant to capture him. You mean I put Virginia's life at risk for no good reason? Damn it!"

The policeman's confused expression suddenly changed to one of belligerence, but Mathew stopped him from hollering at us by showing him his credentials. Evidently, a Pinkerton badge carried some authority with the police.

"Where's McAllen?" I demanded angrily.

Sharp put a hand on my shoulder. "Relax, Steve."

"Why should I relax?"

"Because I know where to find Kelly."

Chapter 42

"Where?" I demanded.

"The Third Ward. Not far from Cortlandt Street dock," Sharp answered.

"The hell you say," the policeman interjected. "We keep the gangs penned in the Sixth Ward."

Without hesitation, Sharp punched the policeman to the ground. Damn. Hitting people had gotten Sharp in trouble before. He had almost hanged for hitting a man in a saloon in Prescott, Arizona. Now he had hit a policeman in New York City. It had happened so fast and so unexpectedly that the policeman's partner looked befuddled. Sharp wagged his finger at the other policeman, confusing him further.

"Just hold a second," Sharp instructed. He looked down at the man on the ground. "We never said anythin' about gangs. The only way he coulda known Kelly was a gang leader was if he was here at Kelly's request."

The policeman on the ground made no attempt to get up. "Horseshit, everybody knows Hugo Kelly's a gang leader."

"We never said his first name either. How many Kellys do ya suppose there are in New York City?"

"Arrest him," the policeman demanded of his partner.

A couple of men in the crowd murmured agreement. In my experience, New Yorkers believed their police were corrupt but still didn't like to see them physically attacked. I wondered how long the crowd would remain passive. Mathew stepped along until he had put himself between Sharp and the most threatening-looking bystander.

The partner who remained standing suddenly got his bearings. "You're under arrest for murder!" he exclaimed with booming authority.

"Murder? What murder?" Sharp asked, incredulous.

The policeman pointed at the dead man in the pathway. "That murder."

"Ya *are* a couple of dunderheads. I wasn't anywhere near the man when he attacked this man an' woman. If I was, I mighta killed him, but I didn't an'"—he waved his hand to encompass the onlookers—"I've got dozens of witnesses."

"Damn it," the policeman on the ground said. "Not for murder. Arrest him for hitting an officer. No one hits a policeman in my city."

"Ya work for Hugo Kelly, so this ain't yer city," Sharp responded. "Seems his gang has a higher claim. Ya just tell yer boss we're comin' for him."

The policeman got up off the ground and approached Sharp's ear, but I was standing close enough to hear.

"You son of a bitch. You ain't going after

anyone. I'm taking you to the station. Just wait. I'm gonna enjoy getting you under my roof. You won't walk upright for a month."

Sharp leaned toward the policeman's ear but spoke loudly enough for the man's partner to hear. "Let it go, flatfoot. I'll spend my considerable fortune on a Pinkerton team to prove you were under the employ of Hugo Kelly. Police don't fare too well in prison."

"You fool. No court will convict the New York police of corruption. Where the hell are you from?"

"Yer right, no court will acknowledge major corruption in yer fine department, but . . . an individual policeman. A scapegoat. Someone to prove the courts will protect people from rotten coppers." Sharp poked him in the chest with his finger. "That, my friend, would be a gift to the city."

McAllen had arrived a few moments before, breathing hard. It took him only a moment to assess the situation.

"Excuse me, sir, I'm Captain McAllen of the Pinkertons. I assure you everythin' this man said is true. He is rich, and he is ornery, and he's vindictive as hell. If he's arrested, I'll personally go with him to the station, and the best lawyer in town will be right behind me. My advice is to let this go."

The policeman rubbed his jaw and glanced at his partner. Suddenly, he went into action.

"Okay, people, back up. The fun's over. This hysterical man just let his emotions get away from him. That's all. No sense making a federal case of it. This man and his fiancée almost got brutally slaughtered. Let's back up and give 'em some room." He rubbed his jaw again and laughed. "No harm done. New York's finest doesn't prosecute distraught victims. Now make way for the police wagon."

McAllen led us to a corner of the park as a team of horses pulled a black wagon into the square to collect the unconscious men and the corpse.

McAllen grabbed Sharp by the upper arm. "Jeff, can you please quit hittin' people?"

"That son of a bitch deserves more than a punch. You heard him. He said Steve and Virginia were goin' to be brutally slaughtered. He was in on the whole plan."

As he spoke, Sharp started to charge back in the direction of the police, but McAllen stopped him with a palm planted firmly in his chest.

"One less corrupt policeman is not goin' to solve our problem," McAllen said. "We never even got close to Kelly, so this ain't over. Calm down and let's figure this out."

"Sharp says Kelly's near the Cortlandt Street dock," I said.

McAllen whipped his head around from me to Sharp. "How do you know?"

"Joseph, ya told me to get close to them

longshoremen. Kelly's not welcome in the Sixth Ward, so he's buildin' a new gang in the Third. Mostly fired laborers an' drunks. A few key followers, but a motley crew for the most part. He's tryin' to set up his old protection racket, but with shipowners this time. He ain't got too far yet."

"Do you know the general neighborhood or exactly where to find him?" Virginia asked.

I didn't like her question. It meant she still thought she was part of this. After our failed attempt, I would never put her life in danger again. Maybe we should just run. Kelly seemed busy with a new enterprise, so I doubted he would follow us. On second thought, he would never let it go. A year from now or five, he could leap back into our lives without warning. We would be unprepared. Complacent. No, we needed to rid ourselves of this fiend now, while we knew where he was and had help readily at hand.

"I don't know where he is exactly, but I know the taverns he uses to recruit," Sharp responded.

"By the docks?' McAllen asked.

"Yep. He arrives close to midnight, after the men are drunk. He acts like he's alone, but he has at least four ruffians in the bar who pretend not to know him. Doesn't fool the locals, but they all play along."

"Why didn't you tell us before this fiasco?" I asked. My tone was unpleasant.

"Because I just found out last night . . . after ya announced to the world ya intended to stroll through Union Square with yer bride-to-be." Sharp's answer was equally snippy. "I went back down to the docks to see what I could learn. I never saw Kelly in these taverns. I was just told about his visits."

"Let's all stay calm," McAllen said. "If he has four guardians, I'll bring six Pinkertons."

"Joseph, you can't arrest him," I said. "He hasn't committed a crime . . . at least not one you can prove."

"I don't intend on arrestin' him. I intend on provokin' him into a fight. It's time to pound this problem into the earth."

Chapter 43

I wanted to go that very night, but McAllen insisted that we needed a day so he could pick his team and plan exactly what we were going to do. McAllen and Sharp spent the next day arranging people and figuring out events. I spent the day arguing with Virginia. She insisted on going with us. I insisted she stay in the hotel. I was resolute. I was forceful. I was logical. In the end, I was even loud.

We spent the late afternoon in used clothing stores, buying a dress for her that would not look out of place around the docks.

The police dropped all charges against us because McAllen's men discovered witnesses who would testify that we were responding to a knife attack. People had also seen the third man draw a gun, but he was released because he claimed Sharp had threatened him. During the encounter, all of my attention had been focused on the man attacking me, and he had kept his knife against his leg. Evidently, the one who had attacked Virginia had brandished his glinting knife with a nasty smirk. We were lucky because if he had been as inconspicuous as his partner, reliable witnesses may have been difficult to find. A young woman attacked by a crazed man waving a big knife made bystanders eager to see the assailant separated from society.

The following evening, we had a leisurely dinner, then dressed in our room for our late night rendezvous with Hugo Kelly.

"I'm still not comfortable with you joining us," I said.

"Until you men butted in, this was a feud between Leadville women and Kelly. I was there at the start and I'll be there at the end."

"The end is not preordained."

"It is if I can get within purse length of that murdering crook." She slung the very weapon over her shoulder. "By the way, there are no gentlemen's rules when it comes to a lady protecting her fiancé."

"Is that what you'll be doing?"

"I'll be protecting our life together. When we leave this city, we won't look back . . . in fear or regret."

"I give up."

"You gave up hours ago. Now come on, let's go down to the lobby and meet Captain McAllen. I hope his plan works this time."

"Union Square wasn't his fault. It was my idea to use us as bait."

She bolted for the door, talking as she went. "When you use the right bait and you get a strike, you're supposed to reel in the catch."

I dutifully followed her out of our suite.

Downstairs, we found McAllen and his team gathered in the same room I had used for my book debut party. It looked almost empty when we entered, I hoped because of its large size and not the scarcity of men. I did a quick count: eight counting McAllen and Sharp. The two of us made ten.

"What the hell is she doin' here?" McAllen demanded as we walked into the room.

"She's coming. What's the plan?"

McAllen looked ready to explode, but then he must have had a change of heart. His next question showed why. "Mrs. Baker, would you be willin' to draw Kelly outdoors, away from the tavern?"

"How?" I asked before she could answer.

"She waits in the tavern until he sees her and then she leaves. That's all. Once he's outside, we do the rest."

"Can I stay with her?"

"Even better. The two of you should stare at him in a challengin' way. You're not in the tavern by accident. You came lookin' for Kelly. It tells him you are now huntin' him and you know his whereabouts. If you get up and leave, he'll likely follow with his gang members. We'll position men inside and outside."

"How many inside, how many outside?" I asked.

"Four and four, but the four inside won't be too far behind Kelly and his men when they leave. That will give us eight against their five or six."

"I count ten," Virginia said.

"After you get clear, you skedaddle. Steve, you stay with her. You'll be her only protection, so stay alert."

"What makes you think he'll follow us out?" I asked McAllen.

"He'll follow," Virginia answered.

"Why do you sound so sure?" Her confidence made me nervous.

"Because I'm going to throw this in his face." Virginia held out her hand to show a tiny pile of fine black dust.

I was incredulous. "You brought Leadville dirt to New York?"

"We came here to see Thomas Edison. The Carbonate Kings have a monopoly on ore refining in Leadville because the equipment costs so much. I though Edison might invent a cheaper way to separate silver from lead."

"Damn!" Sharp jumped off his chair, put his big arms around Virginia, and twirled her in two complete circles. "By God, girl, you're smarter than any of us. Did he have a solution?"

"He promised to look into it . . . after he illuminates District 1."

"Well, why didn't ya tell me? I woulda dug those ditches myself."

"Now, Mr. Sharp, this is my idea."

"Yes, dear, but yer gonna need a minin' expert, an' I know where there's one right handy."

"Of course." She laughed. "Steve and I always intended this to be a partnership with you."

Steve and I? This was the first I had heard of this scheme. I was here trying to get a license for the Edison electric lamp, and Virginia had been working a whole different notion. No wonder she wanted to get friendly with the Edisons. She wanted to use the brain of the greatest inventor in the world. I was stunned and proud.

"Is that all you rich people do? Think about getting richer? I thought we had a job tonight. Let's get back to it." McAllen looked disgusted.

We spent the next hour going over our roles. McAllen was hesitant at first, but in the end, he decided the insult of throwing Leadville soil into Kelly's face would insure his following us out of the tavern. The goal was not an arrest. A street fight seemed more appropriate in the West, but on reflection, I remembered that gangs had been battling it out on New York streets for decades. They just weren't streets I had frequented.

We prepared to leave near eleven in the evening. As we started toward the door, I told McAllen, "You're right, by the way. Rich people always think about how to get richer. It's in our nature."

"You ought to broaden yer interests," McAllen said.

"I would . . . but then I probably couldn't afford to hire you and your team."

Chapter 44

We arrived in separate carriages to avoid arousing attention. The full moon made the dock district a patchwork of light and shadows. Lamps were few, and those that did exist hung outside taverns. Due to the shadows thrown by buildings, moonlight lit one side of the street almost bright as day, while the opposite side sulked in foreboding darkness. The narrow alleys opened with inviting light that quickly faded into a black hole, reminding me of a well bottom.

A Pinkerton Kelly wouldn't recognize scouted the taverns. He would reappear shortly after entering, shaking his head slightly to convey that Kelly was not there. As he proceeded from tavern to tavern, my disappointment grew. We exhausted all of the taverns around the dock, coming up empty every time. We had all been keyed up, ready to end this feud once and for all. Now, I felt energy drain from my body. Damn. I wanted to get past this chapter and get on with our lives.

McAllen had staged a couple of carriages a few blocks away, so he left to bring them to an isolated corner on Liberty Street. We didn't like waiting with a small crowd, and the two carriages couldn't hold ten comfortably anyway, so Virginia and I started walking the three blocks to Broadway to catch our own cab. Mathew came along for our protection.

I no longer used the subterfuge of being somewhat lame and had left my cane at the hotel. This time, I wanted to end it for good and intended to use my Colt if given the opportunity. He had tried to kill us twice. On his third attempt, I would kill him. Unfortunately, it would not be this night. I felt dejected as we walked in silence. I stayed on the inside, fearing the alleys more than the streets. On the street, I could see ahead, but someone could easily leap out of the darkness to surprise us.

Suddenly, I felt a pressure against my abdomen and heard a scratching noise. I recognized the sound from our practice session in the gymnasium. Without a thought, I drew my Colt and was about to shoot the figure who had darted from the alley, but Mathew drove the assailant hard into the wall with a horrendous football block. I felt rather than saw a second assailant swinging around the struggling men to attack Virginia. As he passed in front of me, I fired two times into his chest. Both hit. Then I heard gunfire from down the street and felt debris hit my hat. I grabbed Virginia and roughly drew her into the alley. We pressed our backs against the wall and saw Mathew knock the first attacker's head against the bricks and flip him into the recesses of the alley. Despite having done little physical activity, Virginia and I tried to catch our breath.

"What was that?" she whispered.

"A knife attack . . . and then somebody shot at us from down the street."

"Are you okay?" Mathew asked as he dropped to his haunches.

"Yes, thanks to the bamboo armor." I tried to look deeper into the alley, but it was shielded from moonlight, and I could only make out stacked boxes and litter.

"Are we safe here?" Virginia sounded justifiably nervous.

I gazed into the darkness.

"For the moment. The two who owned this alley are at our feet, but there must be access from the next street over." I tried to think. "Mathew, use this alley to find McAllen. Bring him and Sharp back here, and send the rest of the men to the other end of this street to come in behind whoever's out there."

"My assignment is to stay with you."

"Damn it, we need help. I'm not leaving, and I'm sure as hell not sending Virginia down that alley alone. That leaves you."

"We stick together. McAllen must have heard the shots."

I switched places with Virginia and peeked around the corner. I saw and heard nothing.

"Someone will sneak down this alley . . . soon.

That's where the danger will come from. You need to go now, before someone beats you to the other end. Speed will win this contest."

Mathew hesitated and then decided. He leaped to his feet and sprinted down the alley, knocking down boxes that skittered against the cobblestones. I hoped he was armed, but I hadn't seen him with a gun. I had to trust him. I had my own problems around the corner.

"What will *we* do?" Virginia asked.

"Do you have your gun out?"

She nodded anxiously. She now carried my Remington .38. We had decided before we left the hotel that, despite a plan calling for us to skedaddle, we would wear our bamboo shields and carry guns. Virginia had grown attached to her purse, so she had brought that along as well. Our plan seemed prescient now. Kelly had not given up on inflicting slow, painful deaths on us.

"Stay down and keep low." I did the same. "Watch and listen. If you see or hear anything down that alley, fire a high shot into the darkness. One only. You have five shots before you're out of bullets. Shoot high in case it's Joseph or Jeff. After you shoot, shuffle low to the other side of the alley because the muzzle flash will give away your position. If anyone shoots back, fire again, but aim chest high. Again, one shot only."

"What are you going to do?" she whispered.

"I'll stay right beside you and keep an eye on the

street. McAllen will come. In the meantime, Kelly's men know where we are, but we don't know where they are. No shooting. We stay low and alert until help comes."

"I'm scared."

"So am I. There's no shame in fear. It'll help us survive."

We waited.

I occasionally peeked around the corner, but with the heavy shadows, I didn't spot anyone. I replaced the two bullets I had fired from the five extra nestled in my shoulder holster and added another to fill the sixth previously empty chamber. That left only two bullets not already in my gun. Virginia had no extras. I cursed myself for not bringing more ammunition. We'd have to husband our shots, or we'd be left with a purse as our only defense.

After a couple minutes, I had had enough. "Kelly!" I yelled. "You goddamn coward! How can you lead a gang when you're always hiding behind your men?"

No response. I guessed that he was hoping we thought they had left so we'd step out of the alley. I knew he was still out there.

"You ran in Leadville, you hide in New York. You must recruit drunks and idiots. Nobody else would join you. You're weak. What are you afraid of: one man and a woman?"

"What are you doing?" Virginia asked, a bit breathless.

"Trying to get Kelly mad enough to step into the street. This feud started in the street, let's finish it in the street."

"But what will we do if he accepts . . . if he has men with him?"

"We'll meet him."

"Steve!"

"Don't worry, McAllen can't be long now."

"What if he doesn't get here in time?"

"Then remember what I taught you. Aim careful and squeeze. Fast doesn't win. Accuracy wins."

"I hope he stays hidden."

Then Hugo Kelly came out from the shadows.

"Dancy, come on out . . . bring your woman with you."

I peeked around the corner. Just as I had expected, he stood in the center of the street with nearly a dozen men. I checked the alley, but it was too dark to see. Damn. If I were him, I'd have a couple of men sneak up the alley and come in behind us after we stepped into the street.

I whispered to Virginia, "When we step out, walk briskly, right up to Kelly. Don't stop until you're within arm's reach. There are probably men in this alley who won't hesitate to shoot us in the back, so we need to put some distance between us. Hide your gun. I'll carry mine in plain sight. If you get close enough, hit him with that purse. If shooting starts before you can get close enough, drop to one knee, draw your gun, and shoot for the chest. Kelly first. Then whoever is closest to him on your side. Understand?"

She nodded vigorously.

Virginia was a brave woman. In that moment, I loved her more than ever. It wouldn't be fair for us to die like this. We deserved an entire life together. I wanted to sacrifice myself for her safety, but there was no way to do it. If she stayed in this alley, they would get her. Her best chance, our best chance, was to face this together. If we acted differently than he expected, we might have an edge.

"Deep breath . . . okay, let's go."

I slid my back up the wall, preparing to enter the street, when I heard a scuffle down the alley. I wasn't sure what the noise meant until I heard a distinct groan that could only have come from a man. They were coming, probably stumbling as they scurried in the dark. I quickly put myself between Virginia and the depths of the alley. When I heard nothing more, I bent low and started inching toward the sound. I had to eliminate this threat before we exposed ourselves to Kelly and his men.

I saw only darkness and heard nothing. Then I sensed movement. There were men coming. I saw a piece of lumber, so I slowly slipped my gun back into my holster and picked it up. I didn't have enough bullets to throw random shots down an alleyway. I raised the stick parallel to the ground, intent on jamming it into whatever I encountered. I inched forward. Then I heard my favorite word.

"Steve?"

"Yep, it's me. What took you so long?"

"Some ill-mannered men didn't want us to come up this alley," Sharp said.

"Who's with you?"

"I am," McAllen whispered.

"Mathew?"

"Bringin' men around the other side."

"Okay," I said, turning around. "Let's get Kelly."

I laid the stick back on the ground and drew my pistol. I no longer expected to get close enough to jab anyone with a piece of wood. I had crawled only a couple of feet when I realized that Virginia was no longer at the edge of the alley. I moved fast. Had they captured her? Then I heard the clicking of her shoes against the cobblestones. She was marching toward Kelly. Now I ran the last couple of yards.

As I emerged from the alley, I heard Kelly yell, "Where's your pretty boyfriend? Has he sent his woman to hit me with her purse?" She was walking briskly toward him and his line of men. "Stop!" he yelled. "Stop right there or I'll shoot you, bitch!"

She stopped.

He sneered. "I've seen what you can do with that purse, lady. Just stay back." Then he noticed me. "Ah, I see your boyfriend has decided to come out of his hole . . . and he's brought a couple of friends to our party. My, my, we can settle up right now."

As I hurried forward, I saw Virginia drop her purse and slowly draw her gun from inside her dress. Astutely, she held it at her side, hidden in the folds of fabric. There were three of us plus Virginia against nearly a dozen. She had improved with a gun but was still a mediocre shot. It didn't look like it was going to be a fun party.

My gun was drawn and I saw McAllen carried his Smith & Wesson in his hand. Then I caught something in the corner of my eye that made me feel more confident: Sharp was carrying his Winchester. He must have stored it in the carriage. With his rifle, he could put a bullet in Kelly's forehead even from this distance.

We closed the space and came level with Virginia. I noticed that Kelly and his men held guns in their hands as well. This was going to be bloody. I was ready to just up and shoot Kelly, when McAllen said in his dry, gruff voice, "You men, move aside and you won't get hurt. We only want Kelly. No reason for you to take lead for that snake."

"These are my men. Loyal to me. You're the one about to take lead."

McAllen remained chillingly calm. "Let me ask you men a question. Have you ever been in a gunfight? Not a fight with sticks and pipes and knives, but a fight with loud, noisy guns from a distance. Most men can't hit shit in their first fight. They just blast away until they find themselves dyin' on the ground. The three of us have been in plenty of gunfights. I wouldn't stand with any other two men. When it comes to it, they're cold killers." He paused dramatically. "If you don't want this, go." There was no movement. "Now!" he barked.

A couple of them stepped backwards. As soon as they did, Kelly yelled to kill us and raised his pistol. McAllen and I both shot Kelly in the chest before he fired. I was down on one knee as gunfire became deafening. So many muzzle flashes would disconcert the most experienced soldier. Sharp was smart enough to ignore Kelly and aim at other gang members. He worked the lever on his Winchester so fast that the heavy boom of his rifle almost overrode the pistol discharges. On my second shot, I went to Kelly's left, and McAllen automatically went to his right. We proceeded to shoot anyone who had not stepped away from the fight. Within seconds, billowing gun smoke combined with darkness made seeing impossible.

I stopped shooting. I had only a single shot left, so I ejected two spent casings and loaded my last remaining bullets. I did this from habit without looking at my gun. I kept my eyes on the smoky darkness. Gun flashes still came sporadically from the other end of the street, but they had slowed after visibility became nil. I looked at our party. McAllen and I were both on one knee, but Sharp stood erect. He was calmly reloading.

To my right, Virginia lay on the ground, blood soaking her dress below the waist. Her gun was still in her hand. I scooted over and checked to see where the bleeding was coming from. She was clutching her leg. I took her pistol and touched the barrel lightly. It was hot. She had fired the weapon. I doubted she had shot five times, so I assumed there were still bullets remaining. I raised both pistols just as the smoke cleared.

When it did, two men remained standing. One belligerently yelled, "Kill 'em!" Or I think that was what he was about to yell. He got out only part of the first syllable before he danced backward from a barrage of bullets fired by all three of us. I had fired a single round from both guns and stopped shooting. The other man ran, and we let him go.

I immediately wheeled around to see how badly Virginia was hurt. I found the gunshot wound in her upper leg and quickly checked the rest of her body. No other injuries. She was conscious and managed to look relieved to see me examine her.

"You're all right," she said with wonder.

"Quiet. You've been shot. It doesn't look serious, but don't exert yourself." I unbuttoned my suspenders and double coiled them around her leg as a tourniquet.

"Is he dead?"

"If you lie here quiet, I'll check."

She nodded.

As I approached the bodies on the ground, Mathew and a group of agents came running around the corner. They stopped when they saw the carnage.

I walked over to where McAllen and Sharp stood over seven bodies; five of them appeared dead. Kelly had three bullet holes. I shook my head. One was from McAllen, one was from me, and one was a smaller caliber that could only have come from Virginia's gun. In the heat of combat, she had found her aim. I checked the Remington. Two shots fired. Since I had fired it once that meant Virginia had hit him with one shot. It had been to the left arm, but it had still hit him.

I walked back to Virginia.

"You killed him. One shot, direct to the heart."

She smiled slightly and passed out.

Chapter 45

Virginia recuperated at Edison's home in the city. He and his wife had insisted. The bullet passed clean through her upper leg without hitting bone, and the doctor said she should heal rapidly. Everyone told her how lucky she was to have survived such a dreadful ordeal. She responded cheerfully that her deadly aim accounted for the survival of all of us. When the newspapers wrote the story, she was the heroine who saved her fiancé. I read one of the articles aloud in a mocking tone, and she hit me with her purse. Fortunately, it was not her lead-weighted purse.

None of the rest of us had even been nicked, but Sharp had two bullet holes in his coat. It seemed gang members who grew up in New York City didn't have many opportunities to practice shooting. I was glad our fight wasn't with knives and pieces of timber. The investigation went quickly, and police interviews were perfunctory. I think they feared the city was heading toward a gang war if Kelly had stayed around and were glad to see him buried. The other dead men were no-accounts whose bodies were never claimed. It also helped to have the Pinkerton agency managing the behind-the-scene politics.

Since Virginia was in capable hands, I decided I

could leave her to go on a city tour to sell books. I loaned her my cane and wished her a rapid recovery. When I added that a limping bride might mar an otherwise beautiful wedding, I almost got another blow from her purse. I would have to keep purses out of her reach if I were going to remain satirical.

My book tour lasted four weeks and included Boston, Philadelphia, Baltimore, and several cities in Rhode Island and Connecticut. Sales were brisk but not sufficient for my publisher to pay for a western cities tour. I suspected Mr. Benson did not believe literacy extended beyond the narrow confines of the eastern seaboard.

By the time I returned to New York City, Edison had successfully illuminated the first district. The sagging wires and poles were torn down, and everyone marveled at how subways improved the appearance of the neighborhood. Edison's fame grew even greater, and investors begged to give him money. We had helped, so I had high expectations for an exclusive license.

I knocked on Edison's door, and a new servant opened it with a flourish.

Standing at near attention, he asked, "How may I help you?"

"I'm Steve Dancy. I'm here to see Virginia Baker," I answered.

"Is she expecting you?"

"I should hope so. She's my fiancée."

He bowed his head. "I shall let her know you are calling. One moment, sir."

He closed the door.

Damn, where had Edison found this strutting peacock? Had his enlarged fame gone to his head? In a moment, the servant opened the door again and waved me in with a fanfare befitting a minor royal.

As I stepped inside, I asked, "Are you English?"

"Me, sir?" He looked amused and then added, "I see no reason to burden you with that information. Please follow me."

He strutted off. I decided he was English. Many servants in New York City affected an English accent, but his sounded real. I bet Edison had hired him from an agency that imported domestics for the rich. Somehow a real English butler conveyed cachet in this status-conscious city. He led me to the parlor, which I had visited several times prior to going off to sell books.

Virginia was with Thomas and Mary. She stood and walked straight over to me. She walked smoothly, but I could tell she was working hard not to limp. I went to kiss her on the cheek but instead hugged her. I wanted to feel her body close. After a moment, I whispered in her ear that I had missed her. She pushed back and gave me a welcoming smile that made my heart pound. I wondered how we could get out of there.

"Are you fit for a walk?" I asked.

"Hold on a minute," Edison said. "Don't be in such a rush. I understand these things, but please give us the pleasure of your company for an hour or so. Besides, if I remember correctly, we have a piece of business to discuss."

Virginia took my arm. "Of course we'll stay. At least until supper. I made reservations at Delmonico's, and I have tickets for *The Pirates of Penzance*." She smiled at me. "My welcome home present."

I was impressed. She had already figured out a way for us to be alone, although I had been hoping for more than a meal and a Gilbert and Sullivan opera.

"How is your leg?" I asked.

She looked down demurely. "It works fine—or is getting there—but I'll have an ugly scar."

"No. It won't be ugly. It will always remind me how brave you are."

Her unaffected smile lit her whole face with joy. I couldn't believe she had been worried about a patch of rough skin. If it were on a tactful part of her body, I would have wanted her to wear it as a badge of honor.

Edison coughed to signal that our conversation had become too intimate for company, so I asked about his success in District 1. He held forth for nearly thirty minutes on the wonders of electrical illumination. Then he kiddingly complained that Virginia's fame as the woman who had shot a notorious gang lord made his life's accomplishments as significant as a ditch next to the Grand Canyon. Virginia beamed and told me she had guests or reporters calling on her daily. Even the mayor had praised her in an interview.

Her family had written and telegraphed queries, but Edison had responded that Virginia Baker was a close family friend and unrelated to anyone in Philadelphia. Virginia had never allowed herself to be photographed, under the pretense that other gangs might pursue retribution. The ruse had apparently worked, because no one showed up from Philadelphia.

After tea service, Edison said, "Let's talk business for a moment. You requested an exclusive license for my electric lamp and other inventions for the mining industry. I'm sorry, but I cannot honor that request." I started to protest, but he raised a hand. "What I am willing to do is grant you distribution rights for Denver and points west, with the exclusion of California."

"The territories?"

"Those will be included."

"What's the difference?" I asked.

"Think about it."

I did. "You don't want me to concentrate on mining only. You want me to illuminate the cities of the West, but you've already done a deal for California."

"San Francisco. But it includes options on the

remainder of the state. That leaves a lot for you and Mr. Sharp. You'll have most of the mining in the country like you wanted . . . and Denver, Tombstone, Seattle, and other growing towns."

"Detroit, Chicago, Omaha, St. Louis, and Kansas City?"

"I'll keep them in reserve for you. But you need to prove yourself first."

"Will you give us a contractual option . . . conditioned on performance?"

He pretended to think. "Yes, all right . . . except for Chicago. I'll not put that restraint on myself quite yet."

His comment told me he had plans for the fourth-largest and now fastest-growing city in America. I had no desire to become an electricity mogul anyway, so I accepted this limitation. I was still interested in mining because I liked the energy in the rough camps and towns. Cities were all the same, but I wouldn't turn down an opportunity thrust on me by someone with a national vision.

"What about looking into the Leadville sample Virginia gave you?" I asked.

"Already have someone working on it, but separating the silver from the lead will be a challenge. I can't promise anything."

"Can you promise to look at it personally?"

"I can . . . but that would mean I'd own the process."

"Fifty, fifty—you and Virginia."

He again pretended to think. "Agreed."

I smiled to show I was satisfied. "Now that it's settled, I should tell you I would've paid handsomely for a license."

"I'm glad you reminded me. There's another condition. You'll be required to buy fifty thousand dollars' worth of inventory to be transported to Denver and warehoused by you. You will coordinate with Samuel Insull, who runs my factories. Or rather, he will tell you what you are to buy and in what quantities. All storage, sales, installation, and maintenance will be your responsibility, with strict contractual control over quality and service."

I was suddenly nervous. "You said you had a warehouse full of light bulbs. Are they the latest version of your invention?"

"Don't worry, I'm not going to dump bad inventory on you. My reputation is too important to me. In fact, that's why I'm structuring the deal this way. I retain control. You harm the Edison name, and I can revoke your distribution. I have less control with a license."

I immediately saw that he would not budge from this approach. He had figured out a way to get up-front cash while remaining in control. Control of his reputation was far too important for him to let somebody traipse across the country without retaining leverage on how they conducted business in his name. Instead of being disappointed or angry, I was impressed with his business acumen and reassured that I was entering into a deal with someone who would continue to be enormously successful.

"Mr. Edison, I'm certain that your conditions will be acceptable, but I need to talk to Mr. Sharp first."

He reached behind him and picked up a folio. "Don't just talk. Hire an attorney and have him review these papers. If the deal is satisfactory to you both, sign them and bring them back to me."

I took the folio. "Thank you, Mr. Edison. I appreciate your having already put this in writing." I stood. "Now, if we are going to eat before the opera, I'm afraid we will need to leave."

We made our goodbyes, and the stodgy servant hailed us a cab. I climbed aboard the carriage with mixed feelings. I felt good about the business deal but disappointed about our plans for the evening.

As I settled in the seat, I yelled "Delmonico's" at the driver.

"Are you in the mood for steak?" Virginia asked.

"Not really," I answered.

"Good. Because it seems to have slipped my mind to make reservations at Delmonico's. Does your hotel still serve a decent meal?"

"It does. And with light fare we may be able to get in some recreation before *Pirates of Penzance*."

"Oh dear," she said. "I forgot to buy opera tickets. I must be losing my mind."

I leaned out the window and yelled, "Fifth Street Hotel . . . and hurry!"

The crack of his whip brought Virginia into my arms as the carriage lurched around a corner. We kissed.

Chapter 46

The next morning, I ate breakfast alone. I liked to read at breakfast, so I was not really alone. I had Louisa May Alcott's *Eight Cousins* to keep me company. The story was written with a light, feminine touch that didn't appeal to me, but I wanted to find out how an author remained popular for over a dozen years. At first, I looked at reading her book as research, but I soon became engrossed in the story.

Later today, Virginia would move into a room at the hotel. It would be my room, of course. The Edisons would probably suspect, but as my mother would say, the door would be gently closed. Besides, we were almost ready to return west. Sharp and I needed only a few days to conclude our deal with Edison. It needed to be done soon. I had seen McAllen as he left the dining room after an early breakfast. He was fit to be tied. In fact, if he didn't get away from the crushing crowds, he might whittle down the population of New York. The man had a weakness, and he needed to get to a place where it wasn't noticeable.

A motion brought my attention away from my book to the seat next to me. My mother had sat down. Damn my thoughts for conjuring her up.

"Good morning," she said. "Am I using somebody's chair?"

"Good morning, Mother. No, the seat is open. Virginia is not staying at the hotel."

"Oh dear, I do hope that means you've broken up."

"She'll be moving into my room this afternoon." Her rudeness made me dismiss my initial intent to be circumspect.

"That's unfortunate." She took a piece of my toast and held it without taking a bite. "Mr. Benson says your book is selling well. Seems we have a literary figure in the Dancy family."

"Really, who?" She smiled indulgently, so I added, "I thought you believed my subject matter unworthy of literary aspirations."

She patted my hand. "Stephen, you really shouldn't be so snippy. It's unbecoming."

"Why are you here, Mother?"

"To invite you to dinner this evening. A sort of celebration of your grand tour. Your family is very proud of you."

"No, thank you. I have other plans."

"With that baker?"

"That's her name, not her profession."

"I think it's better if we do not discuss her profession. Besides, family names came about based on what someone did. She certainly had bakers for ancestors. That's not demeaning. It's honest work. I employ bakers for each of our homes."

"Please leave."

Instead, she raised her hand and waved over a steward. After ordering a melon and toast, she smiled sweetly and folded her hands in front of her.

"You don't give up, do you?"

She looked startled. "Of course not. Dancys don't give up. It's not in their nature."

I threw my napkin on the table and stood. "Enjoy your breakfast."

"Stephen, sit down. We need to discuss your inheritance."

I remained standing. "Mother, I can also employ Pinkertons. I discovered that you're not broke, but unless you change your spending habits, you'll probably be destitute by the time you die. As best I can calculate, I have more money than the entire Dancy family. We do not need to discuss my inheritance unless you're asking me to fund it."

"Stephen, you're being difficult. I'm proud you have money. That proves what I've known all along: You are a Dancy. And don't worry about me. I have more assets than a stupid detective could ever discover. But I need to be blunt. This woman is not for you. At least, not as a wife. You need someone that can carry on our family traditions. Tonight, I've invited just such a woman." She leaned in and whispered. "She is young, strikingly beautiful, and unsoiled. I'm sure you will find her exciting."

"You could not have made a worse speech to convince me. I want nothing to do with our family's traditions. I want what makes me happy . . . and Virginia Baker makes me happy. If you ever interfere with my life with her, I will ruin this family." I leaned in next to her ear but didn't whisper. "And don't think I can't . . . because you're right, I *am* a Dancy." I straightened. "Goodbye, Mother."

I walked out of the dining room.

Chapter 47

The train jostled us with a soothing rhythm. I was happy. We were on our way to Denver, where we planned to gather our horses and belongings, stay a couple of weeks, and then leave for parts unknown. We had plenty of time to figure out where we would go next, and we were in no hurry to decide.

Our compartment door slid open, and Sharp and McAllen busted in.

"Well, how are our lovebirds?" Sharp said jovially.

McAllen sat down with his closed-mouth grin. I wondered what he was pleased about until Sharp spoke again.

"When we get to St. Louis, what say we jump this train and board a river boat for New Orleans? Ain't been there in years." He patted Virginia's knee. "You'll love it."

The two of them had obviously just returned from the bar in the dining car.

"Jeff, we left our things in Denver," Virginia said.

"Hell, I ain't sayin' forever. Just a month or so."

"Joseph, don't you need to return to your office?" I asked.

He shrugged. "I can get the New Orleans office to request my services."

"'Sides, Joseph's in the cash now. He needs a vacation."

I was pleased for my friend. "Did Edison give you a bonus?"

"Naw, I got a reward for Hugo Kelly. He was wanted for accessory to murder and extortion in Colorado. He hired a man to kill one of the brothel madams working on State Street. The man was finally caught after Kelly left town and turned against his old boss to escape the noose. A thousand dollars."

"How long did you know there was a reward on his head?" Virginia asked. "I killed him. By all rights, part of that reward ought to be mine."

McAllen looked at me with an expression that said this was my fault. It had seemed a harmless fib at the time. I had no idea there was a reward.

"It does seem she should get something from it," I offered, hoping McAllen would understand that I would reimburse him.

"You got somethin' already," he said. "You think you can gun down people on the streets of New York and walk away clean? No, sir. Not unless the victims were wanted men, and you were helping an official of the law carry out his duties. At least, that's the story my agency used with Mayor Cooper." He leaned forward. "I'm deputized by the United States Marshal's office, so I have authority to pursue wanted murderers across state lines."

Virginia smiled. "Keep it. I was just giving you a hard time. You earned it. If you hadn't come to our aid, we'd be dead."

McAllen tipped an imaginary hat. "Thank you, ma'am. I'd share it between all of us, but you three already seem well fixed."

"I'm glad you did well on this trip." I was thinking Edison had paid his salary while he earned a thousand dollar reward. He had also received some compensation from me. I hoped he was getting together enough money to build his horse ranch. A faraway look in his eyes told me he was thinking hard on something.

"How 'bout that side trip to New Orleans?" Sharp asked, unaware the mood had changed.

McAllen softly said, "Jeff, I think New Orleans can wait a bit. I aim to take my vacation in Durango."

McAllen's daughter Maggie lived in Durango with his ex-wife. She was his only family, and I had seen the longing in his eyes before he came to a decision. My bet was he would bring her a new, spirited horse. She had grown into a young woman, and she rode better than most men. I hoped he would take a long vacation. His line of work was stressful, and he deserved some time with Maggie.

"Are you going to build that horse ranch?" I asked.

"I think I might." After a pause, he added, "I have the money to start, and the agency always needs good horses." His expression became firm. "When we get to Denver, I'll see about gettin' a supply contract."

"Ya thinkin' vacation or retirement?" Sharp asked.

"Retirement," McAllen answered slowly, pronouncing each syllable of the word. "At least retirement from Pinkerton. A horse ranch ain't easy goin'."

"Damn," Sharp said. "Can ya stay put?"

"I think I'm ready. When I was in New York, I hated the place. I like wide-open country, country accomodatin' to horses. The kind of open spaces Maggie loves to ride around." He smiled, showing a full set of teeth. "Yep, I'm ready. I want to start a new life."

I was ready, as well. I reached over and took Virginia's hand. She squeezed my hand in return, and I felt her engagement ring.

"You still like a plain gold band?" I asked. "We could get something fancier in Denver."

"No, thank you." She smiled to herself as she twisted the ring on her finger. "I like the inscription on this one."

"A new ring can be engraved with the same inscription."

"It wouldn't be the same. This is an original."

Now it was my turn to smile. The inscription read, *Search over—I found you.*

From now on, my adventures would include a partner.

Author's Note

This is a work of fiction. Although Thomas Edison encountered difficulties in illuminating District 1, there is no evidence of sabotage. The problems apparently came solely from his insistence on burying the electrical wiring. The Lewis family and firm are fictional. Although the actual illumination of the Wall Street district took place during the time of this story, I have used the novelist's power to compress time. Thomas Edison's contribution to mining included new techniques in blasting, conveying, crushing, and magnetic separation. His greatest mining invention was the electric cap lamp.

Center Point Large Print
600 Brooks Road / PO Box 1
Thorndike ME 04986-0001 USA

(207) 568-3717

US & Canada:
1 800 929-9108
www.centerpointlargeprint.com